PRAISE FOR *NINE ELMS*

"A heart-pounding series launch."

—*Publishers Weekly*

"*Nine Elms* is a taut thriller that sweeps up the reader into the world of Kate Marshall. Kate is a thoroughly realized character with troubles and virtues who will have you rooting for her through to the nail-biting end."

—Authorlink

"A taut thriller that will keep readers guessing, this is a powerful start to a new series."

—*Parkersburg News and Sentinel*

"While there are shades of *The Silence of the Lambs* in *Nine Elms*, due to a connection between an imprisoned monster and an investigator, Robert Bryndza has created wholly original characters and a story that is the very definition of a 'page-turner' and 'unputdownable'!"

—The Nerd Daily

"With *Nine Elms*, Bryndza proves that he's got another blockbuster saga on his hands. Kate Marshall is a bona fide superstar—an appealing mix of strength and vulnerability who shows that the damage of our past doesn't need to define us or defeat us but that it can spark our determination to be smarter, stronger, and singularly successful. That's a hero, and a notion, worth rooting for."

—Criminal Element

"Robert Bryndza's characters are so vividly drawn—even the slightest character—and fully human and uniquely imperfect. His plots are clever and original and cool, and his sense of timing is excruciatingly flawless. *Nine Elms* is Robert Bryndza spreading his already formidable wings to thrilling effect."

—Augusten Burroughs, *New York Times* bestselling author of *Running with Scissors*

"So chilling, with truly terrifying characters and a hard-hitting story line that is gripping from start to finish. I will wait with bated breath for the next Kate Marshall thriller."

—Rachel Abbott, Amazon Charts bestselling author

"Bryndza is my type of author, and *Nine Elms* is my type of book. Twisty, dark, and layered with a protagonist you root for from page one, this is a superb start to what promises to be another standout series."

—M. W. Craven, author of *The Puppet Show*

SHADOW
SANDS

OTHER TITLES BY ROBERT BRYNDZA

Kate Marshall Series

Nine Elms

Erika Foster Series

The Girl in the Ice

The Night Stalker

Dark Water

Last Breath

Cold Blood

Deadly Secrets

Coco Pinchard Series

The Not So Secret Emails of Coco Pinchard

Coco Pinchard's Big Fat Tipsy Wedding

Coco Pinchard, the Consequences of Love and Sex

A Very Coco Christmas

Coco Pinchard's Must-Have Toy Story

Stand-Alone Work

Miss Wrong and Mr Right

SHADOW SANDS

A
KATE MARSHALL
THRILLER

ROBERT BRYNDZA

THOMAS & MERCER

Published by Thomas & Mercer, Seattle

www.apub.com

Amazon, the Amazon logo, and Thomas & Mercer are trademarks of Amazon.com, Inc., or its affiliates.

ISBN-13: 9781542023368 (hardcover)
ISBN-10: 154202336X (hardcover)
ISBN-13: 9781542005708 (paperback)
ISBN-10: 1542005701 (paperback)

Cover design by Caroline Teagle Johnson

Printed in the United States of America

First Edition

For Maminko Vierka

Hell hath no limits, nor is circumscribed
In one self-place, for where we are is hell,
And where hell is there must we ever be.

—*Christopher Marlowe*

PROLOGUE

28 August 2012

Simon gasped and choked on the brackish, freezing water as he swam for his life. The reservoir was huge, and he churned through inky-black water in a frantic front crawl, farther into the darkness and away from the drone of the boat's outboard motor. The cloudy night sky meant no moon, and the only light came from Ashdean, two miles away, an orange glow that barely reached the reservoir and the surrounding moorland.

His trainers, heavy Nike Air Jordans, which he'd laced up tightly before leaving the campsite, were like lumps of lead on his feet, and he could feel them, along with his wet jeans, weighing him down. It was late summer, and where the icy water met the balmy night air, a thin rippling mist hung atop the water's surface.

The boat was small and sturdy, and the man he'd seen beside it on the edge of the reservoir had been in silhouette. Simon's flashlight had illuminated the body the man was lifting into the boat. A limp form bound tightly in a white sheet covered in blotches of blood and dirt.

It had all happened so fast. The man had dropped the body in the boat and attacked him. Simon knew it was a man, even though he was only a shadow. When he knocked the flashlight from Simon's hand and struck him, there was a nasty, sharp smell of sweat. Simon briefly fought back, but he was ashamed how he panicked and ran into the water. He should have run in the other direction, back into the thick woodland surrounding the reservoir.

Simon struggled to breathe but pushed himself to swim faster. His muscles burned from the effort. His swimming training had kicked in, and he was counting one, two, three, his head coming up for air on the fourth stroke. Each time he reached four, the drone of the outboard motor was closer.

He was a strong swimmer, but his injuries slowed him down. He could feel a rattle as he inhaled. The man had struck him in the ribs, and the pain was throbbing. He was taking big breaths as he swam, but he'd swallowed water, and the air wasn't getting to his lungs.

A wall of fog came at him, low across the surface of the water, and it enveloped him in a cold blanket. Simon thought this might save him, but suddenly the boat roared up directly behind him and struck him on the back of his head. He snapped forward and was plunged underwater. He felt pain as the outboard motor propeller gouged his flesh.

He thought he was going to black out; he could see stars, and his body was numb from the impact. He couldn't move his arms. He kicked hard, but his waterlogged feet and legs didn't seem to respond to his effort, moving almost lazily. He came back to the surface, surrounded by mist, and a calm voice in his head spoke to him.

What are you fighting for? Sink down and drown, where it's safe.

He coughed and spat out the brackish water. His ears were ringing, blocking out any sound. The water around him rippled, and the bow of the boat appeared through the mist again. As it caught him under the chin, he heard his jaw crack, and he was thrown up and backward so he was lying on the surface of the water. The boat ploughed over him—he felt the hull on his chest and then the blades of the outboard motor gouge the skin, against his ribs.

Simon could no longer move his arms or legs. His head and face were numb, but the rest of his body was on fire. He'd never felt pain like it. The water felt warm on his hands. It was his blood, not the water. His blood was warm, and it was pouring out into the water.

He smelled petrol from the outboard motor, the water shifted again, and Simon knew the boat was coming back for him.

He closed his eyes and let the air out of his lungs. His last memory was being enveloped by the cold, black water.

1

TWO DAYS LATER

Kate Marshall took a breath and dove into the cold water. She came back to the surface and bobbed for a moment, the rocky Dartmoor landscape and gray sky hovering above the waterline in her diving mask; then she sank down into the reservoir. The visibility underwater was good. Kate's teenage son, Jake, was first in and was treading water below her, the air bubbles rising from his regulator. He waved and gave her a thumbs-up. Kate waved back, shuddering as the cold trickled into her wet suit. She adjusted her regulator and took her first tinny breaths of oxygen from the tank on her back. It tasted metallic on her tongue.

They were diving at Shadow Sands, a deep man-made reservoir, a couple of miles from where Kate lived near Ashdean in Devon. The algae-covered rocks they'd jumped off banked steeply away, and the cold and gloom increased as she followed Jake deeper. He was now sixteen, and a sudden growth spurt in the past few months had made him almost as tall as Kate. She kicked out strongly to catch up to him.

At thirteen meters, the water took on a gloomy green hue. They switched on their headlamps, casting arcs of light around them that didn't manage to penetrate the depths. A huge freshwater eel appeared out of shadows rippling between them, its blank stare caught in the light of their lamps. Kate shrank away from it, but Jake didn't flinch, watching with fascination as the eel ribboned close to his head and back into the shadows. He turned to her, raising eyebrows behind his mask. Kate pulled a face and gave him a thumbs-down.

Jake had been staying with Kate for the summer, arriving after he sat his GCSE exams. In June and July they'd taken scuba lessons from a local diving school, and they'd been on several diving trips out to sea and to a sunken cave on the edge of Dartmoor with a phosphorescent, glowing wall. The Shadow Sands reservoir had been created in 1953 by flooding a valley and Shadow Sands village, and Jake had seen online that it was possible to dive down and see the sunken ruin of the old village church.

They were diving at the top end of the reservoir, a mile away from the sluice gates that drew water through two enormous turbines to generate electricity. There was a small area that was cordoned off for diving. The rest of the reservoir was strictly out-of-bounds. Kate could hear the low hum of the far-off hydroelectric plant, which was an ominous sound in the cold and dark.

There was something eerie about floating above what once had been a village. She wondered what it looked like down there. Their headlamps were lighting up nothing but silt and murky green water. She could imagine the once-dry roads and houses below them, where people used to live, and the school where children played.

Kate heard a faint beep and checked her dive computer. They were now at seventeen meters, and it beeped again with a warning to slow their descent. Jake reached out and grabbed her arm, making her jump. He pointed downward, to the left. A large, solid outline was emerging from the gloom. They swam toward it, and as they drew closer, Kate could see the huge curved dome of a church tower. They stopped a few feet from it, their headlamps illuminating a mass of freshwater crustaceans covering the dome. Below the dome, Kate could see the bricks of the church tower furred green with algae, and the arched stone windows. It was eerie to see this man-made structure, which once towered so high, so far down in the water.

Jake unclipped a waterproof pouch containing a digital camera from his belt and took a few photos. He looked back at Kate. She checked her dive computer. They were now at twenty meters. She nodded and followed him to the window. They hovered outside for a moment, the silt in the water thicker as they peered into the vast, empty cavity of the old bell tower. Crustaceans covered every inch of the inside walls, bulging out in places. In spite of the thick layer, Kate could make out the contours of the curved vaulted ceiling. The tower had four windows, one on each face. The window to the left was teeming with crustaceans, and the window to their right was almost completely blocked up, leaving a small arrow slit that reminded Kate of a medieval castle. The window opposite was clear, looking out into the dim green of the water.

Kate swam through the window into the tower. They stopped in the center, and she swam up to get a closer look at the vaulted ceiling. One of the beams that would have held the church bells ran across one side of the ceiling. The crustaceans had covered this, and they had matched the ceiling's arched contours. A huge freshwater crayfish, more than a foot long, appeared from under the beam and scuttled across the ceiling toward her. Kate almost yelled out in shock as she jerked back, grabbing at Jake, her arms flailing in slow motion. As the crayfish passed above, its legs rattled on the shells of the tightly packed crustaceans. It stopped above them. Kate's heart was now pounding. Her breathing increased, and she drew hard on her oxygen supply.

The crayfish's antennae twitched, and it scuttled across the vaulted ceiling and vanished through the window opposite. Kate noticed something floating outside the window where the crayfish had escaped. She swam closer, her headlamp lighting up the heels of a pair of bright-red trainers. They shifted in the water at the top of the window.

Kate felt a surge of fear and excitement. She kicked out, and using the stone arch, she slowly pulled herself through the window. The shoes were directly above the opening and connected to the feet of a dead body, suspended in the water, like it was standing up, next to the church dome.

Jake had followed her through the window, and he jolted back, his head hitting the wall of the tower. Kate heard his muffled cry, and a spray of bubbles from his regulator crowded her vision. She reached out and grabbed him, unable to get a proper grip because of his oxygen tank. She pulled him away from the tower. Then she looked back at the body.

It was a young man. He had short dark hair and wore blue jeans with a silver buckled belt. On his wrist was a smart-looking watch. The remains of a ripped white T-shirt floated in strips around his neck. He had a well-built, athletic frame. His head was flopped forward, and his face, chest, and bloating belly were covered in cuts and lacerations. What most unsettled Kate was the look on his face. His eyes were wide open, with a look of fear. He was still, but suddenly his neck shifted and pulsed. She felt Jake grab at her again, and for a horrible moment, Kate thought the boy was still alive. His head twitched, and his jaw swung open as a black, shiny eel appeared between his broken teeth and emerged, seeming to ooze from his open mouth.

2

"Why were you diving today?" asked Detective Chief Inspector Henry Ko.

"Jake, my son, wanted to dive here. The water level has dropped in the heat . . . We thought we might see the sunken village," said Kate.

She was sweating under her wet suit, and her hair was sticky and itchy from the water. Jake was slumped against a front wheel of Kate's blue Ford, staring into the distance, his wet suit rolled down to his waist. He was very pale. Kate's car was parked on a grassy bank beside the reservoir. Henry's squad car was a few feet away. The grass bank ended ten meters in front of the cars at the reservoir's original water level, but since the drought there was a twenty-meter expanse of exposed rocks sloping down to the water's edge. The rocks were green with algae, burned to a crisp by the hot sun.

"Can you point out where the body's floating?" said Henry, scribbling in a notepad with a pencil. He was in his early thirties, athletic, and very well spoken. He looked like he should be prowling a Milan catwalk rather than attending a murder scene. His jeans clung to his muscled legs, and three buttons were undone on his shirt. A silver necklace nestled between his bronzed pectorals.

A young policewoman in uniform stood beside him with her peaked cap under her arm. She had long jet-black hair, tucked behind her ears, and her smooth, creamy skin was flushed from the heat.

"The body is underwater. We were twenty meters down. Diving," said Kate.

"You know the exact depth?" he asked, stopping his scribbling and looking up at her.

"Yes," said Kate, holding up her wrist with the dive computer. "It's the body of a young boy. Nike Air Jordan trainers, blue jeans with a belt. His T-shirt was ripped to shreds. He looked around Jake's age, eighteen, nineteen, maybe . . . There were cuts and lacerations on his face and torso." Her voice cracked, and she closed her eyes. *Is the dead boy's mother out there?* thought Kate. *Is she worrying, wondering where he is?*

Kate was an ex–police officer. She thought back to all those times she'd had to inform relatives a family member was dead. The deaths of children and young people were the worst: knocking on the door, waiting for it to be opened, and then seeing that look on the parents' faces, the realization that their son or daughter wasn't coming home.

"Did you see if the boy had injuries on his front or back, or both?" asked Henry.

Kate opened her eyes. "I didn't see his back. His body was facing us, floating against the structure of the church tower."

"Did you come into contact with anyone else? Boats? Other divers?"

"No."

Henry crouched down next to Jake.

"Hey, buddy. How you doing there?" he said, his face creased in concern. Jake just stared ahead. "Do you want a can of Coke? It'll help with the shock."

"Yes, he would. Thank you," said Kate. Henry nodded to the police officer, and she went off to the squad car. Kate crouched down next to Henry.

"That lad. He wasn't wearing diving gear," said Jake, his voice wobbling. "What was he doing down so deep, with no gear? He was all beaten up. His body was black and blue." He wiped a tear from his cheek, and his hands were shaking.

The police officer returned with a can of Coke and a tartan blanket. The can was warm, but Kate cracked it open and held it up to Jake. He shook his head. "Have a tiny sip. The sugar will help with shock . . ."

Jake took a sip, and the officer put the tartan blanket over his bare shoulders.

"Thank you. What's your name?" asked Kate.

"Donna Harris," she said. "Keep rubbing his hands. Get the blood moving."

"Donna, put in a call for the marine dive team. And tell them it could be a deep dive," said Henry. She nodded and placed a call on her radio.

The air was heavy and humid, and dark-gray clouds were forming low in the sky. At the far end of the reservoir sat the hydroelectric plant, a long, low concrete building. A faint rumble of thunder came from behind it. Henry tapped the pencil on his pad.

"Are you both qualified to dive? I know the reservoir is strict, especially with the depth and the fact that the water feeds the hydroelectric dam."

"Yes. We took our dive certificates at the beginning of August," said Kate. "We can dive to twenty meters, and we've logged thirty hours in the water whilst Jake's been staying with me over the summer . . ."

Henry flicked back through the pages of his notebook, a frown creasing his smooth forehead.

"Hang on. Jake is *staying* with you?" he said. Kate felt her heart sink. She would now have to explain Jake's living arrangements.

"Yes," she said.

"So, who lives at the address you gave when you called the emergency services . . . Twelve Armitage Road, Thurlow Bay?"

"I do," said Kate. "Jake lives with my parents, in Whitstable."

"But you're Jake's real, erm, biological mother?"

"Yes."

"His legal guardian?"

"He's sixteen. He lives with my parents. They were his legal guardians until his sixteenth birthday. He's about to start sixth form college in Whitstable, so he's still living with them."

Henry peered at Kate and Jake.

"You've got the same eyes," he said. As if this were the confirmation he was looking for. Kate and Jake shared the same rare-colored eyes: blue with a burst of orange emerging from the pupil.

"It's called sectoral heterochromia, where the eyes have more than one color," said Kate. Donna finished on the radio and came back over to join them.

"How do you spell *sectoral heterochromia*?" asked Henry, looking up at her from his pad.

"Does it matter? There's a young boy's body under the water out there, and it looks to me like a suspicious death," said Kate, starting to lose her temper. "He was covered in cuts and bruises, and he must have died recently, because a body will float a few days after sinking. The pressure at that depth and the cold water will slow down decay, but as you know, eventually, a dead body always floats."

Kate had been rubbing at Jake's hands as she spoke. She checked his fingernails, relieved to see some color returning. She offered him more Coke from the can, and this time he took a big gulp.

"You seem well informed," said Henry, narrowing his eyes. They were beautiful eyes, the color of caramel. He was so young to be a detective chief inspector, thought Kate.

"I was a detective constable in the Met Police," she said.

A faint recollection moved across his face. "Kate Marshall," he said. "Yes. You were involved with that case a couple of years ago. You caught that guy who was doing the copycat murders of the Nine Elms Cannibal case . . . I read about that . . . but, hang on. You were working as a private investigator?"

"Yes. I caught the original Nine Elms Cannibal back when I was a police officer in 1995. I caught the copycat killer two years ago working as a private investigator."

Henry flicked back through his notepad, a look of confusion on his face.

"You told me earlier you work as a lecturer in criminology at Ashdean University, but you're saying you used to be a police officer, and you also moonlight as a private detective? What should I write in my report as your occupation?"

"I was asked to help solve that one cold case two years ago. I was a one-off private investigator. I'm a full-time university lecturer," said Kate.

"And you live alone, and Jake lives with your parents in Whitstable . . ." He stopped with his pencil hovering above the page and looked up at her again. His eyebrows had shot up into his hairline. "Whoa. Your son's father is the serial killer Peter Conway . . ."

"Yes," said Kate, hating this moment, having experienced it many times before.

Henry blew his cheeks out and bent down, peering at Jake with renewed interest. "Jeez. That must be tough."

"Yes, family get-togethers are difficult to organize," said Kate.

"I meant it must be tough for Jake."

"I know. It was a joke."

Henry looked at her for a moment, confused. *You're nice to look at, but you're not the sharpest tool in the box,* she thought. Henry stood up and tapped the pencil against his pad.

"I read a fascinating study about the children of serial killers. *Most* of them go on to live pretty normal lives. There was one in America, her father raped and murdered sixty prostitutes. Sixty! And now she works in Target . . . Target is a shop in America."

"I know what Target is," snapped Kate. He seemed oblivious to how insensitive he was being. Donna had the decency to look away.

"It must be tough on Jake," he said, scribbling in the pad again. Kate had a sudden urge to grab the pencil and snap it in half.

"Jake is a perfectly normal, happy, and well-adjusted teenage boy," she said. At this point, Jake gave a moan, leaned over, and threw up on the grass. Henry jumped back, but one of his expensive-looking tan leather shoes was caught in the firing line.

"Bloody hell! These are new!" he cried, stomping off to the squad car. "Donna, where are those wet wipes?"

"It's okay," said Kate, crouching next to Jake. He wiped his mouth.

Kate looked back out across the reservoir. A low bank of black clouds was moving over the moor toward them, and there was a rumble and a flash of lightning.

How did that boy die?

3

After Kate had signed her police statement, she and Jake were free to leave. On the way out of the reservoir car park, they passed two large police vans and the coroner's van.

Kate watched them in her rearview mirror as they pulled up at the water's edge. The image of the young boy suspended in the water came back to her, and she wiped a tear from her eye. Part of her wished she could stay and see his body brought safely to the surface. Kate reached out and grabbed Jake's hand. He squeezed hers in return.

"We need petrol," she said, seeing the tank was low. She stopped at the petrol station close to her house, pulled past the pumps, and parked at the back. "You should put some dry clothes on, love. There's toilets here, and they keep them nice and clean."

Jake nodded, his face still pale. She wished he would say something. She couldn't bear the silence. He scraped back his wet hair, which was now shoulder length, and tied it with an elastic band he kept on his wrist. Kate opened her mouth to say how terrible elastic bands were for his hair but closed it again. If she nagged him, he would only clam up more. Jake got out of the car and grabbed his dry clothes from the back seat. She watched him trudge away to the toilets, his head hung low. He'd been through so much, more than most sixteen-year-olds.

Kate pulled the mirror down and looked at her reflection. Her long hair was now shot through with gray. She looked pale and every one of her forty-two years. She flipped the mirror back up. This was Jake's last day before he went back to her parents. They had planned to get pizza after their dive, and then they were going to go down on the beach below Kate's house, make a fire, and toast marshmallows.

She would now have to call her mother and tell her what had happened. It had almost been a perfect summer. They had almost been a normal family again, but now there was a dead body.

Kate tipped her head back and closed her eyes. The average person in the world didn't stumble on dead bodies, but here it was, happening again to Kate. Was the universe trying to tell her something? She opened her eyes.

"Yeah, it's trying to tell you to pick nicer places to take your son," she said out loud.

She took her phone out of the glove compartment and switched it on. Kate found her mother's phone number and was about to press "Call," but then she opened her internet browser and googled "missing teenage boy, Devon, UK." The data signal wasn't great out by the petrol station, surrounded by the Dartmoor hills, and her phone ticked over for a minute before the results loaded. There was nothing recent about a missing teenage boy. There was a report about a seven-year-old on the Devon Live website. He'd gone missing for an afternoon in Exeter town center, and he'd been reunited with his family after a tense few hours.

She then googled "DCI Henry Ko, Devon, UK." The first result was from the local paper.

DISTINGUISHED DEVON & CORNWALL

CHIEF SUPERINTENDENT PASSES THE BATON

The article was from the previous week, about the retirement of a Chief Constable Arron Ko. It said when he'd joined the police in 1978, he'd been the first Asian officer in the Devon and Cornwall borough.

There was a picture at the bottom with the caption "Chief Constable Arron Ko was presented with his retirement gift—a pair of silver engraved handcuffs and the Police Long Service and Good Conduct Medal—by his son, Detective Chief Inspector Henry Ko."

Henry was standing with his father in front of the Exeter police station with the framed award. Arron Ko was portly and overweight in comparison to his handsome son, but Kate could see the resemblance.

"Aha. That's why you're so young to be a detective chief inspector. Nepotism," said Kate. She disliked the jealous voice in her head, but she couldn't help but compare herself to Henry. She'd worked hard for four years, sacrificing everything to gain promotion to the plainclothes rank of detective constable when she was twenty-five. Henry Ko was only in his early thirties and was already a DCI, two ranks higher than detective constable. She thought back to her days in the police, her life in London.

Detective Chief Inspector Peter Conway had been Kate's boss in the Met Police when they'd been working on the Nine Elms Cannibal serial killer case. One night, after a visit to the crime scene of the fourth victim, Kate had cracked the case, discovering that Peter was the Nine Elms Cannibal. When she'd confronted Peter, he'd almost killed her.

In the months leading up to this fateful night, Kate and Peter had been having an affair, and unbeknownst to Kate, she was four and a half months pregnant with Jake. By the time she had recovered in hospital, it was too late to have an abortion.

The newspapers had a field day with the story. It had destroyed Kate's credibility within the police, and her career came to an abrupt end. After Jake was born, she struggled. The trauma of the case and the sudden unplanned motherhood and postnatal depression piled onto her, and she started to drink heavily.

Kate's parents stepped in several times over the years to look after Jake, but her drinking grew worse, and she ended up in rehab. Kate got clean, but it was too late. Her parents were awarded custody of Jake when he was six, and for the last ten years they had remained his legal guardians.

Sobriety had been hard. She had rebuilt her life and got to see Jake on school holidays and weekends, but his childhood was almost over. She still felt the loss like sharp shards of glass. The loss of Jake, and of the career she had loved as a police officer.

There was a knock on her window, making Kate jump. Jake was now dressed in his skinny black jeans and a blue hoodie. He had more color in his cheeks. She wound down the window.

"Mum, have you got a couple of quid for a pasty and a bar of chocolate? I'm starving."

"Of course," she said. "You feeling better?"

He nodded and smiled at her. Kate returned the smile. She grabbed her purse, and they went into the petrol station.

As hard as she tried, she couldn't shake the image from her head, of the young boy floating under the water. It was frustrating that she would have to wait and see if there was anything about him in the news.

4

SIX WEEKS LATER

Kate emerged through the creaky wooden doors of Ashdean Community Center and paused to take in the view over the rooftops to the waves churning up and smashing against the seawall. A howling wind was blowing, and it whipped her hair around her head. She took a pack of cigarettes from her bag and teased one out, ducking back under the awning to light up.

There were around twenty or thirty people at her Alcoholics Anonymous meeting on this cold October evening, and they nodded good night as they passed. She watched as they hurried to their cars, heads bowed against the freezing wind.

The cold quickly got the better of her. Kate took a final, hasty drag of the cigarette and dropped the half-finished butt on the ground, extinguishing it with her heel. She started walking back to her car, not looking forward to going home to an empty house. The road was now dark and deserted. Her car was parked at the end of the road in a gap between the terraced houses. When she reached it, there was a white BMW squashed in next to her old blue Ford. The door of the BMW opened, and a thin, pale-faced woman got out.

"Kate?" she asked with a London accent. Her brown hair was scraped back from a high, bony forehead, and she had deep-set eyes with dark circles, reminding Kate of a raccoon. She recognized the woman as a newbie from the AA meeting.

"Yes. Are you okay?" she said, having to raise her voice above the roar of the wind.

"Kate Marshall?" The woman's eyes were running from the freezing air. She wore a long plum-colored puffa jacket, the type that looked almost like a sleeping bag, and she had on bright-white trainers.

Kate was surprised to hear the woman use her full name. She had spoken at the meeting, but she'd used only her first name, as was customary at AA. *This woman's a bloody journalist*, thought Kate.

"No comment," said Kate, opening her car door and intending to make a quick getaway.

"I'm not a journalist. You found my son's body . . . ," said the woman. Kate stopped, her hand on the car door. "His name was Simon Kendal," said the woman, looking Kate directly in the eye. Her eyes were a piercing green and filled with sadness.

"Oh. I'm sorry," said Kate.

"They told me he drowned."

"Yes. I saw the local news report."

"That was bullshit," she cried.

Kate had followed the story, not that the local news had dwelled on it, but they'd reported it as a closed case. Simon Kendal had been camping with a friend; he'd gone in the water and drowned. His body had then been mangled by one of the maintenance boats that regularly patrol the reservoir. The local news also mentioned that it was Kate who found the body. This was why Kate's first thought had been that this woman was a journalist.

"His body was all battered up. They didn't want me to see him in the morgue . . . Look at this," shouted the woman above the wind. She took a small plastic photo album from the pocket of her coat, fumbled with it, and found a picture of a handsome young man standing by a swimming pool, soaking wet in a Speedo. He had two medals around his neck. "That's my Simon. He was UK regional champion. Swimming. He was going to compete professionally. He only missed out on qualifying for the London 2012 Olympic swimming squad cos of an injury . . . A stupid injury . . ." She was flipping the photos and talking fast, as if Kate's attention needed to be captured. "Simon wouldn't have jumped in the water with all his clothes on, at night!"

"What's your name?" asked Kate.

"Lyn. Lyn Kendal . . ." She came closer and looked up at Kate, beseechingly. "What do you think happened? I know you used to be a police officer. I read about you being a private investigator."

"I don't know what happened to Simon," she said. The truth was, in the last few weeks, the story had been filed at the back of Kate's mind. She had been preoccupied with work and Jake, who had been very distant since his return to Whitstable.

"Aren't you curious?" Lyn was shaking. She wiped her tears away with an angry swipe of her hand. "You teach crime. You were an investigator. Isn't my son's death worth questioning?"

"Of course," said Kate.

"Can we talk somewhere, please?" asked Lyn, brushing the strands of hair from her face as they were whipped by the wind. Kate wondered if Lyn was sober. The woman looked a wreck, which was understandable.

"Yes. There's a small café, Crawford's, on Roma Terrace, at the top of the promenade. I'll meet you there."

5

Crawford's coffee bar was the oldest in Ashdean and Kate's favorite. There were photos of Joan Crawford and Bette Davis on the black lacquered walls, and a huge smoked mirror hung on the wall behind the Formica counter, reflecting back the giant copper coffee machine, the faded red leather booths, and the view out over the dark promenade. It was empty on this cold, windy Wednesday night. Kate arrived first and chose a booth at the end.

Across the road, the tide was in right up to the seawall, and from her vantage point, Kate was able to see down the length of the promenade. The waves were breaking up over the wall and spraying froth and shingle over the parked cars. A white BMW roared up the road and pulled neatly into the space behind Kate's battered Ford. Lyn got out, opened the passenger door, and grabbed a bright-green plastic folder and her long jacket.

"Did you order?" asked Lyn when she slid into the booth opposite Kate.

"No."

Lyn put the green folder down on the table, and then she took her mobile phone, a pack of Marlboro 100s, and a gold lighter from her jacket pocket. She then took off the coat, balled it up, and sat on it. Lyn was a tiny woman, and Kate wondered if she'd done that to match Kate's height so she wasn't having to look up at her.

Roy Crawford, the elderly man who had owned Crawford's since the 1970s, came over to their booth. He was a large man with long white hair tied back in a ponytail and a pink, clean-shaven face.

"What can I do you for?" he said, smiling and popping on the pair of half-moon specs that dangled from his neck on a chain.

They each ordered a cappuccino, and he scribbled down on a pad with a flourish.

"I know it's a simple order," he said. "But I'd forget me own head if it wasn't screwed on. I'm ever so sorry, but it's no smoking. To think the Labour Party were the ones to ban smoking." He rolled his eyes theatrically, then left them alone.

Lyn nervously smoothed back the wisps of hair from her high forehead.

"Tell me about Simon," said Kate. Lyn seemed relieved to cut to the chase.

"He was away with his mate Geraint, from university. They were camping at the site near the Shadow Sands reservoir," she said.

"Are you a local?"

"I'm London born. My late husband was from round here, and I've lived here for twenty years. He died of a heart attack." Kate went to say sorry, but Lyn put up her hand. "Don't. He was a bullying arsehole."

"What does Geraint have to say about Simon?"

"They'd been out at the beach for the day. They arrived at the campsite late, pitched the tent, went to sleep. He woke up the next morning, and Simon's sleeping bag was empty. He thought he'd gone for a pee, but as the morning wore on, Geraint couldn't find him."

"Had they been fighting?" Lyn shook her head. The coffee machine in the corner started to hiss, and there was a tinkle of spoons and china cups. "Was it just the two of them camping?"

"Yeah. They were best mates; they never argued. There wasn't a scratch on Geraint. All his clothes were dry."

"Had they been drinking?"

Lyn put her hand up.

"I've already thought of the obvious questions. When they did the postmortem, they ruled accidental drowning. Simon had no alcohol in his bloodstream . . ."

Roy came bustling over with their coffee.

"Here we are, ladies," he said. "You enjoy, but I'm closing in half an hour."

"Thanks," said Kate. Lyn waited impatiently until he'd put their coffees down and was out of earshot.

"Accidental drowning," repeated Kate. She thought back to the battered body floating in the water.

"Simon was sober. He was a very strong swimmer. Even if he had gone swimming in the reservoir, he'd have had his wits about him. He wouldn't have gone in wearing his clothes and shoes. The campsite is half a mile upriver from the power plant, and it's another half a mile upriver to where you found him. He trained most days, a hundred lengths in an Olympic-size pool. That's more than three miles. He also swam in the sea."

Kate put her cup down and sighed.

"Did the coroner rule *definitively* that he drowned?"

Lyn's face crumpled. "Yes."

"And they think the injuries on his body were caused by a boat patrolling the reservoir?"

"I just keep seeing that in my mind. His beautiful body, just in the water, being run over."

Kate wanted to reach out and take Lyn's hand, but she could see Lyn was angry and proud.

"When was Simon reported as a missing person?" asked Kate.

"Geraint phoned me the afternoon of the twenty-eighth of August and told me he couldn't find Simon. I then phoned the police, who told me Simon couldn't be listed as officially missing for the first twenty-four hours, so he officially became a missing person on the morning of the twenty-ninth."

"I found Simon's body on the afternoon of the thirtieth."

"The police *decided* Simon got up in the night, went swimming next to a hydroelectric dam, and drowned . . . He wouldn't have done that!" said Lyn, slamming her fist on the tabletop. "He knows, knew, about currents. The conditions of water. The hydroelectric dam sucks in the water from the reservoir. It's a no-swimming zone. There are signs up all around the campsite. He was due to go back into training after being off for months with an injury. He was sober! He wouldn't have risked his future."

"I'm sorry to ask, but was he depressed?"

"No. No. No. He was not depressed. He was on holiday with his best friend, for fuck's sake! They got along like a house on fire. He'd been looking forward to it all summer . . ." Lyn was now very agitated and tearful. She pulled a tissue from her sleeve and blew her nose. "I'm sorry," she said.

"No, don't be sorry. You have every right to feel . . . To feel."

"You know that feeling where everyone is dismissing you and not listening?"

"It's been the story of my life," said Kate ruefully.

Lyn's shoulders dropped, and she seemed to calm down.

"That's how I bloody feel. I understand that Simon was in the water and a boat could have run over him, but the police don't seem to be interested as to why or how he ended up in the water in the first place."

"How did you find me?" asked Kate.

"I googled you." Lyn opened the folder and took out a printout of a *National Geographic* article. It was from two years ago, and there was a photo of Kate and her research assistant, Tristan Harper, standing in front of Ashdean's gothic university building, which towered behind them like a miniature Hogwarts castle. They had been interviewed after they solved the Nine Elms copycat murder case. It had been an exciting time, and Kate had believed that she and Tristan might forge some kind of career as private investigators. "I tried to find you online, if you had an agency."

"No," said Kate, hearing the disappointment in her own voice.

"I just want to find out what happened to Simon. You have a son. You've had to protect him from all the crap slung at you over the years . . . There are loads of private detective agencies around, but you—I want you to help me. Will you?"

Kate had seen too much bad in people. The best of friends could suddenly turn on each other, she thought. A detective had to always use logic. If Simon and Geraint had been alone, the first logical conclusion was that Geraint had done it.

Lyn closed her eyes. "It's bad enough my son has been taken from me. I want to know why he was in that water in the middle of the night. I'm not the kind of woman who begs, but please." Her eyes filled up with tears. "Please. Will you help me?"

Kate thought how she would feel, if their roles were reversed and Jake had been found in the water, his body covered in cuts and bruises.

"Yes," said Kate. "I'll help you."

6

Early the next morning, Tristan Harper ran up the steps from the beach and came to a stop on the promenade, leaning over to catch his breath. The dawn was just breaking over Ashdean, the sky was now light blue, and lights were coming on in the long row of terraced houses lining the seafront.

A black Labrador loped past on the beach below and splashed into the calm sea to chase a stick. The tide was out, exposing craggy seaweed-covered rocks. The dog's owner, a tall guy in skinny jeans wearing a yellow waterproof jacket, saw Tristan in his running gear, did a double take, and smiled. Tristan smiled back, then crossed the road and let himself into the small flat he shared with his sister, Sarah.

He was handsome, with short brown hair, brown eyes, and a tall, athletic frame. He pulled off his T-shirt, revealing a washboard stomach and muscular pectorals. On his back was a beautiful eagle tattoo, the eagle shown from reverse with its wings spreading across his shoulders. On his chest was the same eagle, but seen from the front, its head down and amber eyes glowing on his breastbone. Its wingspan stretched to each shoulder. His biceps and arms were adorned with more tattoos. He went to the mirror and checked a wrap of cling film at the top of his left tricep. The film was coming away from the skin. He debated for a moment, then gently peeled it back to reveal his newest tattoo, a plain black band that was healing nicely.

"Cool," he said, admiring himself for a moment. "Not too shabby."

He showered, dressed, and walked the short journey along the seafront to the university building. He didn't get the chance to talk to Kate until the last lecture of the morning, History of Forensics. As the students were filing out of the lecture theatre and he was packing away the slide projector, she came over.

"I've got something I want to run past you. Fancy a coffee?" she said.

Over the past few weeks Tristan had noticed Kate had been withdrawn and a little distant, and it didn't look like she was sleeping much. He was pleased to see today she looked happier and well rested.

"Sure. I'll meet you there after I stash this projector back in storage," he said. "I'll have a caramel macchiato."

"Yuck," she said. "I bet you're going to put sugar in it too."

"I know I'm sweet enough, but yeah," he said with a smile.

Tristan joined Kate at the Starbucks on the ground floor a few minutes later. She was sitting at one of the tables under the long window looking out to sea. She handed him a cup.

"Thanks," he said, taking the seat opposite her. He took off the lid, and Kate watched in amusement as he added four sugars. He took a sip, nodded his approval, and got the diary from his bag. This was where he put down the details of all Kate's work commitments: when specialist lecturers came to visit, equipment hire, and when the students sat exams.

"This isn't *officially* work stuff," said Kate.

"Oh?"

Tristan listened as Kate told him about her meeting the previous night with Lyn Kendal.

"She gave me this folder. It's not much to go on," finished Kate. "She also left five thousand pounds in cash inside. She'll pay us another five thousand pounds if we find out what happened to Simon."

"That's a lot of money. Do you think it's her savings?" he asked, raising an eyebrow.

"I don't know. She seems well off."

Tristan opened the folder and took out the paperwork. It contained a cutout of the story from the local newspaper and photos of Simon Kendal. Mostly details of his swimming championships. Tristan read through the article.

LOCAL TEENAGER DROWNS IN RESERVOIR

Simon Kendal, 18, reportedly got into difficulties after trespassing into Shadow Sands reservoir, near Ashdean.

Police were called to the moorland beauty spot on Thursday. An underwater search team examined the area and later recovered the man's body.

Police have said they do not believe his death was suspicious.

Det Ch Insp Henry Ko said: "My sincerest condolences are with Simon's family at hearing this heart-wrenching news."

Mike Althorpe, leisure safety manager at the Royal Society for the Prevention of Accidents, said: "We understand the temptation to want to go swimming, especially during the hot weather. But open water sites can be very dangerous with strong currents and underwater debris that you cannot see from the bank."

"Does it seem like the local paper really wants to push the idea that Simon drowned?" asked Tristan.

"They're taking the lead from the authorities," said Kate. "But yes. They don't mention he was a champion swimmer."

Tristan looked through the photos of Simon with his diving team. He felt excited at the prospect of working on another real-life investigation, and on a practical level, the money would be very helpful. His sister was about to get married and would be moving out of the flat they shared after her wedding in December. He would be taking sole responsibility for the rent and bills when she was gone.

"We've got lots in the diary," he said. "The History of Forensics class are turning in their dissertations in two weeks, as are the 1970s American Serial Killers students. We've got the field trip to London for the Criminal Icons course, also in two weeks . . ." He wanted to add that Sarah's wedding was in six weeks, and that would create all kinds of drama, he was sure.

"I have a feeling that we're going to find it was an accident," said Kate. "If Alan Hexham did the postmortem, which I suspect he did, then I don't doubt the results."

"The friend, Geraint, could be interesting to talk to, though," said Tristan.

"Exactly," said Kate. "I've left a message with him, asking if we can talk to him on Saturday. I'm hoping he'll call me back. I'm going to see Alan Hexham at the morgue tomorrow morning. He's going to let me see the file on Simon Kendal's postmortem."

"What time?"

"He can only see me early, before nine."

"I've got to do equipment hire tomorrow morning, and I'm not great at the morgue, especially so soon after breakfast."

Kate smiled and nodded.

"Okay, I'll do that one on my own," she said.

"Count me in for Saturday; hopefully this Geraint will want to talk."

"Yes. I'm going to try and get the police report from Alan. I'd love to know what Geraint told them. It would be a good opportunity to challenge his story and see if it stands up a few months later."

7

Kate arrived at the Exeter morgue just before eight the next morning. She signed in at the small office and was shown into the examining room. Jemma, one of Alan Hexham's assistants, was working on the body of a young girl lying on one of the stainless steel mortuary tables.

"Morning, Kate," said Jemma, looking up from her work. Kate had known Alan Hexham ever since he'd come to be a guest lecturer for one of her criminology modules. He was now a regular lecturer, and he often provided cold case files for Kate's students to study.

Jemma was a junior mortician, a few years older than Tristan. She was a tall and well-built young woman—strength was essential in a mortician—and she was an expert in reconstruction. Kate stopped to look at the body of the young girl. Her face was crisscrossed in neat stitches, and Jemma was rolling up two small balls of cotton wool on the edge of the steel table. She lifted the dead girl's right eyelid, placed the cotton wool ball in the empty eye socket, then did the same with the left eye.

"She was in a head-on collision on the M6; they didn't recover her eyeballs, and most of her brain was . . . missing," said Jemma, standing back to inspect her work. "We've been working all night to put her back together. The family want to view her."

"You've done an amazing job," said Kate, peering at the young girl. She thought back to her time spent as a police officer in road traffic and all the accidents she'd seen. Motorway head-on collisions were the most horrific, and they usually meant a closed casket for the victims.

"I've packed her head with cotton wool, glued the skull back together as best I could. The rest is stitching. And she's going to look even better when our mortuary cosmetologist arrives."

"Can you give me her number?" joked Kate, seeing her tired face reflected at the end of the stainless steel table.

"I nearly asked her to do my makeup for my brother's wedding, but I was worried she'd use her work brushes on me," laughed Jemma. "Alan's in his office, at the back."

"Thanks," said Kate. She moved past a long line of refrigerator doors to Alan's small office at the end. The door was ajar, and he was sitting at his desk, surrounded by piles of paperwork and scribbling on a pad with his phone under his chin. He was a huge bear of a man with a kind face and long graying hair tied back in a ponytail.

"Great, thanks, Larry," he said, ending the call. He looked up and saw Kate. "Come in. I've only got a minute, I'm afraid. I've got to dash off."

"No problem, thanks for seeing me," said Kate.

Alan threw his phone onto the desk and stuffed the last piece of a McDonald's Egg McMuffin in his mouth and tossed the balled-up wrapper into his wastepaper basket. He took a file from a pile on his desk and opened it. Kate could see the postmortem photos of Simon Kendal on top.

"Simon Kendal," said Alan, chewing and swallowing. "He was on a camping trip with his friend by Shadow Sands reservoir. I wasn't on duty the day this lad was brought in, but another coroner was called in to do the postmortem."

"Is that normal?" asked Kate.

"It can happen. This mortuary can be commandeered for use by other police forces, for various reasons . . . Was Simon Kendal anyone special?"

"Special?"

"Child of a politician? VIP?"

"No. Just an ordinary kid. A student. It doesn't say why another coroner was brought in?"

"No. As I said, there could have been all sorts of reasons why someone else did the postmortem . . ." Alan slid his glasses up on the top of his head and peered closer as he flicked through the file. "Simon Kendal didn't have any alcohol in his bloodstream. He was healthy. No disease. Very little body fat. Incredible lung capacity."

"He was a swimmer, training for the Olympics," said Kate.

Alan's brow furrowed.

"And yet he drowned." He flicked back through the file and started to examine the postmortem photos. He stopped on a photo and peered at it very closely.

"What is it?" asked Kate.

"His right lung was punctured. See, here," he said, holding out the file and indicating a close-up photo of a puckered circular wound on Simon's rib cage.

"I was told his body was run over by a boat with an outboard motor propeller," said Kate.

"Who told you that?"

"Lyn Kendal. Simon's mother. And the police told her."

Alan examined the photo again and looked up at Kate, raising a bushy eyebrow. Then looked back at the report.

"He was a muscular lad, with well-built lats . . . Would an outboard motor propeller puncture through all that flesh in that way? *And* through the rib cage to the lung?" Alan seemed to be talking to himself more than to Kate. "Hmm. No. Not without ripping a huge rent in his side . . . An outboard motor blade is curved. This wound looks more like a sharp object penetrated the flesh. Rapidly, stabbed in, and then out again." He mimed a stabbing motion with his finger.

"Do you think the cause of death is wrong?"

"What? No, no, no," said Alan hastily. "When a postmortem is conducted, we present the facts, and then it's the police who use the information to form a theory . . ."

That's not really answering my question, thought Kate. Alan was being loyal to this unnamed colleague, not wanting to accuse one of his own.

Alan flicked through the pages of the report to a chart at the back.

"Although if this poor lad fell in the water, drowned, and was then mangled postmortem by the outboard motor of a boat, why did he lose so much blood?"

"How much blood did he lose?"

"He'd bled out, considerably. Lost half the blood volume in his body. As you know, if a person is injured and the heart is still pumping, the blood loss is greater." He closed the folder with a snap and looked troubled. "I think you should leave this with me."

Kate had been reading snatches of the report as Alan turned the pages. She'd seen two signatures on the last page: Dr. Philip Stewart and DCI Henry Ko.

Alan got up from his chair, now towering over her. He rubbed at his eyes and slid his glasses back onto his nose.

"And you say the boy's mother is questioning the cause of death?"

"Yes. She doesn't believe he drowned."

"I would rather you didn't share what I've told you until I've had the chance to look at this."

Kate nodded. "Of course."

"Right . . . Yes." Alan looked at his watch and picked up his coat. Kate could see he was troubled. He was straight down the line, honest and highly respected. He pulled on his coat and gathered up his phone and car keys. They went to leave, and Kate hesitated by the door.

"Alan. Off the record. Do you think Simon Kendal's death was an accident?"

"Off the record. And I *really mean* off the record. No. I don't think it was an accident. Now. I have to go," he said.

Kate had never seen him look so worried and pale faced. She just wished she had more power and resources to follow the clues. She missed being a police detective.

8

Tristan knocked on the door of Professor Rossi's office, and a slim young woman with long dark hair and black-rimmed glasses opened the door. She wore skinny jeans and a red sweater.

"Hi. Is Professor Rossi in today?" he asked.

"Yes. Hello," she said. She spoke with a soft Italian accent.

"Oh. Hi," said Tristan.

"You were expecting some crazy old Italian lady?"

"No . . . ," said Tristan. That was exactly what he had been expecting. Professor Magdalena Rossi was a new professor lecturing in philosophy and religion. Both her name and subject didn't match the beautiful, cool young woman in front of him. "Well, maybe. Hi. I'm Tristan Harper."

They shook hands.

"It's nice to meet you. I'm still the new girl; even after all these weeks, I haven't met everyone."

"Don't worry, I feel the same."

"How long have you been the new girl?" she said.

Tristan smiled. "I've been working here a little over two years. I've seen you around, I think. Do you have a yellow scooter?"

"Yes. A Vespa."

"You drive fast."

"Well, I am Italian," she said with a grin. She held eye contact for a beat longer than Tristan felt comfortable.

"Right. I've got your slide projector," he said, indicating it on the trolley beside him.

"Thank you, you can bring it in," she said, opening the door wide. Her small office was filled with old wooden furniture, and every inch of the walls was covered in paperwork. A small window looked out over the sea, which today was choppy and gray. Tristan wheeled the trolley inside. "Just park it there, next to my desk. I was about to make a coffee—would you like one?" She indicated a little capsule coffee machine on the bookshelf.

"No, thank you. I should get going," said Tristan. He pulled out his phone and checked to see if there was a message from Kate after her meeting with Alan.

"Are you sure? A shot of espresso won't slow you down."

Tristan was about to say no, when he noticed a map fixed to a pin board on the wall. It was of Shadow Sands reservoir and the surrounding moors. A card saying LOCAL MYTHS AND LEGENDS was pinned underneath with newspaper articles featuring famous Devon and Cornwall legends that Tristan recognized: the Beast of Bodmin Moor, King Arthur's pool, Cornish giants, the Hound of the Baskervilles. But there were also a few handwritten notes with queries: *WOLF MAN of BODMIN MOOR—find him, FOG PHANTOM—too new?*

Magdalena followed his gaze.

"Are you doing a project about the reservoir?" he asked.

"No. Why?"

"I just recognized it. I'm local," said Tristan, not wanting to go into the details of Simon Kendal's death. He stepped closer to the board.

Underneath *WOLF MAN of BODMIN MOOR—find him* were two photos of a giant paw print. The first photo showed it in situ on a muddy, tree-lined footpath. The second photo was a close-up. The paw print looked like it was from a large dog; Tristan could see the outline of the paw pads and long claws. What shocked him was the large, hairy human hand next to it for comparison; the paw print was three times the size of the hand.

"That's not my hand, by the way," said Magdalena. Tristan jumped. She was now beside him holding two steaming espresso cups. She was small and fine boned. The top of her head came up to his shoulder. Her rich black hair was neatly parted and smelled fresh, of fruit shampoo. Tristan thought she had an earthy beauty.

"Thanks," he said, taking one of the cups. "Is this for a new module?" he asked, indicating the corkboard.

"No. It's for my thesis. I'm studying the origins of urban legends. Devon and Cornwall are rich with study material. I took the photos of the paw print on a farm out near Chagford on the edge of Dartmoor. The farmer swears that one night he saw a beast-like figure, standing on two legs, ten feet tall next to a fence in one of his fields."

"What did he do?" asked Tristan, sipping at the strong and bitter coffee.

"He did what I'd do. He went inside and locked the doors. He didn't dare venture back out until the next morning. That's when he found this footprint."

"What the hell leaves a footprint like that?" asked Tristan. He reached up to touch the photo, and the arm of his sweater shifted up, showing an inch or two of the sleeve tattoo covering his forearm.

Magdalena paused for a moment, and he noticed her staring at his tattoo. It was a black-and-white block of trees, set against the night sky.

"It's probably a lion, or a lynx, or some crossbreed," she said. "You must have heard all the theories of rich Victorians bringing back baby lions and tigers from voyages abroad and then turning them out into the wild when they got big and dangerous."

"Yes."

"That's the logical conclusion."

Tristan downed the rest of his espresso. The huge paw print made him shudder.

"What's the Fog Phantom?" he asked, seeing a series of tiny black-and-white photos from a stretch of empty road surrounded by trees. Pockets of fog clung to the depressions in the tarmac as the road banked down and then vanished around a bend.

"That's a work in progress. I had a chance conversation with a local girl in the pub. She told me a story about young people going missing on a stretch of the A1328, the road which runs close by to the Shadow Sands reservoir. Every time there's thick fog . . ."

"Really? I haven't heard of that," said Tristan.

"I think she's—what do you say in English?—an unreliable narrator . . . probably a better idea to pitch as a movie than to put in my thesis."

"Like that movie *Candyman*. You know, you say his name five times into the mirror and he appears behind you with a hook."

"That's based on a story by Clive Barker, a very good one."

Magdalena took a sip of her coffee, and they were silent. Tristan felt the urge to tell her of the death of Simon Kendal, but he didn't. She smiled and reached over, sliding up the sleeve of his sweater to reveal his forearm. "I like your tattoo," she said, tracing her fingers over his skin. "Sometimes they can look tacky, but this is real artwork."

"Thanks. I have a great guy I go to, in Exeter . . ." He felt himself blushing, and goose pimples appeared on his skin. Magdalena smiled and gently pulled his sleeve back down.

"Are you a postgraduate?"

"No," said Tristan, feeling embarrassed. "I assist Kate, Professor Marshall. And I seem to be the only one who knows how to mend these old slide projectors."

"I've heard about your adventures with Professor Marshall," she said, not breaking eye contact. She had beautiful brown eyes and full lips.

"There's that, too, yes, but officially I'm on the payroll, not an academic or nothing, anything."

She smiled.

"How was your espresso?"

He looked down at the cup.

"Um . . ." He laughed. "I'm more of a Starbucks kind of guy."

Magdalena laughed.

"You're talking to an Italian. That's not coffee. What's your usual drink in Starbucks?"

"Caramel macchiato," he said with a grimacing grin.

"Oh my Lord."

"You haven't been here long, and most people here end up having meetings in the Starbucks downstairs. I'm sure you'll be converted."

"Perhaps we should get some Starbucks sometime?" she said, cocking her head and looking up at him from under her thick fringe of hair. "You could convert me."

"Oh," he said, realizing she was flirting.

"Yes, Tristan. I'm asking you out . . . Is that something you'd be interested in?" Her confidence had taken him aback, and he didn't know what to say. "Can I have your number?"

"My number?"

"Yes. You can probably tell. I'm not the kind of girl who sits waiting by the phone."

"Of course."

He put his espresso cup down on her desk as she handed him a ballpoint pen and a small notebook open to a blank page. He scribbled down his phone number. His phone pinged, and he took it out of his pocket. He saw it was a message from Kate.

"I better go—that's Professor Marshall," he said.

"I'll call you." She smiled.

"Great," he said. "And thanks for the coffee."

He waited until he was outside Magdalena's office, and then he looked at the text:

GERAINT JONES HAS AGREED

TO MEET US TOMORROW AT 11 AM

Tristan hurried off to call Kate, and his meeting with Magdalena went to the back of his mind.

9

Geraint had asked to meet them at a local snooker club close to his student halls on the outskirts of Exeter town center.

Kate and Tristan found it at the end of a run-down parade of shops, and they parked outside. A tall, stocky lad with shoulder-length strawberry blond hair was waiting for them under a faded green awning that read **POT BLACK SNOOKER CLUB.** He wore black Doc Martens boots, grubby jeans, and a denim jacket with an equally grubby sheepskin lining. He had a pleasant, round face and was trying to grow a beard, but all he had was a fluff of downy hair on his chin.

"Do you play snooker?" Geraint asked Tristan as he flashed a membership card at the front desk and signed them into the club.

"No," said Tristan.

"I don't either," said Geraint in a low voice. "I come here cos you can have a cigarette with your pint." He had a soft, lilting Welsh accent, and his eyes were a little glazed. Kate wondered whether he had already been drinking. He led them through a chipped, grimy door, and they emerged into a long, low room with dark-green walls. The rows of snooker tables were empty, apart from two elderly gents playing a game at one by the bar. The snooker tables each had a large lamp above with a red velvet fringed shade. They cast a dim light over the room, catching the haze of cigarette smoke. "What can I get you to drink?"

"I'll have a pint of Foster's," said Tristan.

"Do they have cappuccino at the bar?" asked Kate, seeing this was a working men's club.

"They're more likely to have Al Pacino at the bar," deadpanned Geraint.

"Black coffee, then," she said, warming to him.

"Sit yourselves down. I'll be over," he said.

Kate and Tristan found a table farthest from the bar, under a wall display of polished trophies in glass cabinets.

"How come you can smoke in here?" asked Tristan when they sat down.

"It's a members' club. You can still smoke in members' clubs," said Kate, getting out her pack of Marlboro Lights. It was quite peaceful and chilled, with just the murmured chatter of the elderly men and the click-clack of the snooker balls.

Geraint came back with their drinks and sat opposite them both, keeping his coat on. He downed half his pint in one go and then lit up a cigarette.

"I first want to say, sorry about Simon," said Kate. Tristan nodded.

"Evil-Lyn's put you up to this, has she? Digging around?" he said, exhaling and fixing Kate with a stare.

"She's not put us up to anything. She's concerned with the circumstances of Simon's death."

"You know that's what Si called her. Evil-Lyn. Like in the cartoon *He-Man*." He smiled for a moment and then wiped a tear from one of his eyes. "Fuck it." He downed the rest of his pint and raised his glass at the bar.

"Simon didn't get on with his mum?" asked Kate.

"No. The coroner and the police ruled it was an accident. Does Lyn think she knows more? She wasn't there. She just doesn't like me and wants to make trouble for me."

"What do you think happened to Simon?"

"I think Evil-Lyn killed him . . . Not directly, but she put so much pressure on him with the swimming. She was a pushy mother, to say the least. She spent a fortune hiring a trainer. A right bastard, he was; he drove Si half-mad. It should have been Lyn training for the Olympics. She wanted it more than Si."

"Lyn said that Simon got injured last year, and he didn't make the Olympic team," said Tristan.

"He hurt his foot last Christmas, something stupid, fell off the pavement outside a pub."

"Was he drunk?"

Geraint nodded and stubbed out his cigarette in the ashtray.

"Drunk with you?" asked Kate.

Geraint smiled and nodded again. He lit up another cigarette.

"Which would explain why she doesn't like me," he said, exhaling smoke up at the ceiling. "She thought I was a bad influence, but it was the first time in months that Si had been out on the lash, and even then, he only had a pint. He was a lightweight. It was a silly accident. Si tripped, landed on the curb in a load of broken glass. There was blood everywhere. I helped him to the A&E. They patched him up and x-rayed him. He'd chipped a bone in his foot, and it put him out of action. He couldn't train for six weeks, which meant he lost condition. He was a dead cert for competing in the London Olympics. Lyn had a sponsor lined up, but come June, he just failed to qualify for Team GB by a matter of seconds."

"Jeez. That must have been tough," said Tristan. Geraint nodded.

"Not only did his dream of being on the Olympic team go down the shitter, Evil-Lyn was on the warpath. She'd mortgaged the house to pay for his training over the past couple of years. If Si had qualified, a sponsor would have taken over those costs and paid off her loan . . . She demonized Si after that. She was pushing him to train harder and always going on about how he'd missed his biggest opportunity. That's enough to make anyone suicidal."

"Was Simon suicidal?" asked Kate.

"I don't know, but he wasn't in a good state of mind, started likening the pool where he trained to a concrete hole full of chlorine."

"What made you pick the campsite by the reservoir?"

Geraint smiled ruefully.

"We were meant to go camping in the Gower, in West Wales. It's gorgeous there for surfing and camping, but Evil-Lyn changed her mind at the last minute and told Si he could only have two days off from training. He trains, trained, here in Exeter. Shadow Sands is obviously a lot closer than the Gower. And there're a couple places nearby. Benson's Quarry is good for swimming and diving. Loads of fit birds, girls hang out there . . . You been there, mate?" he added to Tristan.

"No," said Tristan.

"You should check it out, especially on a hot day. Lots of hot girls in just their bikini bottoms . . ." The barman appeared with a fresh lager for Geraint. "Thanks, mate," he said, downing half of it in one gulp and lighting another cigarette. Kate exchanged a glance with Tristan, who was still sipping at his first pint.

"Was the Shadow Sands campsite empty when you and Simon arrived?" asked Kate.

"Yeah. The weather was shit. And so is the campsite. It's beside the reservoir, but it has a huge fence with razor wire blocking off the water. It's like something out of Auschwitz. And the toilets were half-boarded-up and caked with shit. There was stuff left over from druggies. We got to the campsite about eight, eight thirty in the evening. We'd been to Dawlish Beach nearby, surfing, and we ended up forking out for a cab to the campsite. We were hungry, and it was getting dark when we arrived . . . I don't know why we didn't just get a youth hostel. It was one of those holidays where you plan something, then stuff changes, and you try to keep the whole idea of a camping holiday alive . . ." He took another gulp of his pint. "But you end up in a shithole like that."

"Were you drinking that night?" asked Kate.

"No. We forgot to get the booze in. And all we had for dinner was cold baked beans, right out the tin, and Mars bars. It turned into a gloomy night. I wish we'd had booze. Si went into a dark mood."

"How did you know his mood was dark?" asked Tristan.

"He was withdrawn. August had been tough for him. You couldn't move for hearing about the Olympics, could you? We'd had a great day, though. We met some girls on the beach. One swapped numbers with Si. She had a fat friend for me," he added with a grin. "We were going to meet them the next day to go diving at Benson's Quarry. There was a group of them going there."

"Did you see any other campers or walkers that night?" asked Kate.

Geraint shook his head.

"It was eerie. Creepy. The roar from the power plant seems to block out all other noise. It's not loud, but it's constant, and gets into your head."

"Did you see any boats on the reservoir?"

"No. I just wanted to bed down, sleep, wake up, and get the hell out the next morning. We pitched the tent, and I must have fallen asleep around nine or ten, I can't remember. Si kept saying his body was aching and he felt rough. He only had a couple of days off before he had to go back to training. I don't think he was eating properly. I didn't see him eat the whole day on the beach, and he hardly touched any of the beans or chocolate. I woke up around seven the next morning, and Si wasn't there. His sleeping bag was empty."

"What did you do?"

"Nothing at first. I thought he'd gone for a piss or a number two. I went outside and made some tea on the little gas stove and waited. Then I phoned him a few times, but his phone was off. That's when I . . ." He hesitated.

"What?" asked Kate.

"I searched through his bag for his mobile. It wasn't there, but I found a bottle of pills. Citalopram. They're antidepressants. I was shocked, cos I always thought Si was, you know, dealing with stuff."

"Do you think Lyn knew he was on antidepressants?" asked Kate. Geraint shrugged.

"I googled citalopram. It's strong stuff, and there're side effects, which would affect his performance swimming. I don't know if Lyn would have wanted him to be taking them."

"What did you do after you found the pills in his bag?" asked Tristan.

"I went around the site, checked the woods, the horrible toilets again."

"And there was nothing suspicious alongside the fence, by the edge of the reservoir?" asked Kate.

"Suspicious, like what?"

"Was there any blood on the grass or the fence? I've seen how much damage a razor wire fence can do to someone if they try and climb it."

"I walked the fence alongside the water for quite a way in both directions; in fact, in one direction, I went through the trees and all the way along to the power station. There was no holes in the fence, nothing," said Geraint.

"When did you raise the alarm that Simon was missing?" asked Kate.

"Just after lunch. I called Evil-Lyn. She was worried, told me to keep in touch. I had to charge up my phone, so I walked back to the power plant and went into the visitors' center and had a coffee."

"What's in the visitors' center?"

"It's an art gallery. It's on the edge of the reservoir. You can have a coffee looking out. It was really surreal to be there and drinking coffee, knowing Si had gone off somewhere. I was still there later in the afternoon about five o'clock when Lyn rang me back to say she'd called the police and reported Si missing. I still didn't want to believe it. I hoped that he'd gone off with that bird we'd met the day before . . ." Geraint swirled the last of his pint in the glass and downed it. His eyes were wet with tears. He rubbed them away. Kate noticed a red stain on the sheepskin sleeve of his jacket.

"Did you hurt yourself?" she asked.

"What? This?" he said, peering at the faded stain on his sleeve. "No. This is old, from that night Si injured himself and cut his ankle. I helped him to A&E." He stared at the bloodstain for a moment longer, then rolled up his sleeve, tucking the stained sheepskin inside.

Tristan mouthed if he should get him another pint, but Kate shook her head. Geraint was already slurring his words, and they needed to ask more questions.

"So. Lyn called the police. What did you do?"

"I went back to the campsite, late afternoon, packed up our stuff, and I got a cab back to my student halls. The next afternoon, the police rang my mobile. I thought they'd found Si, but they asked me to come down to the station and make a statement about him being officially missing, which I did. I was there for seven hours. They were hard on me, asking the same shit over and over, trying to catch me out. Then they let me go in the evening."

"Did they question you with a solicitor? Or was it more informal and you left a statement?" asked Kate.

"They kept saying I was free to go at any time, but . . . I've got a criminal record. I went to juvenile detention when I was fourteen. I got a year for glassing this arsehole who attacked me in a pub. I also got into a bit of bother a couple of years back in a club; again, it was self-defense." He shrugged. "Just cos I stick up for myself when drunk arseholes come at me, doesn't mean I'd kill my best mate for no reason."

"What happened after you left the police station?" asked Kate.

"I had a couple of phone calls from Evil-Lyn. Asking questions. She wanted Si's stuff back, his bag. The second time she phoned, she was drunk . . . she was asking me all this stuff. Were me and Simon gay?

Were we having sex with each other . . . That's a no, by the way. The third time she phoned, she was proper roaring drunk and screamed at me that I killed him cos I was jealous, and I had a history of violence."

"And what did you say?" asked Tristan.

"I stuck up for myself. I know her son was missing, but she was just vile on the phone . . . I don't know if she's got many friends. Si is—was—an only child. His dad's dead. They don't have much other family. After the third call I switched my phone off. There were loads more missed calls from her when I switched it back on the next morning. She said she'd called the police and told them to question me again . . . She shook me up, she was so insistent and confident."

"Did the police speak to you again?" asked Kate.

"I got a knock at the door that evening. It was the police. I thought they'd come to arrest me, but they told me Simon's body had been found in the reservoir and he'd drowned. They said they'd officially ruled it was an accident."

Geraint's bottom lip began to tremble, and he looked away.

"Can you remember when exactly this was?" asked Kate.

Geraint turned back and wiped his eyes. "Must have been four or five days later."

"Can you be sure? The exact date?"

"I went to his funeral on the fourteenth of September, which was exactly two weeks after the police came around, so that would make it . . . the thirty-first of August."

How could the police rule so fast on accidental drowning? thought Kate. If only she'd found Simon's body the day before.

"Can you remember what time of day the police came over on the thirty-first?" she asked.

"Afternoon. Just after lunch, around two," said Geraint. "They were only there a few minutes, told me on the doorstep. Si was dead, it was an accidental drowning, and that I was no longer under any suspicion."

"They came to the conclusion that fast?" said Tristan, echoing Kate's thoughts.

Geraint shrugged.

"I don't trust the police. Never have and never will. But if they say I'm innocent, I'm not going to argue . . . Although how could a strong swimmer like Simon drown?"

10

"It doesn't add up," said Kate when they were in the car going back to Ashdean. "I found Simon's body on Thursday, the thirtieth of August, late in the afternoon. I called the police, and they arrived pretty quickly, but the dive team couldn't have brought up his body until later that evening. Then a doctor was brought in to do the postmortem on Simon's body the next morning . . ."

"The morning of the thirty-first of August," said Tristan.

"Yes. A postmortem takes time, a few hours. Then reports have to be written. The reports go back to the police officer assigned to the case. More decisions have to be made. If the postmortem was done at nine a.m., how could the police be knocking on Geraint's door within five hours to tell him that Simon's death was an accident and that there will be nothing further pursued?"

"What if Geraint was lying to us?" said Tristan. "And the police still think he's a person of interest?"

"No. When I went to see Alan Hexham yesterday, the report in the file said it was accidental drowning. Alan was concerned. He didn't do the postmortem. Another doctor was brought in."

"Something fishy's going on," said Tristan. The road from Exeter to Ashdean followed the coastline, winding farther inland through empty ploughed fields and bare trees where a low mist was hung in the air. Kate's phone rang, and she picked it up with her free hand.

"Speak of the devil. That's Alan Hexham."

"Shall I put it on speaker?" asked Tristan. Kate nodded and handed him the phone.

"Hello, Kate?" boomed Alan through the speakerphone.

"Hi, Alan. I'm here with Tristan," she said.

"Oh. Hello, hello. Look. I'm just calling you about the Simon Kendal postmortem. I wanted to say thank you."

"What for?" asked Kate.

"You alerted me to some worrying inaccuracies in the case file. Simon Kendal was camping with his friend, and it made me think. Tent pegs."

"Tent pegs?" repeated Kate.

"Yes. The picture I showed you. That puncture mark on Simon's rib cage. It had been mistakenly identified as being caused by an outboard motorboat propeller, but I think it was caused by the beveled edge on a sharp object. A metal tent peg would fit that description as a potential weapon . . ." Kate and Tristan exchanged a glance. Alan went on, "I gave this information to DCI Henry Ko, the SIO on the case."

"Do you know why it was ruled so quickly as accidental drowning?" asked Kate. "We've been putting together a timeline . . ."

"Kate. I'm sorry I can't comment on the cause of death right now."

Tristan glanced across at Kate. Alan sounded very uncomfortable.

"Okay. Alan, the only person camping with Simon was his friend Geraint. Are the police now saying Simon's death is suspicious?"

There was a long pause.

"I can't comment on that either."

"So, Geraint is now a suspect?"

"Kate. I'm calling you as a courtesy. I can't comment anymore, and I'm not party to what the police decide . . . Now, I really must go now," he said and hung up the phone.

Kate saw a lay-by up ahead and pulled into it. It was next to a large, desolate-looking field that had been freshly ploughed for the winter. They were silent for a moment.

"Did we just read Geraint completely wrong?" asked Kate.

"If we did, he's a bloody good actor," said Tristan. "With such control."

"No, if he was controlled, he wouldn't be walking around with Simon's blood on his jacket and then be so calm when we asked him about it," said Kate. "And there's the whole question of how Simon got into the water. Was Geraint with him? The campsite is fenced off from the reservoir. Did they walk a couple of miles around to the other side of the reservoir? Did Simon climb the razor wire? Did they both climb it? I remember Simon's hands. There weren't any cuts or bruises on his skin. Geraint was unscathed too. It doesn't add up."

"Do we know for sure they even went to the campsite in the first place?" said Tristan. "We're just taking Geraint's word for it."

"Exactly. And why didn't I think of tent pegs? It's so bloody obvious as a murder weapon!" Kate thumped the steering wheel. The horn blared out over the field, scaring a group of crows, who took off into the sky cawing.

"Did Alan say anything when you saw him? If the police found a tent peg at the campsite?"

"No, he didn't. And even if they did find a tent peg, I doubt there would be much forensic evidence left on it after so many weeks out in the elements."

"It still doesn't answer the question: Why were the coroner and the police so quick to rule Simon's death as an accident?" said Tristan.

Geraint stayed at Pot Black Snooker Club for another hour, and he sank a few more pints. When he left, the cold outside hit him, and he felt unsteady on his feet as he walked home. He had a bedsit in a block of flats a mile from the snooker club. The road where he lived was a mix of scruffy terraced houses and two-story postwar concrete blocks of flats. As he drew close to home, it started to rain, and he hitched up his jacket collar so it covered his head. He didn't see the police cars outside his building until he rounded the bins on the corner of the small car park out front.

There were three police cars, and six police officers grouped under the concrete awning over the main entrance. The lights were on in the hallway, and he could see one of his neighbors, an elderly lady who lived at the end of his floor, talking to the police. She looked up and saw him.

"There. That's him," she said, indicating him with her unlit cigarette. Geraint didn't know why he made a run for it. He could have stood his ground. The booze was coursing through his veins, and the blue flashing lights still turning on top of the squad cars put him in a panic.

"Stop! You! Stop where you are!" shouted one of the police officers, but they needn't have bothered. Geraint lost his balance on the corner by the bins and tumbled onto a wet pile of black sacks, feeling something large inside one of the sacks push into his belly. The police officers piled on him like a rugby scrum before he could catch his breath, pinning his hands behind his back, slapping cold cuffs on his wrists, and reading him his rights. As they pulled him up to his feet, the ground seemed to give a horrible lurch, and he saw stars, then threw up.

"Jesus Christ, what a state," said a voice. A slim Asian officer got out from one of the police cars and came over to them. He was in plain clothes: skinny jeans, a white polo shirt, and a bright-yellow Ralph Lauren–branded waterproof jacket. Geraint thought he looked dressed up and ready for a night out.

"It's cos you all piled on top of me," said Geraint. He coughed and heaved again, spitting on the ground, his hands still cuffed behind his back.

The Asian officer came close and looked him in the eye, challenging him. Geraint thought he was going to punch him; then he took out his police ID card.

"I'm Detective Chief Inspector Henry Ko. Geraint Jones, I'm arresting you for the murder of Simon Kendal . . ."

"What the fuck?" started Geraint, hearing the shock in his own voice.

"You do not have to say anything, but anything you do say can be used as evidence in a court of law," said Ko.

"I want a solicitor," he said.

"You'll get one . . . Process him. But don't put him in my car," said Ko. The police officers led him away, and he was shoved into the nearest police car.

11

Kate dropped Tristan back at his flat, and they agreed to meet the next day and keep in touch if there was any more news about Geraint.

Kate lived in a large, old two-story house at the end of a road running along the cliff edge. It was a few miles outside Ashdean, in a small hamlet called Thurlow Bay.

Next to Kate's house was a surf shop, which served the campsite nearby in the summer. It was run by Myra, her friend and her sponsor in AA.

Kate's house was comfy and lived-in—*grandma-ish,* Jake called it. The furniture in the living room was chintzy, and the walls were covered in bookcases stuffed with academic books and novels. An old piano sat against one wall. The house came with her job as lecturer at Ashdean, and she'd been renting it for eight years. Her favorite part was the living room and the row of windows that looked over the cliff top out to sea. The kitchen was slightly more modern than the rest of the house, with blond wood countertops and cupboards painted white.

Kate unpacked her shopping in the kitchen, then opened the fridge. She kept a jug of iced tea on the top shelf. She took out a crystal tumbler, filled it half with ice, and topped it up with the sweet iced tea. Then she sliced a lemon, adding a sliver to the top of the ice. Preparing her iced tea in this way had the same ceremony as making a cocktail, without the alcohol. Alcoholics Anonymous frowned on any sort of crutch or replacement, but Kate found this worked for her. It helped to keep her sober.

She took a long drink of the cool sweet tea and pulled out her phone. Should she call Lyn? It was coming up to five p.m. The issue of the tent pegs as a potential murder weapon came back to her again. If Geraint had stabbed and killed Simon with a tent peg, where was it now? She thought of the reservoir and the day she and Jake had gone diving. It had seemed bottomless, an endless darkness beyond her lamp.

She sent Jake a quick text message, asking if they were still Skyping later. She waited a few minutes, and when there was no reply, she opened the fridge again and topped up her glass.

What she wouldn't give for a whiskey. A Jack Daniel's and Coke. The smoky depth of the whiskey flavor, mixed with the sweetness of the cold, fizzy Coke.

She took a sip from the freshly filled glass.

Nope, it wasn't the same. The problem with sobriety was that once you had it, there was always that niggling feeling that you could cope with a little drink now and again.

She sat down at the table and lit up a cigarette. Did she buy Geraint's whole melancholic Welsh rogue act? Was it an act? She wished she could be at a desk, down at the station with HOLMES, the police database, at her fingertips. With a few keystrokes she'd be able to find out whether the police knew the whereabouts of the camping gear and whether they'd seized it as evidence.

There was a knock on the back door, and it opened. The roar of the sea below the cliff grew louder, and the wind blew through the kitchen, causing the notes and pictures stuck to the fridge to flap and sway.

"I saw your light was on," said Myra. She was in her sixties with wrinkled olive skin and bleached blonde hair that was short and scraped back. She came into the kitchen, closing the door behind her. She slipped off her welly boots and put them on the piece of newspaper Kate kept by the door. "I can see you're on the iced tea," she said, taking off her waxed jacket and hanging it over a chair. She was dressed typically Myra-style in old, baggy jeans and a Def Leppard T-shirt. Her big toe was showing through a hole in the fluffy pink sock on her left foot. The dark-blue sock on the right foot was less threadbare.

"I could murder a Jack and Coke. Really, really murder one," said Kate.

"I could double homicide a Newcastle Brown Ale with a shot of Teacher's," said Myra, going to the kettle and switching it on. "And I'm holding twenty-six years' sobriety in my hand."

Kate put her head forward on the table. Myra came over and patted her on the back.

"You know the score. Hunker down. Grit your teeth. Imagine you're having really great sex," she said.

"I hate it."

"Really great sex?"

"No, not that that's happened for a while. The cravings."

"Grit, grit, grit those teeth, love, and grit some more," she said, rubbing Kate on the back. "I'll make us a cuppa, and let's get high on chocolate Hobnobs. Talk to me. What's caused this?" asked Myra, filling the kettle and then taking down the teapot from the cupboard.

"It's that lad who died, Simon . . . The police now think his best friend killed him."

"What do you think?"

"I think it's possible, but it's a bit too convenient."

"Convenient for who?"

"That's the big question."

12

When Tristan arrived back at the flat, he heard his sister, Sarah, in the front room talking to her fiancé, Gary. He'd hoped to have the flat to himself and a bit of peace and quiet to think after the meeting with Geraint.

The hall led into a small living room. Every inch, including the furniture, was crammed with boxes, piled high, of duty-free alcohol.

Sarah and Gary were sitting at the dining table in the corner, working on the seating plan for their wedding. The TV was on in the background.

"Hey, Tris. Do you mind if my friend Georgina from work sits at the top table next to you?" asked Sarah, looking up from the plan.

"That's cool," said Tristan. He took his phone and wallet from his pocket and put them in the bowl on the mantelpiece.

"Hi, how's it going?" he said to Gary.

"Can't grumble. I get to spend the rest of my life with this one," said Gary, swooping in for a kiss with Sarah. She batted him away, scribbling on the seating plan with a pencil.

"Right. I'll pencil in Georgina. Just in case," she said. Tristan ducked into the small kitchen and grabbed a can of Coke from the fridge.

"Just in case what?" he said, coming back into the living room.

"In case, I don't know, you decide to invite someone," said Sarah, sitting back, retying her ponytail, and allowing Gary to plant a kiss on her cheek.

"What about Kate?"

"I'm not having that woman come as a glorified seat filler," snapped Sarah.

"Kate won't be a glorified seat filler. She's my boss, and my friend."

"Tristan. This wedding is costing twenty-seven fifty, plus VAT, per plate," said Sarah, tapping her pencil on the seating plan. "We're being very generous and having a free bar," she added, indicating the boxes piled up around the room.

"Kate doesn't drink," said Tristan.

"No, but she'll pull focus . . . Darren from work is obsessed with true crime books, *and* people might think you're her toy boy."

"I'm not her toy boy."

"I don't want to spend the whole reception telling people that. I want them to admire me in my dress, which isn't cheap, either, and it's not the kind of thing I can wear twice."

Gary looked at Tristan and raised his eyebrows awkwardly. He was forty, fifteen years older than Sarah. When Sarah first met Gary, his hair had been going gray, but he now sported dark hair and had taken to wearing a shoe with a slightly thicker heel. Gary was a head shorter than Sarah.

"I'm going to have a shower," said Tristan.

"You'll need to turn on the immersion heater," Sarah shouted after him as he went upstairs. Tristan heard Gary murmuring for her to calm down.

"No, Gary. It's my wedding, and I'm not going to compromise!"

When Tristan came back downstairs twenty minutes later, Sarah and Gary had cleared the wedding plan away and were sitting on the sofa watching TV. They looked at him expectantly. Sarah was grinning.

"What?" said Tristan, squeezing past the boxes to the kitchen to get himself something to eat.

"Your phone rang when you were in the shower," said Sarah.

"Was it Kate?" he asked, hoping she had some more news.

Sarah's face dropped briefly.

"No. It wasn't Kate. I didn't recognize the number, so I picked up. I thought it might be something important . . . It was *Magdalena*."

"Oh. Right," said Tristan, remembering she'd said she'd call.

"She sounds very Italian."

"She *is* Italian."

"She wants to know if you can call her back about having a coffee," said Sarah, now almost ecstatic with glee.

"Okay, thanks."

"Who is she? And where did you meet? Is it serious? Is she attractive? She sounded attractive, didn't she, Gary?"

"I didn't really hear, cos you were on the phone to her, not me," said Gary.

Sarah shot him a look.

"Trust me, Gary. She *sounded* attractive, and Tristan is also attractive. I can say that, as his sister, so I'd expect him to attract someone who is equally attractive."

Gary grinned.

"Thank you," he said.

"What?"

"Well, ergo, you are attractive, so it must make *me* attractive . . ."

Sarah ignored him and turned back to Tristan.

"Tell us about Magdalena."

"She's a professor from work who asked for my number," said Tristan.

"A professor! Ring her back," said Sarah, holding out Tristan's phone.

"Can I finish my tea?" he said, annoyed that Sarah was sticking her nose in. He wanted to go and have a quiet coffee with Magdalena and decide how he felt.

"Speaking as a woman, I don't like it when men play games. Gary never played games with me, did you, Gary?" Gary opened his mouth to say something, but she was scrolling through Tristan's phone. "I told her you'd ring back. Here. It's already ringing."

Tristan snatched his phone and ended the call.

"Jesus! Back off, Sarah."

He left the room, slipped on his shoes and grabbed his coat from the hallway, then went out the front door, closing it behind him. He huddled under the porch. It was now cold and dark on the seafront, and the wind was blowing off the sea. He dialed her number, cupping his hand over the phone. Magdalena picked up after a few rings.

"Hello, thank you for calling back," she said. "Does your sister always answer your phone so *thoroughly*?"

"Sorry about that. I was in the shower," he said.

There was a pause. He was about to ask her about the Shadow Sands reservoir when she said, "I know I suggested Starbucks, but would you like to go to the cinema? I'm a real David Lynch fan. They're showing *Eraserhead* at the Commodore on Sunday evening."

"Yes, that would be great," said Tristan.

"Text me your address, and I'll pick you up at seven thirty," said Magdalena, and she hung up. He stared at his phone for a moment, feeling unsure. It was now an official date.

He crossed the road and went down the steps to the seafront. There was something very lonely about being around people who didn't have to hide their emotions. Sarah and Gary drove him crazy, but he envied the way they didn't censor themselves. He walked along the dark beach, hearing the waves hit the shingle, enjoying being lost in the darkness, out of the reach of the streetlights along the promenade.

Just as he reached the other end of the beach, his phone rang, making him jump. It was Kate.

"Tris, are you at home?" she said.

"No. Why?"

"The local ITV News has just started. They're trailing a headline about Geraint being arrested for the murder of Simon Kendal."

Tristan stayed on the phone and hurried to the greasy spoon café at the end of the seafront, where they always had the TV on. The café was almost empty. He ordered a cup of tea and a bacon sandwich and asked the waiter to change the channel to ITV News.

He watched as footage was played of Geraint being taken, handcuffed, out of a police car and into Exeter police station. They showed a picture of Simon Kendal at one of his swimming competitions.

"Police have arrested twenty-year-old Geraint Jones in connection with Simon Kendal's murder and have seized property which they believe is connected to his murder." At this point the officers were shown emerging from the front door of a block of flats with camping gear, and there was a lingering close-up of tent pegs wrapped in a clear plastic evidence bag. "And they have recovered a jacket which they believe contains a trace of the victim's blood. Simon Kendal and Geraint Jones were camping at the Shadow Sands campsite on the night of August twenty-seventh, when Simon Kendal went missing. His body was later found in the Shadow Sands reservoir."

The report showed some stock footage of the empty campsite and the reservoir from the point of view of the power plant. The news concluded with a reporter outside Exeter police station, reading out a number the public could call to give information.

"They pulled that together quickly," said Tristan.

"Yes, they did," said Kate on the other end of the phone. "Whoever arrested him wanted to put lots of info out into the public domain."

"It looks pretty damning," said Tristan. His bacon sandwich arrived, but suddenly he didn't feel hungry. "Tent pegs wrapped in plastic and paraded past the TV camera. Do you think they've got his coat with Simon's blood on the sleeve?"

"We should assume so if the police briefed the media about a blood sample on Geraint's clothing," said Kate.

"How does it work with the police? I thought they had to keep details of a case confidential."

"This is a managed leak. The police are using the press to set the narrative."

"Do murder cases need a narrative? I thought it was about facts," said Tristan.

"It should be, but there's something odd going on. They quickly ruled Simon's death an accident, and when I got Alan Hexham to look over the postmortem report and he saw something fishy, things changed, and it's in the press as a murder investigation . . . They made sure the news camera got pictures of the tent pegs, the potential murder weapon. I'm sure they're hoping that someone as poor as Geraint won't be able to afford decent legal representation . . ."

"If the tent pegs have been sitting in Geraint's flat, wrapped up in plastic . . ."

"Then any forensic material would have been preserved, unless they've been cleaned," said Kate.

"I'm sure Lyn will be happy. They've changed the cause of death from accidental to homicide, I presume. That's what she wanted," said Tristan.

"I know. But I don't want us to take her money. I don't think anything has been solved. It's just opened up more questions," said Kate.

After Tristan ended the call, he stared at his face reflected in the window of the café. He thought of how lucky he was in comparison to Geraint. It put his problems into perspective. What would it be like to be suspected of murder?

It made him shudder.

13

On Sunday morning Kate got up early, pulled on her swimming costume, and left the house through the kitchen door, working her way down the cliff for her early-morning swim. It was a crisp morning, and the sun glinted golden off a bank of low clouds, scattering diamonds across the water.

She'd taken up sea swimming after reading that it could combat depression. It had taken courage to keep swimming all year round, but the cold water was addictive. The positive feeling when she emerged after a swim stayed with her most of the day.

She waded into the rolling surf and dove headfirst into a breaking wave. The cold water woke her up, and she swam out for a few minutes, then stopped and floated on the surface, enjoying the rolling motion of the waves and feeling her hair zing at the roots as it shifted and fanned out in the water. With her ears submerged, she listened to the strange clicks and noises under the water, the soft echo of the pull of the surf on the rocks.

Kate felt such freedom in the sea, and it made her think of Simon Kendal. When had he first started swimming? Had he felt this same freedom? The joy of just being in the water on his own terms, to swim, to stop and float? Geraint had told them that Simon grew to hate his early-morning training sessions and the feeling of being trapped in the pool—what did he call it?—*a concrete hole full of chlorine.*

Kate had never heard of a swimming pool framed in that way by an athlete. She felt disturbed by the case—not only Simon's death but Geraint being the prime suspect. He'd demonstrated such fondness and brotherly love for Simon. What would Geraint gain from killing him? Violence manifested itself in many ways. When violence came with an uncontrolled flash of rage, it was messy and unplanned. Like Geraint's fights in pubs and bars, when he was defending himself. If Simon's body had been found stabbed repeatedly at the campsite, or dumped in the woods, Kate would have been more inclined to believe Geraint was the perpetrator. But how had Simon ended up in the middle of the water, so far from the campsite? If Geraint had stabbed him with a tent peg, where was the trail of blood to the water? There wasn't a clear path from the campsite to the water; it was blocked by a high fence topped with razor wire. How had Simon climbed the fence with a stab wound, and why didn't he have the cuts and lacerations associated with razor wire?

When Kate came back up to the house, her phone was ringing, and she hurried to pick it up, still dressed in her towel. It was Lyn Kendal.

"Kate. Thank you," she said excitedly. "I didn't expect a result so quickly. I'm really impressed."

"They've arrested Geraint. They have ninety-six hours to formally charge him," said Kate.

"They've charged him. I just heard."

"Did the police call you?"

"Yeah. A policeman, Henry Ko, phoned me up . . . Did you know that bastard Geraint is on probation for attacking a bloke in a club?" Kate perched on the edge of the sofa, still wrapped in her towel. She felt her heart plummet in her chest. Lyn went on. "It was an unprovoked attack. This bloke had started seeing Geraint's ex-girlfriend. Did you know?"

"No."

"Nor did I . . . Simon never said anything. Who knows what Geraint is capable of? It always worried me that Simon could get involved . . . with the wrong sort." Lyn started to sob. Kate tried to pull her thoughts together.

"Lyn. There's so much of this case that doesn't add up."

"Henry said that you raised some kind of issue about Simon's post-mortem, and that's what led them to the new evidence, the, er, the tent peg being a murder weapon . . ." She started to cry again.

"Yes. Did you tell Henry Ko that you'd asked me to look into the case?"

"No. I didn't."

"Did Henry Ko give you any other information? Have they been able to prove a tent peg is the murder weapon?"

"He said they're DNA testing all the camping gear they seized . . . I'm just relieved that the police are now doing their bloody job. I wanted to phone and thank you," she said between sobs. "Can we talk again in a few days? This is all a lot to take in. I need some time."

"Yes. Of course," said Kate. She sat for a few moments after Lyn ended the call.

Alan Hexham must have spoken to Henry about Kate looking into Simon's death. Alan was a straight-down-the-line guy. He'd offered help to Kate in the past, but his ultimate loyalties were to his job and to the authorities. Kate suspected she'd soon get a call from Henry Ko. The police didn't like it when private investigators sniffed around.

She looked out the window. A low bank of clouds now obscured the sun, and a layer of mist was forming above the sea.

Kate shivered. The cold had seeped into her bones. She went upstairs and took a long, hot shower.

14

Magdalena Rossi wheeled her yellow Vespa motor scooter through the cramped tiled hallway of the flat she shared with two postgraduate students, out the front door, and onto the road.

Her flat was perched on a quiet street high above the seafront. Her bright-red coat, blue jeans, and green patent leather walking boots were a splash of color against the gray pebble-dashed houses. Magdalena pulled on her crash helmet with mirrored visor and swung her leg over the seat, pushing off with her foot. She let the Vespa freewheel down the steep hill toward the seafront, enjoying the sensation of speed.

At the bottom, she leaned into the curve as the road turned sharply to the right onto the promenade. Halfway along the beach, by the boarded-up ice cream hut, she stopped to kick-start the engine. She didn't see any sign of Tristan as she sped past his flat. There was a little buzz of excitement in her stomach about their forthcoming date. He was delicious. Very sexy. She'd shown a picture of him to her housemates, Liam and Alissa, and they both agreed.

Magdalena pushed the thought of Tristan to the back of her mind so she could concentrate on her field trip. The previous night's forecast had been for coastal fog, and it was correct—the air was thick with damp and fog forming out at sea, punctuated by the far-off blast of the foghorn.

Her project had started with the farmer who'd found the huge footprint. After she visited him to take photos, they had gone for lunch at the local pub to talk further. Through the farmer she got talking to the locals about the Beast of Bodmin Moor, and then the conversation moved on to other local legends. Two of the barmaids had stories about a young man and a young woman, residents of the local children's home, who had vanished in the fog on the same stretch of road leading out of Ashdean. One of the barmaids had given her the phone number of a third woman who could tell her a story about the fog abductions, but even after Magdalena left a couple of messages, there hadn't been any answer.

The barmaid had also told her own story of the fog.

It comes up from nowhere and it gets you, disorientates you into a blind panic, she'd said. The barmaid told how she'd been out picking blackberries by the cliffs one cold June day, when a fog rolled in from nowhere. She'd spent an hour stumbling blind and lost and had nearly fallen over the cliff and down to the rocks and crashing waves below.

Magdalena wanted this to be the starting point for her research project. This was evidence enough that it wasn't a fog phantom causing these people to vanish. They could have got lost, or fallen into the sea, or into the undergrowth. There were footpaths and fields along the coast. Lots of places to fall and meet an untimely end. Today, she was planning to get some good photos of the sea fog rolling onto the land. Magdalena also harbored a fantasy that she would find the remains from one of these victims, stumbling across a pile of bones tucked away in some ditch or crevice on the cliff, still partially dressed in clothes they wore the day they went missing.

Magdalena took the A1328 out of the town, and soon the houses and shops thinned away to fields and trees. This was the coast road linking Ashdean to Exeter.

The cliffs were to her left, hidden behind a thick line of trees over the fields, freshly ploughed for the winter. As she passed a dirt track in the break between two fields, she slowed. Fog was rolling up from the cliffs and heading toward her down the track.

She did a U-turn and turned off onto the dirt track. There were huge tire prints, left by a tractor, and she found it was easier to drive along the compacted mud, smooth and silky and pressed into perfect ridges.

Magdalena had heard the English phrase "rolling fog" and thought it was silly. A ball rolls, not fog, but today the fog was coming toward her in just that way, rolling, as if it were being poured out in a huge mass, pushing forward along the track, turning over, with wispy fingers curling outward. It was as if it were alive, and the living mass was feeling its way toward her.

Magdalena turned off the engine and kicked out the Vespa's stand. She was fumbling in her bag for her camera when the wall of fog seemed to pick up speed, and she was enveloped in the white chill. She breathed in the cold, slightly salty taste of the fog, wet on her tongue, and felt the moisture condense on her hair and eyelashes.

Magdalena was a practical woman. She didn't believe in urban myths, and during her course of study, she'd remained logical. Ghosts, goblins, and mythical creatures didn't exist. But as she was enveloped by this mass of fog so thick that she couldn't see more than a few feet in front of her, she panicked. The Vespa didn't want to start, the engine coughing and sputtering with a *rih, rih, rih* sound. The fog carried on rushing past, burying her deeper.

It's just condensed water, she said to herself.

The Vespa finally came alive with a roar, and she pushed off, riding for a good thirty seconds, having to use the tire tracks to stay on the path. Suddenly, she emerged from the whiteness back into the fields, wispy fingers of fog trailing out behind her.

She carried on at full speed for another thirty seconds before she slowed and came to a stop. Her heart was pounding against her chest, and her breath was quick. She parked the Vespa and got up on the grass shoulder and took some shots of the fog advancing toward her.

Next to the grass shoulder was a ditch, overgrown with dead reeds and gorse. She parted the undergrowth and peered into the ditch. It was deep, and in the shadows, she could see only an oily black patch of water.

If she fell into the ditch and drowned, or even if she fell and broke a bone, would anyone hear her calling? This was the middle of nowhere. She would be swallowed up by the undergrowth . . . Could there be a dead girl or guy down there? A poor soul who had stumbled wrongly in the fog? The body slowly rotting in the mud?

She took a few shots of the ditch, focusing the lens, and then she saw something move in the water. She leaned closer. There was a sudden movement, a flapping of wings against her face, and she screamed as a duck flew up from between the reeds into the sky above.

Magdalena sat back, the dry reeds prickling through her jeans. Her coat was warm, but the fog had left a thick layer of moisture on her hair and soaked through to her scalp. She was hungry and cold and feeling a little spooked, so she decided to head back to Ashdean.

At the end of the track, she turned back onto the road. The fog was starting to disperse from the sea, and the air was hazy. There was a cream-colored Volvo parked farther along the road. It was caked with dirt and jacked up on its back wheels.

An old man was heaving a spare tire out of the boot. As she passed on her scooter, she saw he was dressed in baggy blue corduroy trousers, boots, and a tweedy jacket going threadbare at the elbows. A mass of gray hair poked out from underneath a flat cap, and he had a bushy gray beard and thick-rimmed glasses.

In her rearview mirror she could see the old man was struggling to move the tire. He kept dropping it. He stopped and clutched his back. She thought herself smart and savvy, but she came from a small town in the north of Italy, where elderly people were afforded a great deal of respect. What would her mother say if she left this old man to struggle on the side of the road? She checked her mirror again.

"No, no, no," said Magdalena under her breath. She slowed, did a U-turn, and started back.

"Can I help you?" she said to the old man as she drew level to the car. She slipped up the visor on her helmet. The old man was panting and had the tire against the back wheel facing the road.

"Oh, that's very kind," he said with a thick Cornish accent. "I just . . ." He stopped to gather his breath, which sounded ragged. "I just need to get the tire round the other side. I think I ran over some glass or a tack."

The old man dropped the tire, and it rolled across the road, just as a lorry came along. The lorry driver had to slow and swerve around the tire lying in the road, honking the horn loudly. The lorry sped past them with a whoosh of dust.

Magdalena parked her scooter behind the Volvo, took off her helmet, and hooked it over the handlebar. There was a small jack under the back wheel of the car. She picked up the spare tire and came back over to the man. It was heavy, but she could manage. "Please. Round the side there," he said, indicating the rear-wheel axle next to the shoulder.

"Thank you," he said, following her. "I've got the wrench." He picked up a torque wrench from the open boot of the car, and a cloth.

The Volvo was parked right up against the high grass, which was lined with a ditch. The front mirror on the driver's side protruded over the grass between the road and the ditch and blocked her way to the front. The old man was now standing between Magdalena and her Vespa. She saw through the grimy windows that the back seat was covered in old blankets.

"Let me just move so you can get to the tire," she said, going to squeeze past him. The old man blocked her way. He suddenly seemed to stand up taller, and she noticed how broad he was. He had a large gnomic nose, and his eyes behind the thick glasses were an odd color.

"Do you like to party?" he said. His voice was now different, smooth and oily, without any accent.

"What?" she replied.

He punched her hard in the face, grabbing her camera on its strap as her head snapped back. She saw stars and was dazed. It took her a second to realize he was looping the camera strap around the Volvo's roof rack. It tightened around her neck.

"Noooo!" she cried, but her mouth was thick and numb and covered in blood.

"Do you like to party?" he repeated, pushing a small brown bottle up under her nose. A chemical smell overpowered her and seemed to explode in the back of her head. Blood rushed around her body, and her legs buckled. The camera strap broke her fall, catching under her chin and choking her.

It was as if Magdalena were outside her body as she watched the old man calmly pick up her scooter and toss it into the ditch. The undergrowth seemed to swallow it whole. She was hanging by her neck. The camera strap was tight around her throat, and her feet scrabbled underneath her as she tried to get purchase on the ground and stand.

He came back and put his face close to hers.

"Do you want to touch the stars?" he purred, his voice soft. His eyes were an odd purple blue. He pressed the small bottle under her nose. She felt another explosion in her head, and a falling sensation, and then there was darkness.

15

Kate returned to work on Monday feeling despondent. She'd checked the news the last two mornings, but there was nothing more about Geraint being charged with murder, or the progress the police were making on the case.

It was a full day of lectures and meetings, so she didn't get the chance to speak to Tristan until Tuesday afternoon. They were coming back up the stairs to her office, at the top of one of the towers in the campus building, when they heard two male voices echoing down the stairs, speaking in a low murmur.

"Who's in your office?" said Tristan.

Kate shook her head and moved past him and up the last turn of the spiral staircase. The door to her office was ajar, and she found DCI Henry Ko sitting at her desk, peering at some paperwork. An older man with a portly frame and a jowly face was holding a book from the shelf in his hand. He wore a creased, ill-fitting suit.

"Can I help you?" she said, staring between the two men. Tristan appeared behind her a moment later.

"You? No," said Henry. "Tristan is the man we're looking for." He got up from Kate's desk. The other officer put the book back on the shelf. "I'm DCI Henry Ko. This is DI Merton . . ." They both pulled out their police ID cards. Kate turned to Tristan and saw the look of alarm and confusion on his face. "Where's Magdalena Rossi, Tristan?"

"Who?" asked Kate.

"Professor Magdalena Rossi; she works here. I thought you'd know that, *Professor* Marshall," said Henry.

"She's a visiting professor. She lectures in philosophy and religion," said Tristan to Kate.

"When did you last see her?" asked Henry.

"Last week. Friday. I delivered some equipment to her office," said Tristan.

"And you spoke to her on the phone on Saturday, and you were due to meet her Sunday night," said DI Merton, speaking for the first time.

"She didn't show up," said Tristan. Kate was watching, confused as to why the police were suddenly interested in a visiting professor, and why Tristan would be meeting her.

"What does this have to do with you poking around my office without a warrant?" asked Kate. Henry opened his mouth to protest. "You should have a warrant if you're going to go through my stuff."

"We were shown up here by one of the administrators downstairs," said Henry. "Magdalena Rossi was reported missing yesterday afternoon. She went out on Sunday and never returned home. Your assistant here was the only person Professor Rossi was due to meet."

"She was supposed to come by my flat, Sunday night at seven. We'd arranged to go to the cinema, but she never turned up," said Tristan. Kate could see he was starting to shake.

"Where were you between one p.m. Sunday and nine a.m. Monday?" he asked.

"I was at home Sunday morning with my sister and her fiancé. I went to the gym after lunch; then in the afternoon, the caterers came around to our flat."

"Caterers?"

"My sister's getting married in a few weeks. They came to give us a tasting menu. I then got ready to meet Magdalena, but she never showed up."

76

"Did you phone her? Or go round her house and see why she stood you up?" asked DI Merton.

"I phoned her a couple of times, but it went to voice mail. In the end I went out with my sister and her fiancé for pizza."

"Which pizzerie did you go to?" asked Merton.

"The proper word is *pizzeria*," said Kate. He ignored her.

"Where did you go?"

"Frankie and Benny's, on the high street," said Tristan.

"What time did you go?" asked Henry.

"Eight, maybe just after."

"What did you eat?" asked DI Merton, moving closer to Tristan and, realizing the height difference, peering up at him.

"I had . . . an Italian hot pizza."

"What about the other two diners?" fired back DI Merton.

"I can't remember; four cheese, I think. Sarah will have the receipt . . ."

"That's enough," said Kate. "Is this your strategy? If Tristan can't remember what food everyone ordered, that's grounds for, what? Arrest?"

"Arrest?" said Tristan.

Henry stepped back and folded his arms. A look passed between him and DI Merton.

"We'll need to verify all of this," he said.

"It shouldn't be difficult," said Kate. "Tristan was with his sister, then a caterer, he went to the gym, came back, and went out to a restaurant. Lots of witnesses and CCTV you can call on. Where did Professor Rossi go missing?"

"If we knew that, she wouldn't be missing," said DI Merton. Kate rolled her eyes at his petulance.

"Did she tell anyone where she was going?"

"She told one of her housemates she was going on a field trip, to take photos on the A1328," said Merton.

"Doesn't a portion of the A1328 run between the cliffs and the Shadow Sands reservoir?" said Kate, seeing that stretch of road in her mind and thinking of Simon Kendal. "Have your officers done a search?"

"We're searching the beach, and maintenance boats regularly patrol the water on the reservoir," said Henry.

"A maintenance boat will only find a body when it floats. As you remember, I found the body of Simon Kendal deep underwater," said Kate. "Did Magdalena have her belongings with her when she went missing?"

"She left her house with her camera, bag, and mobile, and she was driving her moped. Are you sure Magdalena didn't drop by your house, Tristan?" asked Henry. Kate didn't like his accusing tone.

"Tristan has already told you he was busy for most of Sunday. Wouldn't it be a better use of your time to confirm his alibi?" said Kate to Henry. "You rushed to rule Simon Kendal's death an accident, then had to backtrack. Professor Rossi could have had an accident on the moor. She could have fallen into the reservoir. She could have decided to leave of her own accord. Tristan's able to prove where he was during the period she went missing. If you want to talk to him again, you need to phone and make an appointment. I'm sure he will be happy to assist you with his solicitor present."

She went to the open office door and indicated they should leave.

"Just out of interest, have you charged Geraint Jones with the murder of Simon Kendal?" she asked Henry as he passed.

"Yes," he said.

"Good luck proving how Simon and Geraint levitated over a razor wire–topped fence from the campsite into the water."

Henry gave her a hard stare.

"We'll probably want to talk to you again," he added, pointing at Tristan with his notebook. DI Merton gave them a nod and followed Henry out.

Kate closed the door. Tristan slumped onto the small sofa under the window.

"What do you mean *with a solicitor*?" he said.

"I'm reminding them that they need more than a hunch to come and harass you."

"Do the police think I'm a suspect?"

"Suspect for what?" said Kate. "They don't even know if she's missing or if she's run away. There's no body!"

"I have a criminal record, you know that," said Tristan.

"You have a caution for smashing the window of an abandoned car as a drunken teenager. It's nothing like being on probation for attacking someone in a club, if that's what you're thinking," said Kate. "Tell me, what's going on with you and this Magdalena, Professor Rossi?"

Tristan outlined how he'd met her, the myths and legends project she was working on, and their subsequent phone call. Kate felt concerned for Tristan, but a curiosity was prickling the back of her head. The Shadow Sands reservoir had come up again.

"Why didn't you mention any of this?" she said. "I mean, that she was working on a project to do with the reservoir?"

"I didn't know her project was directly linked to the reservoir. She had a map of the reservoir up on the wall in her office, but lots of other stuff about myths and legends. I was going to ask her more about it when we went to the cinema."

"Where's her office?" asked Kate.

"On the other side of the building, top floor," said Tristan.

"Can you show me the map?"

Tristan looked at Kate. "Her office will be locked, if the police aren't in there now."

"You have keys, don't you? For when you do the equipment deliveries and pickups," said Kate.

The corridor was quiet outside Magdalena's office. Kate tried not to look as if she were "keeping watch" as Tristan searched for the key on a large bunch. There was a thin, oblong window of glass in the door, and Kate could see that the office was dark inside.

"This one, here we go," said Tristan as he turned the lock and the door opened. He went in first and flicked on the lights. Kate followed and closed the door behind them.

The light was already fading outside, and the fluorescent strip lights glared off the polished wood furniture and made the view of the sea and the sky a dark blue. Kate looked around at the desk, strewn with books and folders. It looked like the offices of most of her colleagues, apart from the little coffee machine in the corner. Most professors liked to use their coffee breaks as an excuse to get out of the office. She wondered if Magdalena was shy, or if she hadn't yet got to know any of her colleagues.

"Here's the project," said Tristan, indicating the corkboard. Kate looked at the photos, newspaper cuttings, and map of Shadow Sands reservoir.

"And you say she didn't mention the reservoir?" asked Kate.

"No. I asked her, but she said she was concentrating on the surrounding area. She went to meet a farmer near Chagford, who found that footprint in the mud on his land," he said, indicating the photo. "Then they went to the pub, and she got talking to a couple of local girls who said they'd heard stories of young people who went missing in the fog around the A1328 . . ."

"Which runs by the reservoir," said Kate, looking at the map again. She reached up and unpinned it from the corkboard and checked the back. It was blank. "Did she give you any names, the farmer, the girls at the pub?"

"No."

Kate had a look around the rest of the office, then searched under paperwork and checked the large paper blotter on the desk. Tristan joined her.

"Anything?"

"The folders are all student coursework," she said. She opened the three drawers in the desk, but they were filled with office supplies and a couple of romance novels in Italian. Kate looked at the desktop computer. It was password protected, and most professors brought their laptops in from home. "Can you see anything, like Post-its or notes, anything?"

"No."

"Did she tell you where she lived?"

"No, but we can find out from the staff directory."

Kate checked her watch.

"Yes. Let's go and knock on the door."

On the way out of the office, Kate took some photos of the corkboard, and Tristan grabbed the trolley with the slide projector.

"In case anyone asks, I opened the door and collected this," he said.

"The Fog Phantom who abducts young women," said Kate, reading off the board.

"And there was thick fog on Sunday," said Tristan.

"That's a troubling coincidence," said Kate, shuddering.

16

It was dark and very cold when they arrived at Magdalena's house. A tall Australian guy answered the front door. He was a typical surfer with shoulder-length blond hair. He wore board shorts and a T-shirt, despite the cold weather. He looked a little bleary eyed, as if he'd recently woken up.

"Hi. We're Magdalena's colleagues," said Kate. They both showed him their university ID cards. "We're sorry about what's happened. We're here to find out who's taking care of her research papers and books."

Kate knew they were winging it, and crossing a line, but they were only looking for details of the people Magdalena had talked to about the Fog Phantom.

"Yeah. It's intense. Magdalena's a really nice girl. The police have just been here," said the guy. "Are you police?"

"No. We work with Magdalena at the university," said Kate.

"Right. Sorry. I haven't got my contacts in. The police came and took a load of her stuff."

"Did you get their names?" asked Tristan.

"They said their names, but I can't remember. There was a mixed-race Asian guy. He was pretty cute."

"What's your name?"

"I'm Liam."

"What exactly did they take?" asked Kate.

"Her laptop, schoolbooks, research papers. They even took some of her clothes; half of her wardrobe is empty, and she didn't have a lot of stuff to begin with."

"Did they give you a paper to sign?"

He shook his head.

"They all flashed their badges and were gone within half an hour . . . Do you really think she was abducted?" he said.

"No one knows. Did she seem like she was acting odd before she left?" asked Kate.

"I didn't see her. Sunday I was in bed all day until the evening. I did hear her wheeling her scooter down the corridor at some point, early, could have been. My other housemate, Alissa, has been away for a couple of days. I don't know Magdalena all that well—we live our own lives—but we get along. I really hope she's not hurt. Do you think it's some psycho?"

"Can we come in and check if her students' coursework papers were taken?" asked Kate, feeling bad for lying.

"Sure. Knock yourselves out," he said, stepping to the side to let them in. "I'm gonna grab a shower; just close the door on your way out."

Magdalena's room was large and looked out over the seafront and Thurlow Bay. There was a double bed, a wardrobe, and a desk unit with shelves. The charger was still lying on the desk for her laptop, and the bookshelves were empty. Kate noticed a line of dust where the books had been.

"Can the police take stuff when it's a missing person?" asked Tristan.

"Yeah. They can remove things if needed for evidence, but they would need to record what they are taking," said Kate. "It looks like Henry Ko just came in, flashed his police ID card, and grabbed a load of stuff."

"Why would they take her books?" said Tristan.

"We don't know exactly what was on these shelves. They could have taken personal papers, diaries. Her laptop," said Kate, feeling her heart sink that there was nothing personal left over.

They came back downstairs, and Kate peered into the living room. It was empty of furniture, apart from a large TV and six beanbags dotted around. They went and had a look in the kitchen.

"It's so clean. Even the stove top," said Tristan. Kate gave him a look. "That's not an observation about the investigation. Just an observation."

Kate noticed the fridge. It was covered in magnets and takeaway menus. Tucked among it all was a Post-it with two names and phone numbers. The first name was Barry Lewis; the second was Kirstie Newett. Kate took a photo of the Post-it with her phone. Then she googled "Barry Lewis."

"Okay. I think he's our local farmer," said Kate, holding up the search results. There were four entries, and the third was the owner of Fairview Farm on the edge of Dartmoor.

"Kirstie Newett is a pretty common name. There's seventeen Facebook profiles, and lots of Google search results coming up," said Tristan, working on his phone.

They heard the bathroom door open, and Kate moved to the bottom of the stairs.

"Hello? Liam?"

He peered over the banister. His long hair was wet, and he was wearing just a towel around his waist.

"Yeah?"

"Sorry. Did Magdalena talk about a woman called Kirstie Newett?"

"Nope."

Tristan joined Kate at the stairs and looked up.

"What about a project on local myths and legends?" asked Kate.

"Yeah. She was nervous about meeting this local dude, a farmer who had found a weird footprint."

"Barry Lewis?" asked Tristan.

"Yeah. She went to see him in the day, but then they went to the pub, and she called me just to check in when she got there; she said the pub was full of a few weirdos."

"When was this?"

"First week of October. I offered to go meet her, but she called me later from the pub and said it was all cool, and she came home . . . That time." His face dropped at the realization.

"Liam, do you remember the name of the pub?" asked Kate.

He reached up and ran his fingers through his wet hair.

"It was something old English. The Old . . . No . . . the Wild Oak, near Chagford."

"Thanks. This is my phone number, in case you remember anything else," said Kate, writing on a piece of paper and climbing a few stairs. Liam reached down and took it.

"Shouldn't I be calling the police, if I remember anything about Magdalena going missing?" said Liam.

"We're just concerned for Magdalena."

"Concerned colleagues," added Tristan.

"Did the police want an alibi from you?" asked Kate.

"Yeah. I had a guy staying Sunday and Monday. He vouched for me," he said with a sheepish grin.

When they came back out onto the street, the wind was blowing up from the sea below.

Kate checked her watch.

"Shit. I have an AA meeting in ten, and then Jake is Skyping me . . . Can I call you later?"

"Sure," said Tristan.

"Are you okay? Don't worry about the police."

Tristan nodded, but Kate thought he still looked troubled.

"I've come across police officers like Henry Ko many times. They use macho bullshit to compensate for the fact they're not much good at

85

their jobs. It's not like you had anything to do with Magdalena going missing . . . Do you want me to drop you home?"

"No. Thanks. I'm going to walk home. It's not far. I need some air," he said.

"Okay. I'll call you later about these names."

Kate got into her car and watched as Tristan walked to the end of the road and turned down toward the seafront. He didn't seem fine. He was hunched over and withdrawn. She would have to keep an eye on him. She started the car and then set off for her AA meeting.

17

When Tristan got home, his heart sank to see Gary and Sarah sitting together on the small sofa in the living room. The sound was up loud, and they were watching the quiz show *Eggheads*.

"Hey, Tris, there's a couple of slices of pizza in the kitchen," said Sarah, not taking her eyes off the TV.

He navigated around the boxes of duty-free wedding booze to the kitchen. There was a supermarket-brand pizza box on the counter and a couple of anemic-looking slices left in the grill pan. There was nothing more depressing than frozen supermarket pizza. And why did they put *Italian Style* on the box? Where else did pizza come from? He put a couple of slices in the microwave. He could hear Gary and Sarah muttering about something in low voices. Tristan wished he could come home to peace and quiet so he could think. In six weeks Sarah and Gary would be married and living in their own place, and Gary wouldn't be a constant presence.

When the microwave was done, he put the pizza on a plate, took a can of Coke from the fridge, and went through to the living room. The small dining table in the corner was strewn with wedding paperwork. *Eggheads* was finishing on TV.

"Don't get pizza sauce on my wedding plan," said Sarah. Tristan put his plate on the chair and gathered up the papers into a pile. He sat down and started to eat.

"We had a visit from the police today; they came into the bank," said Sarah. They were now looking at him intently from their spot on the sofa.

Oh crap, thought Tristan. He should have thought that the police might contact her. "They wanted to confirm we all went out for a meal on Sunday night."

"Which we did, that wasn't a problem," said Gary.

"Why didn't you tell us that girl Magdalena has been reported missing?" asked Sarah.

"I only found out a few hours ago when the police came to talk to me at work," said Tristan. Gary switched the TV channel to the ITV early-evening news.

"They said she was planning to go out on Sunday for a ride on her scooter and she never came home . . ."

"Here, it's on the news," said Gary. He turned up the volume, and they watched the news report.

"Look, her mum and dad have flown in from Italy," said Sarah. "Aren't the Italians well dressed? They must be in their sixties, and they're beautifully turned out."

A woman and a man, both small with dark hair, were pictured at a news conference organized by the Devon and Cornwall police, sitting behind a long table with two police officers in uniform. They looked bereft. A picture of Magdalena flashed up, taken in a vineyard. She was smiling and wore a long red dress. Her long dark hair tumbled over her bronzed shoulders.

"She was a nice-looking bird. Shame you didn't get to date her before she went missing," said Gary.

"That's very insensitive," said Sarah.

"Just an observation."

"One we don't need."

Tristan chewed on the cardboard pizza. His appetite was gone, and he was shaking. This was all too close for comfort and real. They watched the news conference as the police outlined a timeline of the night and day before Magdalena vanished. Then they showed a grainy CCTV image from the early hours of Monday morning, taken on Jenner Street, which ran along the end of Magdalena's road. There was a series of time-lapse images between one and four thirty a.m. that made his stomach lurch. They showed a tall young man walking up and down the empty street, twice between one and one fifteen a.m. and then returning at four thirty a.m.

"That looks like you, Tris," joked Gary. Tristan swallowed a chunk of the dry pizza. He could feel the color drain from his face.

"Tris? Is that you on Jenner Street?" asked Sarah.

"Erm, no," he said, coughing.

"Where's the remote?" Sarah grabbed it from Gary and used the "pause live TV" function. She ran the news report back to the part where they showed the CCTV images.

"Sarah," said Tristan, starting to panic. He felt the pizza crawling in his stomach. She was now standing up in the middle of the room, peering at the TV.

"Tristan. That's your tracksuit. The black one with the red, green, and blue stripes . . . and your white, red, and blue Adidas vintage cap you bought from America. That's what you were wearing when we went out for pizza on Sunday night." Sarah ran it back again. "He's even got your gait."

"What do you mean, gait?" asked Gary, getting up and standing beside her.

"The way Tristan walks. His body language." She left the TV report playing as an appeal number flashed up on-screen asking for any information. "What the hell, Tris?" she said, turning to him. Tristan could feel his legs shaking. He couldn't control them. He hadn't even known there was a CCTV camera on Jenner Street. Sarah and Gary were both staring at him, but he couldn't think of what to say. "Say something! What the bloody hell are you doing on police CCTV . . ."

"It's not police CCTV," said Tristan, hearing his voice wobble. "It's Jenner Street."

"It's on the bloody news! If I've recognized you, I'm sure someone else will!"

"I just went for a walk," he said. "I couldn't sleep."

"Tristan. The police came into the bank! I told them that we went for dinner Sunday evening and then you were in all night until Monday morning. I gave them a signed statement!"

"I didn't ask you to," he said. Tristan thought how the police had treated Geraint and arrested him with flimsy evidence. He was terrified.

"I could have perjured myself at work!"

"Sarah, love, you weren't under oath," said Gary, reaching out to try and grab her hand. "I'm the assistant manager; I can protect—"

"What normal person gets up in the middle of the night and goes for a walk, in October?"

Sarah and Gary were now in his face, and the walls of the cramped and tiny living room seemed to be closing in on him.

"You know what, Sarah? You're the only *normal* person in the world, you just judge everyone."

"Now come on, mate, that's enough," said Gary.

"Or what?" said Tristan, standing. He was more than a head taller and able to look down on Gary, at the overhead light bouncing off the top of his shiny bald patch.

"That's enough! You are both going to sit down. *Sit*," said Sarah. Gary obediently sat back on the sofa. "Tristan."

He rolled his eyes.

"Tristan. You need to phone this number or go to the police and explain what you were doing. I don't for a moment think that you had anything to do with this, but why did you make us lie?"

"And, Tris. They're gonna want to know what you were doing for three and a half hours near Jenner Street," said Gary. Sarah's mouth opened as it seemed to dawn on her that he wasn't walking through Jenner Street; he was hanging around.

"What *were* you doing for three and a half hours in the middle of the night on Jenner Street?" said Sarah. "Why did you walk past Magdalena's road three times?"

They were both looking at him now, as if he were capable of something horrible, like kidnapping or murder. Tristan could feel the pizza lurching in his stomach. He bolted out of the living room and up the stairs and only just made it to the bathroom in time before he threw up. He heaved and coughed, holding on to the toilet bowl and seeing stars. There was a knock at the door.

"Erm, mate, it's Gary . . . Mate. Are you okay?"

"No."

There was a pause, and he could hear the sound of Gary breathing through the thin door.

"Sarah has asked me to ask you to come back down to the lounge. She wants you to tell her what's going on. We'll stand by you, mate."

Tristan flushed the toilet, got up and yanked the door open, pushed past Gary, and went downstairs back into the living room.

"Sarah . . . ," he started. She came out of the kitchen wiping her hands. She looked scared.

"What?"

He opened his mouth to say more, but Gary appeared in the living room doorway.

"Listen, Tris . . . Mate. I hope you don't mind me saying. You're acting a little wacko for my liking," said Gary, putting up his hands. "Perhaps, Sarah, you should come and stay at my place tonight until Tristan calms himself down."

"Can I have a minute with my sister?"

"I'm not comfortable with that," said Gary. It was all too much for Tristan. He wanted to explain to his sister first, without bloody Gary, who was always there, in the way, popping up like some irritating idiot. He opened his mouth to speak, but he had nothing. He grabbed his coat and left the house, slamming the door. He started up the seafront, against the howling wind, with tears in his eyes.

18

Kate emerged from the AA meeting an hour later and found a message from Jake to say he'd been invited to the cinema, and could they do another day. It was the second time he'd canceled talking to her.

As she was driving back along the seafront, the weather was horrible, and she wasn't looking forward to the cold, empty house waiting for her. Kate saw a young man sitting on the seawall, alongside the university building. As she passed, a wave slammed into the wall, and a jet of water shot up twenty feet beside the young man, and she saw it was Tristan.

"What are you doing?" she said, pulling in to park at the curb. She got out of her car and hurried over as another wave broke, shooting up a jet of water, which soaked him. There was a large drop down to the rocky beach below.

"Tristan! What the hell are you doing!" she shouted. He turned his head, and it took a moment for him to realize it was her. "Are you drunk?" She saw another black, inky wave below roll toward the seawall, and they were both soaked as it slammed into the concrete. Kate pulled Tristan backward, over the wall, and managed to hold him up. He seemed to come to his senses. His hands were like ice. They both stood there, soaking wet. "Tristan! What's going on?" His face crumpled and he started to sob. Huge, heaving sobs. She was shocked and upset to see him like this. "It's okay," she said, leaning up to hug him. Another wave hit the wall, and they were doused in spray. "Come on. My car's over here."

As they walked to her car, he wouldn't stop sobbing. She helped him inside and found some old blankets from the back. They sat for a few moments as his sobs slowly subsided.

"It was on the news, about Magdalena," he said. He went on to tell her about the CCTV images and then started to explain that he'd gone to visit someone. He broke down again.

"Why does it have to be so difficult? Why can't I just be normal?" he sobbed. "I haven't told anyone . . . and I can't cope anymore." He hung his head, unable to look at her, his bottom lip trembling. Kate took his hand.

"Tristan. I think I know, and it's fine, it doesn't matter," said Kate. She squeezed his hand. He was shaking all over. "Is saying it out loud going to make things any worse?"

There was a long silence.

"I'm gay," he croaked. He cleared his throat again. "I'm gay." He started to sob, harder.

"It's okay. It doesn't matter. Do you hear me?" said Kate, leaning over to hug him, feeling his chest and shoulders heave with the sobbing. "It doesn't matter," she said, hating the way of the world, that Tristan had to feel like this about himself.

He let out a long breath, as if he were breathing out for the first time in months. Kate found him a tissue, and he blew his nose.

"You don't seem surprised," he said. His eyes were still bright red, but he was calmer.

"I wondered. I've never seen you that interested in girls, and you could have your pick. There're so many girls in the faculty who would give their left eyeball for a date with you."

"My sister's getting married, and she's acting like it's going to be a huge crisis if I don't bring a girl to her wedding."

"Couldn't you bring a guy?"

Tristan looked at her.

"She would never forgive me."

"Tristan. I don't want to bad-mouth Sarah, but this is your life. This is who you are."

"Kate. She's not bad, she's just different. She thinks differently."

"So are you, so am I. We're all different. That's the world . . . When did you know you liked guys?"

"When I was thirteen, I watched that movie *Ghost*, and there's that scene at the beginning when Patrick Swayze and the friend both have their shirts off, and they're hammering down that wall with Demi Moore . . . I didn't know gay people in my life, growing up, and being gay isn't great, according to my family, to my old friends."

"Tristan. There are millions of gay people in the world. And it's totally normal. It drives me crazy that you even feel like you have to announce to me that you prefer guys. It's such bullshit . . . So, you were going to meet a guy and got caught on the CCTV?"

He nodded.

"I met this guy walking his dog on the beach the day before, and we got talking. We swapped numbers, and he invited me over to his place, you know."

Kate nodded.

"I left the flat around one in the morning, walked up to his door. Bottled it, went around the block, then came back. The second time I knocked on the door, and I stayed until four thirty a.m. And then I came home."

"Okay. Is he handsome?"

"Very."

"What's his name?"

"Alex. He's an art student. Long dark hair, beautiful brown eyes . . ."

Kate was so pleased that Tristan felt he could talk to her.

"Do you think you'll see him again?"

"I don't know."

"Is he out?"

"Yeah. His housemate was there too . . . Nothing like that," he added quickly. "He works at night. He's a painter. We all had a cup of tea before I left."

"They need to tell the police that's why you were there."

"I don't see why they wouldn't . . . Oh God. I have to tell Sarah, and Gary."

"I think that you'll breathe a huge sigh of relief when you've told them."

"What if Sarah hates me, or doesn't like it?"

"If she hates you, then that's her problem, not yours. If she's willing to shun a brother because he doesn't conform to her way of thinking, then that's her loss to take." Tristan stared out of the window and nodded wearily. "You weren't going to jump off that wall, were you?"

He shrugged. "In that moment, I quite liked the idea of being swept out to sea. I've heard drowning can be quite peaceful."

"When I started out in the police, I was a WPC, as women police officers were called back then. I was called out to West Norwood, in South London. There had been a huge rainstorm when this kid was mucking about in a stream near the cemetery. There was a sudden surge of floodwater, and he was carried to a storm drain, where his arm got caught in a grate. His arm swelled up, trapping him. I got there as the water was rising. We called for an ambulance, but it didn't get there quick enough. I tried to get him free, but I had to watch helplessly as the water rose up, over his head. I tried to give him air, but the water was moving so fast . . . I saw his face as he drowned,

Tris. It wasn't peaceful. You do not need to kill yourself because you happen to love men instead of women. Do you hear me?"

Tristan was quiet. He nodded. "What do I do?"

"You need to tell your sister. And tomorrow, we need to talk to the police and get this whole thing with the CCTV cleared up. We don't want it to distract from them finding out why Magdalena went missing."

19

Magdalena lay in the dark. She had no idea how much time had passed.

When she'd first woken, she'd thought she was in hospital. The bed she lay on was comfortable, firm, and dry underneath her back, and as she drifted in and out of consciousness, an unease permeated her sleep, a far-off memory of something . . . wrong.

The pitch black was confusing—she hadn't known it was real, and it had taken longer for her to come fully conscious. When she did, the panic overwhelmed her. There was no difference when she opened her eyes and when she closed them, and she couldn't smell anything. Her nose was blocked—it was crusted with blood. He'd punched her. And her neck was sore from the camera strap.

"No!" she cried out loud. Hearing her voice gave her a sense of space. "No! No! Help!" she said. Her throat was so dry and parched, but she kept saying words. *Help. Help me. Help!* The sound bounced around.

She put her arms out into the darkness and felt them move in the empty air. There was a wall on one side with smooth tiles. She listened. Silence. Feeling her body, she was unhurt, apart from a fat lip and bloody nose. She still had on all her clothes, but no shoes. Her phone was gone from her pocket. Her necklace and earrings and watch were also missing.

Magdalena sat up slowly, keeping one hand on the smooth, cold tile to her right. Keeping her arm outstretched to feel for anything above.

There was cold, empty air all around her. As she put her feet over the side of the mattress, she panicked, and then her feet touched the cool surface of the floor. For a minute she'd thought the bed was somewhere high up and she was about to tumble into a dark abyss.

Magdalena listened for a long time, trying to hear the silence. Listening for any cues, any hints as to where she was. Her heart wouldn't stop thudding in her chest. Breathing through her mouth was loud.

She liked to think she was a strong, practical woman, but she felt on the edge. A few times she had to swallow down an almighty scream that wanted to rip its way out of her chest. She placed the palm of her hand on her breastbone, and she started to tap rhythmically, along with the sound of her heartbeat. It didn't calm her, but it stopped the scream from escaping.

Standing up made her dizzy, and she had to try it twice before she felt safe on her feet. Slowly, slowly, she started to feel out her surroundings. A few paces led to a wall.

To her right was more tile. She could feel in places where it was smooth and cold, but in others it was grubby and sticky. She put her face a little closer to smell, but her nose was still blocked. She traced her hands back along the walls and found a sink and a tap in the opposite corner. To her joy, when she turned the tap, water came out. She let it run, enjoying the sound and feeling the cold water on her hands. She winced as she bathed her nose, trying to unblock it. She felt doubly blind not being able to smell. She managed to breathe a little through her nose, and a faint smell of damp came to her.

The water tasted pure, and she drank and drank; so acute was her thirst that she had to drink it, even if she wasn't completely sure that it was safe. It had strong pressure, and it must come off the mains. She dried her face and carefully felt her way around the other side of the room, back to the bed. The damp smell had intensified, and was now like rotting vegetation, but everything she touched was smooth and dry. The bed was a box bed, made of a frame and material with no space underneath. When she started to feel around on the other side of the bed, she fell out of a doorway.

Magdalena hurt herself, falling on her hip bone onto the cold, hard floor. It felt damp outside, and as she sat, she debated whether to continue searching. She cleared her throat. Magdalena was surprised how fast she was getting used to using sound to determine her surroundings.

Carefully, she felt her way along. There was a wall on each side, with a width of just a few paces. She was in a corridor. The walls were smooth, not tile but plaster, and sticky in places. She crossed the corridor and felt her way along the wall and found a door. It opened outward with a creak. This room was small and smelled of mold. Her knees crashed into something hard and cold, and as she reached down, her hands felt a curved bowl and then water. She pulled her hand back. It was a toilet. Magdalena felt a moment of joy. A toilet. There was no seat, and just cold porcelain, but she sat and relieved herself, feeling more human and less like an animal. She felt around hopefully for a toilet roll or a holder but there was none.

Where was she? And what was this? She felt around for a flush, and a long pipe at the back of the bowl led up to an old-style box cistern on the wall. The chain had been removed, but there was a plastic lever that she could reach if she stood on the edge of the bowl.

She was about to pull it when she stopped. It would make a noise.

She pulled her hand away, stepped down off the bowl, and came back out of the room. Should she close the door or leave it open? The door opened outward, and she decided to leave it open so she could find it again. She felt along farther and found that the corridor ended with a wall that felt different. Cold to the touch, and it took her a moment of feeling around with her hands before she knew it was metal.

It was the outline of cold steel doors, with a crack down the middle. They opened. Magdalena pushed her fingernail in between the two metal doors and tried to lever them open, but they were thick and solid.

There was a whirring sound, and she felt a rumble through the metal. She stepped back.

It was a lift.

The sound was getting louder; the rumbling came through the concrete floor under her feet. It was coming down toward her.

Groping at the wall, she hurried back down the corridor, hearing the lift come closer. She ran straight into the open door of the toilet. It swung inward when she hit it and slammed closed. She felt her fragile nose crack, and the pain was intense. She had a warm taste and the sensation of blood.

Magdalena heard the lift arrive with a faint ding. She started back down the corridor toward the room with the bed and the sink. The doors opened with a whir. Her breathing was ragged from the exertion, and then she coughed, spitting blood. It echoed in the corridor. A draft came from the open lift doors, but it was still pitch black. Then there was a click, and a strange sound. She'd heard it before in a movie, or on a TV show. A sort of mechanical whistle.

Night vision goggles.

With panicked breathing, Magdalena felt her way along the walls. She was disoriented, and she tried to stay calm, but little whimpers came out of her mouth.

When she found the doorway, she groped around inside and felt the edge of the doorframe. If there was a door, she could somehow barricade herself inside against whoever, or whatever, had come down in the lift.

There was no door. She could just feel the cold wall and two empty hinges. Magdalena retreated into the room and fell back on the bed as she heard the soft sound of footsteps coming toward her.

20

Tristan had gone back to the flat, on Kate's insistence, and told Sarah and Gary that the pictures on the CCTV camera showed him walking to Jenner Street to meet a guy.

"To meet a guy for what? Drugs?" Sarah asked. She was sitting on the sofa with her arms crossed, looking nonplussed. Gary sat beside her, with his hands crossed over his protruding belly.

"No. Not drugs. I was going on a date, well, not quite a date. His name is Alex. He's an art student. I went to his flat to, er, have sex with him. I'm gay. I've been gay for a long time—well, not a long time. All the time."

Tristan put his shaking hands in his pockets. He was standing up in front of the television. A little like he was doing a recital for them.

Sarah stared at him. Gary's eyes went wide. He kept looking to her, to see how to react. A moment passed, and she calmly got up, went to the kitchen, and closed the door.

"Are you sure, mate?" said Gary. "You don't *seem* gay." Tristan could see the wheels turning in Gary's head, running over memories of their interactions, searching for any clues of homosexual behavior. "I thought you had a date with that girl who's gone missing. She phoned you."

"Yes. She asked me out. I shouldn't have said yes."

"But you've got nothing to do with her going missing?"

"No. Nothing."

"Well, that's something," said Gary, anxiously looking to the closed door to the kitchen, where they could hear Sarah crashing around, tidying up the dishes. "You should speak to her."

Tristan nodded. He took a deep breath, opened the door, and went into the kitchen. He closed it behind him. Sarah was at the sink, furiously scrubbing a dirty saucepan with a Brillo pad.

"Don't you have anything to say?" asked Tristan.

"I just don't know why you want to throw your life away," she said, rinsing the pan and slamming it down on the draining board.

"What do you mean?"

"You have a very good job with a final salary pension scheme. You are about to take over the mortgage on this flat, and you've got the police questioning you about a woman who's gone missing," said Sarah.

"That's not what this is about."

"You already have a criminal record. And you didn't stop to think about me. I've basically lied to the police for you. God knows what will happen next. I've worked my backside off to better myself."

Tristan stared at his sister's back as she furiously scrubbed at the dishes.

"I'm sorry. It can be fixed. I will tell the police you didn't know that I left the house."

"Do you do that often? Sneak out at night to visit with . . . ," she said, turning to him and fixing him with a stare.

"A couple of times I have," said Tristan, wishing for a hole in the floor to open up and swallow him.

"Does it make you happy? Behaving like that?"

"What do you define as being happy?"

"Having a family! Settling down!"

"I don't want kids."

"Who will continue the family name?"

"Us Harpers are hardly a glittering dynasty. Dad ran off when we were small, God knows where he is. Mum enjoyed shooting up more than she enjoyed her two children."

"Don't you dare talk about Mum like that!" said Sarah, still holding the sponge. She was livid. Tears were in her eyes. "She was mentally ill, and when you mix that with drugs . . ."

"Sarah. We're not talking about Mum. I'm telling you something about me . . . I'm gay. I just want you to love me and accept me for who I am."

"I will always love you, Tristan, but don't expect me to accept it. I have *a right* not to accept it . . ."

Tristan felt tears in his eyes, and he wiped them away. Sarah glanced back at him, then looked away. "Your timing is classic," she added with a bleak-sounding laugh. "What are people going to say at my wedding when you show up being all gay?"

"Your wedding is about you and Gary."

"No. It will be all about you. The whole day will be spent having to explain *you* to people."

"Explain me to people? I'm still the same person. And your reaction says more about you than it does about me."

"Oh, now I'm homophobic?" Sarah shouted.

"I don't know. Sounds like it."

"You're choosing a life that will never make you happy."

"I'd rather live my life than yours," he shot back, and instantly regretted saying it.

Sarah dumped a couple of plates in the sink with such force that they broke. She started to wash the intact plates, in between pulling out shards of china.

"That poor girl, she could be lying in a ditch somewhere or fallen foul of some rapist . . . ," Sarah said, almost muttering to herself. "I wonder how Magdalena would feel if she knew that you were off doing God knows what with some other man. You're going to go to the police first thing tomorrow and explain what you were doing and that you lied to me."

"I didn't lie to you."

"You led me to believe."

"No, I didn't. I went out at night. I just didn't tell you. You assumed."

"It seems I assumed a lot of good things about you."

Tristan sighed. This was going nowhere. He had hoped that he would be able to explain things to Sarah and that she would understand. It broke his heart that they were now so far apart.

"I'm going to stay at Kate's for a few days," he said.

"Oh, of course. I thought *she* would be involved," said Sarah.

"I love you, Sarah, you hear me?" he said. She kept her back to him and carried on crashing around with the dishes.

Tristan came out of the kitchen and closed the door. Gary was lying on the sofa with one eye on the TV.

"Listen, Tris. Sarah's not homophobic. She loves them colored cups they do for Pride at Costa Coffee. She washed one out and kept it at work for her tea. She washed it so many times it ended up falling to bits."

He looked at Gary and didn't know how to react to that.

"I think Sarah needs you," he said. "I'll straighten it out with the police, about her statement."

Gary nodded. Then Tristan went and packed a bag. He didn't see either of them as he left the house. Kate was waiting for him outside in her car.

"You okay?" she asked when he got in.

He nodded, feeling like a huge weight had lifted from his chest. He could breathe easier.

"How about Sarah?"

"I don't know. I need to give her some space," he said.

21

The man stepped out of the lift wearing night vision goggles. The corridor and the two doorways glowed green through the lenses. He was surprised to see Magdalena in the corridor. She had ventured out quicker than many of his victims. This was only the second full day.

He watched her as she ran for it, crashing into the open door and then getting up again, dazed. He adored that blank look in their eyes, blind from the darkness. Their eyes were black through the night vision goggles, and their pupils showed up as bright spots of white.

She couldn't see, but she left a spot of blood on the corner of the toilet door. It was another addition. The bloodstains of his other victims decorated the walls and doors. Blood spatter like graffiti. He loved how it showed up green through the goggles.

He held back and watched her flail and feel her way back down the corridor. Why was it that the guys he'd captured always tried to get past him into the lift, yet almost all the girls ran toward the dead-end room—like those stupid horror-movie heroines who scream and run past the open front door and upstairs when the monster chases them?

He followed Magdalena into the room at the end of the corridor and watched her as she backed into the corner of the room and stayed, like a hunted animal staring out into the blackness.

He was always addicted to the fear in their eyes. So many women masked their emotions. He never knew what they were thinking. He hated that about them. The bitches were always trying to outsmart him. But here, in his dungeon, he was the monster, and he could see they were terrified.

He carried a broom in his hand. An ordinary broom, but he'd switched the head for that of a toy broom. A toy broom was softer, and the bristles were longer. It thrilled him that something so silly could screw with their senses in the dark. He moved closer to Magdalena.

"Who are you?" she said into the darkness. Her face was beautiful, but she had a strong nose, which was now bent out of shape and bleeding over her teeth and chin. She spat blood onto the floor. "Please? Why are you doing this?"

God, they asked such stupid questions. As if he were going to list his plans and tell them his name. He suppressed a laugh and extended the broom handle, letting the bristles lightly touch her face.

She cried out and swatted it away, slapping herself in the face in the process. He quickly pulled it back, out of her reach, as she swiped and clawed with her hands in large arcs.

"Leave me alone!" she shouted. "Please!"

He stood still and quiet. He waited and watched as she opened her eyes and tilted her head, trying to see. She reached out with her arms, waving at the air in front of her. It was like watching a wildlife show, observing his victims. Everything was stripped away from them. All pretense and affectation. They didn't worry about the way they were being seen, blubbering, crying, and often shitting themselves. They wanted to survive.

After a minute more he held the broom up, and again, he let the bristles swipe over her face.

Magdalena suddenly screamed and ran at him. It took him by surprise, but he was prepared. He lifted the broom up high and pivoted to the right, sticking his foot out. With the speed and force of how she was running at him, she tripped and went down hard, hitting the concrete floor with a horrible thud and sliding into the concrete bed base, cracking the top of her head. She was still.

No, please don't be dead, not this soon, he said under his breath. He moved closer, skirting around her still form on the floor. He gingerly reached out with the broom handle and nudged her in the hip. She didn't move. He pushed the broom into the soft flesh between her buttocks and jabbed it in hard. She groaned but didn't move.

She'd fallen with her hair across her face. He lifted the curtain of hair up away from her face with the broom handle and draped it over her shoulder. Her eyes were closed. There was a cut on her forehead where she'd caught the edge of the bed, and the blood running down her forehead was dark green, matching the blood clotting and bubbling in her nostrils as she breathed.

Good. She was breathing.

Very carefully, he knelt down and placed two fingers on her neck. Her skin was soft and, through the night vision goggles, so pure and white. Like ivory. He could feel a pulse, good and strong. He stroked her long neck for a moment and then pulled his fingers back, relieved she was still alive.

This was only the second day he'd been keeping her. There was plenty more fun to be had.

22

The next morning, Kate drove Tristan to the Exeter police station and waited for him in the car park. The road out front was busy in the morning traffic. She'd been waiting for only half an hour when she saw Tristan emerge from the main entrance. His face was difficult to read as he crossed the road.

"Everything okay?" she asked when he opened the door.

"Yeah. I spoke to a plainclothes officer, DC Finch. She seemed clued up and took a short statement. Then she phoned Alex and Steve, who confirmed I was at their house in the early hours of Monday morning, and I gave them the number for Sarah's wedding caterer, and the times I went for pizza with Sarah and Gary. She also said it wasn't a problem about Sarah saying I was at home when I wasn't, if she didn't know I'd left the house. She was very nice."

"Did you see Henry Ko?"

"No. And I did get the impression that the uniform officers thought he was a bit of an idiot."

"Why?"

"I said that Henry came to your office and was kind of aggressive. DC Finch made a joke about Henry watching too many episodes of *The A-Team* . . ." Kate smiled. Tristan went on. "She also said the police have spoken to Liam, Magdalena's housemate, and he said he heard Magdalena wheeling her scooter through the hall on Sunday, midmorning time, and she didn't come back. Which means they now believe she went missing Sunday morning."

"That's good," said Kate.

"Yes. It is. It just makes the row I had with Sarah even more ridiculous."

They set off back to Ashdean. Kate didn't want to press Tristan to talk about the night before. He had slept in her spare room, and she was going to see what he wanted to do next. She felt lucky they could share a comfortable silence without the need to make small talk.

On the quiet stretch of country road a few miles outside Ashdean, a cluster of cars was parked up ahead on the grass shoulder. As they drew closer, Kate slowed the car.

Two police cars were parked next to a scrap-recovery lorry. Henry Ko was standing on the shoulder with two other uniform officers, watching as a mud-spattered yellow Vespa scooter was winched out of the ditch on a crane. Farther along the road, the ditch was being cordoned off by another police officer.

"That's Magdalena's scooter," said Tristan. Kate drew level with Henry and came to a stop, winding down her window. He waved at them to keep moving, then noticed who they were and came to the window.

"My desk sergeant said you've been at the station," he said. He looked like he hadn't slept. All his cockiness had evaporated.

"Yeah. And that's Magdalena Rossi's scooter," said Tristan. It was now being winched up onto the back of the lorry.

"Yes. We just ran the number plate," said Henry as the crane whirred and the scooter came to rest on the lorry and two police officers started to cover it in plastic sheeting. It looked pitiful to Kate, covered in mud, with grass caught on the handlebars.

"What about Magdalena? Have you found her body?" asked Kate, watching the police officers peer into the ditch and the police cordon being strung up.

"No," said Henry. "A farmer was dredging the ditch. He found the scooter . . . Now please, I need you to move along. We need to close the road for forensics."

Kate and Tristan pulled away and carried on back to Ashdean. She watched the lorry with the bike and the cluster of police recede through the back window.

"Shit. That means she really went missing," said Tristan. Kate nodded. A part of her had hoped that Magdalena was one of those people who, one day, decided to up and leave their old life behind.

A moment later, they reached the crest of a hill, and they could see the Shadow Sands reservoir and the power plant below. On the right-hand side of the road, they passed a long, low redbrick building with arched windows and a pillared entrance. It looked like a once-majestic building. The roof had tiles missing at one end, the rows of arched windows were boarded up, and the car park out front was overgrown with brown weeds.

"Wasn't that a nightclub?" asked Kate.

"Yeah. Hedley House. Trashy as hell, and the police were often called out to deal with fights."

"Did you ever go there?"

"A couple of times," said Tristan. "It closed down about eighteen months ago."

"It looks like an old house," said Kate, watching it in the rearview mirror. A flock of birds flew up from a large hole in the roof and took to the sky.

"Yeah, I think it was a manor house at some point," said Tristan.

The road ran right past the reservoir. The sun broke through the clouds, and a shaft of light hit the center of the water and lit up the surrounding moor with a steel-gray light. They passed a road sign that read: **ASHDEAN 2½ MILES**. The road was long and straight. Kate could still see the boarded-up nightclub in the rearview mirror. Abandoned buildings always made her shudder, especially one on such a lonely stretch of road.

"How did teenagers get to Hedley House? Is there a bus?"

"There was a bus to get there, but the buses don't run after ten p.m. It used to be parents and friends who ferried people home. The taxis used to make a fortune on a weekend . . . Some people used to walk home."

"It's probably around three miles from the club to Ashdean," said Kate, her mind starting to whir. "And you never heard stories of teenagers going missing after walking home from the club?"

"No. There was a girl who was raped. I remember the case in the local paper, but they caught him. And he went to prison."

"When was this?"

"I dunno. Five, six years ago."

"Can you remember his name?"

"No. I do remember that he got sentenced to ten years in prison. It was a pretty brutal attack. After that there were fewer girls willing to walk back to Ashdean after a night out."

They reached the end of the reservoir where the River Fowey fed into it with a couple of other streams. And the outskirts of Ashdean appeared over the hill.

Kate turned her mind back to Hedley House nightclub, so close to the reservoir. She was brave in many ways, but she wouldn't want to walk this lonely stretch of road late at night.

"Do you have much work to do after the lecture?" asked Kate.

"No. I could use a distraction, to be honest," said Tristan.

"I want to visit that pub, the Wild Oak. I want to see if those barmaids are working. The ones Magdalena talked to. I want to hear what they told her and what they know about the woman whose number Magdalena had on the Post-it."

23

"Yeah, Magdalena came in here for a drink with Barry Lewis from Fairview Farm," said Rachel, the barmaid at the Wild Oak Pub. Despite the cold weather, Rachel wore a grubby cropped white T-shirt, a short skirt, and flip-flops. Her short, slicked-back hair was dyed red. "She got talking about her project, and I told her about the two people I knew who went missing in the fog."

Rachel placed a small Coke and a cup of coffee on the bar in front of Kate and Tristan. The Wild Oak Pub was six miles outside Ashdean, on the edge of a tiny village called Pasterton. The pub faced the open moor, and through the windows you could see for miles, but the interior was gloomy and run down. It was quiet midafternoon. A few elderly men propped up the bar, and a television in the corner was showing horse racing.

"How did you end up talking to Magdalena?" asked Kate.

"Barry found this big paw print on his land one morning, and he put a photo of it on Facebook. It got loads of likes; the paper reprinted it. Magdalena got in contact with him cos she was doing her project about Devon and Cornwall legends," said Rachel.

"Is Barry local?" asked Tristan.

"Yeah. Nice guy. A regular. Er. That's four twenty," she said, indicating their drinks on the bar. Kate could see her eyeing Tristan up as he took his wallet from his pocket.

"I meant to say, one for yourself," added Tristan.

"Thanks. That's six twenty."

Rachel took the money, gave Tristan his change, and then pushed a highball glass up under a Bacardi optic where a handwritten sign, **£1 A SHOT OR DOUBLE-BUBBLE**, was stuck on with peeling sticky tape.

"We're trying to work out what happened to Magdalena," said Kate. "Can we sit down and talk?"

Rachel eyed them for a second and nodded. She went to a door at the back of the pub.

"Doris! I'm taking my break!" she shouted. Kate and Tristan followed her to a low table with a smoked glass top at the opposite end of the bar from the TV. There was a screen built into the middle, under the glass, where an ancient flickering game of PAC-MAN was running. Rachel went to a plug, yanked it out, and they sat down.

"Why did Barry ask you about local missing people?" asked Kate.

"He didn't. When Magdalena came to the bar, she asked me if I'd ever seen anything weird, like big beasts or ghosts. I told her about two people I knew who'd gone missing when it was foggy," said Rachel.

"Can you tell us?"

Rachel nodded. "You know Hedley House, the old club on the main road?"

"Yes," said Kate.

"I went there a couple of times, when I was younger," said Tristan.

"I used to go there, a few years ago, before I had my little girl . . . There was this guy who was always there on a Friday, had a weird name, Ulrich. He was older than me at the time, nineteen or twenty, I think. He was German, a painter and odd-job man. He'd been here a few years, and he was a bit of an oddball, but he would come to Hedley and have a few drinks. He was always on his own, liked a chat. Never sleazy, regardless of how much he drank. And then one week, he wasn't there. The only reason I questioned it was cos of my mate Darren. Ulrich was putting a new toilet in Darren's flat. He'd taken it out on the Friday and was due to put it in on the Saturday, but he didn't show up. Darren got pissed off, as you would, no loo, and he'd paid Ulrich five hundred quid cash up front. He went round to Ulrich's place, but he wasn't there . . . Darren's a bit confrontational, and he got it into his head that Ulrich had pulled a fast one, so him and a few mates go back to Ulrich's bedsit and they kick the door in. All his stuff's there: clothes, shoes, food in the fridge. The TV was on. There was even a glass of water by the bed and a couple of painkillers, you know. If I ever go out on the lash, I have water and painkillers ready for when I get back."

Tristan nodded.

"I've done that before," he said.

"Did you report Ulrich missing?" asked Kate.

"Darren did. Phoned the police, they took a statement and wrote it down, but they weren't that interested."

"When was this?"

Rachel had to think.

"It was 2008—October 2008, close to Halloween."

"Can you remember his surname?" asked Tristan.

"Yeah, Ulrich Mazur . . ." She spelled the surname for them.

"What happened after you called the police?" asked Kate.

"We never heard anything about him after that, and we still thought he might have done a runner. Plumbing is a cash job, and we heard later that there were a few people he was doing work for that gave him cash."

Kate saw an older woman emerge from the doorway at the back of the bar. She had on jeans and a smart pullover and looked as if she'd just woken up; her short, curly hair was disheveled, and she was straightening it in a small mirror. She greeted the old men and took another order for pints of bitter.

"What made you link Ulrich to these disappearances in the fog?" asked Kate, turning her attention back to Rachel.

"Nothing at the time. A year later, I got to know a girl called Sally-Ann Cobbs. Very young. She'd just been kicked out of the local children's home."

"Why was she kicked out?" asked Tristan.

"She turned sixteen," said Rachel. "They pretty much turf them out. She got a cleaning job at Harlequins and had a bedsit somewhere. I forget where."

"Harlequins is the shopping center in Exeter?" asked Kate.

"Yeah. The shittiest," said Rachel.

"It is a bit of a shithole," agreed Tristan.

"What happened to Sally-Ann?" asked Kate, drinking the last of her coffee.

"Sally-Ann was another one I used to see up at Hedley House. One Friday she was drunk and had hooked up with this guy who wanted to take her home. She was off her face by the end of the night, and I remember them arguing outside the club, in front of the whole taxi line."

"Was he violent?"

"No. Sally-Ann was. She slapped him round the face and stormed off into the night. You've seen it round the club. It's all fields and moorland around that lonely road. That was the last time anyone saw her."

The hairs started to prickle on the back of Kate's neck.

"Did anyone report her missing?" she asked.

"I did. Again, I didn't twig for a while that she was gone. I knew one of the girls Sally-Ann worked with at the Harlequin. She said Sally-Ann hadn't turned up for work for five days. I knew Sally-Ann's rent was due cos she'd told me she was worried about money. I went around to her bedsit, and the landlord was there and about to chuck all her stuff."

"After how long?" asked Kate.

"A week."

"That's not legal."

"It was a dodgy bedsit. Those landlords can do what they want. All her stuff was still there. Photos, clothes, food going off. She'd just topped up her meter for leccy and gas. Her silver Saint Christopher necklace was by her bed. Her mum had given it to her when she was little, before she died . . ." Rachel fumbled at her neck and pulled out a silver necklace with a Saint Christopher. "This is it. That bastard landlord was there with black sacks, ready to put all her stuff on the tip. No doubt he was going to take what little she had of value and sell it. I took what I could, thinking that when she showed up, I could give it back to her, but she didn't . . ."

"Did you talk to the police?" asked Tristan.

"Yeah. They came and talked to me, said that they'd put Sally-Ann on the missing persons list . . . but what good is that when you've got no one to miss you?"

"Can you remember the date when Sally-Ann went missing?"

"Yeah, it was November time, in 2009."

Rachel stopped and pulled a grubby tissue from her pocket and scrubbed at her eyes.

"I'm sorry," said Kate. "What makes you think it's linked to the fog?"

"That night Sally-Ann stormed off outside the club, it was thick fog. And then I remember the last time I saw Ulrich, me and my mates were all squashed in a taxi going back from the club to Ashdean. There was thick fog, and we passed Ulrich walking. We even stopped, but the cab driver said he was full, and we drove away and left him to walk. He was a nice bloke."

She took another sip of her Bacardi. Kate could see the guilt on Rachel's face.

"Last year, this girl called Kirstie Newett started working here. She was a bit . . ." Rachel shrugged.

"A bit what?" asked Kate; she remembered the Post-it they'd found on Magdalena's fridge, but she didn't mention it and let Rachel continue.

117

"She was a bit of a liar. Silly, pointless lies. Saying one thing to someone, another thing to someone else to contradict. She told us she had a new car, when she didn't. She told us she'd bought a house, when she lived in a bedsit. I didn't mind her. Then one shift we were on together, thirty quid goes missing from the till. Doris had just put in a security camera above the till, and it was Kirstie. Doris sacked her . . . This was at lunchtime. That evening, I set off home in my car, and I saw Kirstie at the bus stop with a bottle of cider. I took pity on her, offered her a lift, and I asked her straight why she did it. She said that she was broke and it was a stupid mistake. When I dropped her off at home, she invited me in for a drink. We got talking, and it turned out she used to go clubbing up at Hedley House. And then she starts telling me that one night, she spent all her money and couldn't afford a taxi home, so she started to walk. In the fog. She said halfway back to Ashdean, there was this car stopped in a lay-by, and this old man rolled down the window and asks if she wants a lift. She's three sheets to the wind, dressed in a skimpy little number, and it's freezing cold, so she accepts. As soon as she gets in the car, he offers her some kind of drug to sniff and punches her. She wakes up later sometime, and she's all alone in the dark. He keeps her captive for days in some basement; then he attacks her, chokes her, and she passes out. Then, she says she wakes up in the back of a car by the Shadow Sands reservoir, as this bloke is about to dump her in the water! She said she fought him off and managed to swim away."

"Did you believe her?" asked Kate.

"No."

"Did Kirstie tell the police?" asked Kate.

"Yeah, she told me she flagged down a car on the other side of the reservoir, and the man who stopped was a policeman. He took her to hospital, and then she said she was slung in a mental hospital."

"Did she say which part of the reservoir the man took her to? It's big," asked Tristan.

Rachel thought for a moment.

"Yeah, she said it was the campsite, cos there was a big sign close to the place he'd parked and where she woke up. That's how she knew . . . Again, she was known for telling lies, and I had a drink with her, and then I left, and that was it. I saw her around a couple of times to say hi, but I never saw her again socially."

"What made you think, later, that she was telling the truth?" asked Kate.

"Well, it wasn't until a few weeks ago, when Magdalena was here with Barry. She was such a nice woman. Educated. She said she was doing a study on urban legends, local weird stuff, so I mentioned Ulrich, Sally-Ann, and Kirstie and the fog, and it all started to fit together in my mind. I know that Kirstie could have heard about Ulrich and Sally-Ann going missing, but I don't remember seeing her at Hedley around that time. Magdalena asked me for Kirstie's phone number. I still had a number for her in my phone, which I gave her. Magdalena asked all about the stretch of road near Hedley House, the surrounding area. Then it's on the news, that she's gone missing, right on the day when there's thick fog," said Rachel. "It's all more than a coincidence, don't you think?"

24

When they left the pub, Kate and Tristan sat in silence in her car for a few minutes, listening to the sound of the rain tapping on the windows.

"Jesus," said Tristan.

"It's the campsite link. Kirstie woke up at the campsite," said Kate. "Simon Kendal is attacked at the campsite and ends up in the water. Could whoever's doing this be abducting people and dumping their bodies in the reservoir? Ulrich and Sally-Ann."

"It would make sense, then, for Simon Kendal to be in the water. If he went for a walk at night, he could have ended up on the other side of the reservoir and been attacked; maybe he fought back, or he was thrown in the water. That's been a big problem for me, how he ended up on the other side of the fence."

"What if Magdalena ended up in the reservoir?"

"If you're going to dump bodies, it would make sense to weight them down, especially with how deep the reservoir is. If she wasn't weighted down, her body would float at some point," said Kate. "And then there's this club, Hedley House."

She was trying to piece it all together, but it made her head hurt.

It was coming up to three in the afternoon, and already the light was fading. "I want to have a look at the reservoir and the campsite."

When they drove back to Shadow Sands reservoir, the road took them on a big loop, past the point where the River Fowey fed the reservoir, and the area where Kate and Jake had gone diving. Kate slowed as they passed the visitors' center, which was next to the power plant. It was large, built in the shape of a ship, and surrounded by neat landscaped land overlooking the water.

"That's where Geraint went for a coffee and to charge his phone the day Simon went missing," said Tristan. There were lights on in the huge porthole windows lining the building, but on this gray day, the car park was empty as they drove past.

The power plant was next to the visitors' center, and it was a box shape with a huge dome on either side. A road bridge crossed the point where the water flowed through the turbines, and stopped at a small lay-by on the edge of the road. The roar of the turbines was very loud and grew deafening when they got out of the car.

They walked out onto the end of the bridge, where it ran across the top of the concrete dam.

"Imagine falling off here!" shouted Tristan as they looked down at the huge drop on the other side of the dam. The wall of the dam had a sharp slope to it, and far below, a torrent of murky water was gushing out of two giant sluice gates into a wide concrete channel. The channel carried the water along for a couple hundred meters and then became a fast-moving river that flowed away into the surrounding woodland.

They got back in the car and drove over the rest of the bridge, which tracked alongside the huge wall of the dam for a quarter of a mile. The campsite was farther along a quiet country road, with only a small sign indicating a gap in the trees. A tree-lined dirt track wound its way back down toward the reservoir.

The campsite was rough grass and scrub roughly a hundred meters square, and banked down to the reservoir. At the top was a small toilet block that was boarded up, and it met trees and moorland.

"Did Geraint say if they lit a fire?" asked Tristan, looking around at several scorch marks in the grass.

"I don't think so. He said they had a small gas stove, but they didn't light it, because they had cold beans and chocolate to eat," said Kate.

"What would make Simon get up in the night?"

"He needed the loo. He wanted to phone someone."

"I wonder if the police know where his phone is," said Tristan.

They walked down to the ten-foot-high metal fence lining the water's edge. It was thick and sturdy, with a roll of razor wire on top. There was a bank of mud and rubbish, about ten meters wide, leading down to the water, which was flowing past them toward the power plant. It was gray and cold. The light was already starting to fade, and there was a drizzle in the air.

"The fence is solid as a rock," said Kate, gripping it.

She checked her watch. It was now sunset. She shivered.

"It's bloody creepy here. Imagine if you need the loo and you wake up in the night and have to go over to that toilet block."

They both looked over at the toilet block, which was next to the dirt track and a row of pine trees.

They walked up to it. Tristan got out his phone and activated the light. Kate pushed at the door, and after a shove, it opened with a squeal. There were three cubicles, one with the door missing, and a row of sinks that were coated with grime and full of leaves. A small safety glass window, high on the back wall, was boarded up, and the wind whistled through a gap in the wood, and leaves skittered on the tiled floor.

"Smells just how I'd expected," said Tristan, pulling up the neck of his sweater so it covered his mouth and nose. Kate did the same. They walked past the first two cubicles. Tristan shined his light inside. The first toilet bowl was smashed, and it looked like a fire had been lit inside. The second cubicle had its doors hanging half off the hinges, and bird feces splattered the floor and the cistern. The last door was closed.

A noise made them both freeze. It sounded like a snort. They took a step back from the door, which was closed completely with no gaps underneath.

Kate reached out her hand and put it on the door handle and turned it, but the door wouldn't open. She jiggled it.

"Get away," said a male voice, thick with sleep. It made them both jump.

Shit, mouthed Tristan, stepping back from the door. Kate wondered who the hell would be using this toilet in the middle of nowhere on a dark October evening.

"GET THE FUCK OUT OF IT!" shouted the voice, and the door juddered, as if it had been kicked.

Tristan was already by the exit.

"Kate! Come on!" he said.

"Come back, and bring your flashlight . . ."

"What?" hissed Tristan. Kate was wary, but logically, she thought it could be a drifter, and he might have seen something. She took a small bottle of Mace from her pocket and showed Tristan. Mace wasn't strictly legal, but she always carried it with her. He relaxed a little when he saw it. She held it out in front of her.

"Hello. I'm Kate, and I'm here with, er, Tristan. We're here from the local homeless shelter," she said. There was a long pause.

"I have every right to be here. I'm trying to sleep," said the voice. Kate relaxed a little. She felt such pity for this man, having to shelter in a disgusting toilet block.

"Okay. That's fine. We're just here to check on you," she said. Juggling the little bottle of Mace, Kate rummaged in her handbag and found a bottle of water and a chocolate bar she'd bought from the petrol station when they stopped to fill up the car on the way. She also took out a twenty-pound note. Tristan was now beside her.

"What's your name?" she asked.

"None of your business!"

"I've got some food and twenty pounds here . . . Can you open the door so I can give it to you?"

"Leave it outside!" said the voice. The man had a Cornish burr to his accent.

"I don't want to leave a twenty-pound note outside, in case someone else takes it," said Kate. There was a long pause, and then a rustling sound, a crashing of a stick on the concrete floor. The door shook, and then there was a bang, and it swung open. Kate quickly stowed the Mace in the palm of her hand. A man of undetermined age lay on the floor between the toilet bowl and the wall. He was filthy, his face orange-tinged from the dirt. He had a long, matted beard and shoulder-length hair, which was either tied back or in a clump of knots—Kate couldn't tell. He wore many layers on top, all filthy and stained, and a ripped overcoat. He pushed himself up onto one elbow and blinked up at them. He had a broken bottle in his hand, and he was holding it up at them in half-hearted defense.

"We're not here to hurt you," said Kate.

She could see only one of his feet, with a brown scuffed shoe where long, dirty toenails were poking through the leather. Then she saw the other trouser leg was tied up at the knee and knotted with string. The rest of his leg was missing. The toilet lid was closed and covered with a small square of cloth. On it were a crumpled pack of cigarettes, a box of matches, three onions, and a small red penknife, covered with a layer of dried mud.

"Sorry to bother you," said Kate. It sounded stupid as soon as it came out of her mouth. "I'm Kate, and this is Tristan."

"You told me that already!" the old man cried, and he winced at the flashlight in his face. Tristan lowered it.

"Sorry, mate, didn't mean to blind you," said Tristan.

"Here," said Kate, holding out the bottle of water and the chocolate bar. He snatched them, turning them each over in his hands before placing them neatly on the toilet lid.

Kate was right, she thought. He was a drifter, and this could be a regular place for him. He might have seen something when Simon and Geraint were camping.

She crouched down and held up the twenty-pound note. He went to take it, but she kept it out of reach.

"Do you sleep here a lot?"

"Sometimes."

"Is it busy, the campsite?"

"Never. Though there's often comings and goings in the night . . ."

"What do you mean?"

"There's always kids boozing, foxes, and there's a van. It goes down to the water," he said.

"What kind of van? When? Can you describe it?"

"A white van . . . I don't know. I just try and sleep," said the old man.

"Does the van arrive in the day or at night?" asked Kate, holding the twenty-pound note closer.

"I'm only here at night. I mind me own business."

"That's a nice penknife," said Tristan. It glinted in the beam of the flashlight, and Kate saw there was an inscription on it. She reached out to take it.

"It's mine. I found it," said the old man, about to grab it off the toilet bowl.

"I'll only give you this twenty-pound note if you let me see it," said Kate. The drifter eyed the money and let Kate pick up the penknife. Tristan moved closer to look at it.

As she turned it over in her hands, Kate remembered her brother having a similar one, which he took to Cub Scout meetings, with a tiny blade, which was only good for cutting a piece of twine or peeling an apple. Kate fumbled with the penknife and managed to open it out. Like her brother's penknife, the blade was small with a dull, blunt edge. The handle was caked in mud, and she rubbed it away to reveal an engraving in tiny letters on the handle.

For Simon, on your twelfth birthday.

Tristan and Kate exchanged a look. He lifted his phone and took a photo.

"Where did you find this?" Kate asked the drifter.

"In the mud by the water. Most things in the water are lost or chucked away, so it's not stealing! It's mine. MINE!"

"You're lying. There's a huge fence blocking off the water," said Kate. The drifter still had his eyes on the twenty-pound note between her fingers.

"You can get through the fence! By the track!"

"Where?"

"Along, towards the power station. That's where I found it, in the mud. Can't you see the fucking mud on it?" shouted the drifter.

"Did you see anyone by the water, when you found this?" asked Kate.

"I don't go down there if I see people. They patrol the water with boats. I don't like people. People are cruel." The drifter moved quickly, reaching up and grabbing the knife from Kate, and the twenty-pound note. He shoved them into the folds of his coat, and pulled out a broken bottle with a spur of glass. "NOW GET OUT, DO YOU HEAR ME! OUT!" he shouted, his arm flailing with the broken glass. Kate and Tristan stepped back out of the toilet cubicle, and the old man slammed the door shut, kicking at the wood. There was a click as the lock was turned. Kate knocked on the door, but there was no answer. She knocked again, pleading with him to open the door, but there was no answer.

Kate and Tristan left the toilet block and came back outside, relieved at the taste of fresh air. It was now dark and raining harder.

"We need to confirm Simon had a penknife," said Kate.

"We should check out the fence," said Tristan.

They put up their hoods and walked back down across the grass to the fence. The turbines from the power plant seemed to be humming at a higher pitch, and on the other side the water was rushing past.

They found an opening in the trees leading off to the right, in the direction of the power plant. They had to put their phone lights back on. It led to a thin track. The roar of the turbines grew louder, and Kate saw that there were tire tracks in the soft grass. On each side the track was lined with trees. The tall fence continued on their left-hand side.

After a couple hundred meters, the track widened out to a square of rough ground, and for a few feet there were no trees, just the bare metal fence.

They got up close and started to examine the fence with the flashlights from their phones. Pushing her fingers into the mossy dirt where the fence panel met the ground, Kate found a small piece of metal attached to the fence panel that hooked into a small hole in the tall fence post.

"Hang on, there's something here," she said. Tristan came over, and they fiddled with it for a moment and pulled. The hook suddenly popped out, and the whole bottom panel of the fence came loose. They could lift it up, leaving a half-meter gap. They crouched down and crawled through.

On the other side was a moss-covered bank and some trees with a clear path through them down to the water.

They emerged onto the muddy edge of the reservoir, where there was lots of rubbish, thrown up in several lines with the changing water level.

"The drifter said he found the penknife in the mud by the water," said Tristan.

"If he did, how did he know about the fence?" said Kate.

"Simon or the drifter?"

"Both of them . . ." Kate's voice trailed off, confused.

They looked up at the two huge domed buildings housing the hydroelectric turbines. The red lights were flashing on and off in unison, to warn airplanes.

"Let's go back a bit. Simon gets up in the night; he leaves the tent and goes for a walk . . . ," started Tristan.

"It's dark. Creepy as hell. He's on his own. Screwed up in the head. He's got that penknife, but it's a silly little thing, almost a toy. Maybe he grabs one of the sharp metal tent pegs as well, to protect himself, feel safe," said Kate.

"He walks down here and somehow finds there's a gap in the fence, to get down to the water's edge."

"What if someone was here, doing something at the fence? And Simon saw them?" said Kate.

"He scared someone, and they attacked him? And Simon ends up being stabbed with the tent peg."

"Yeah."

"So, Simon scared someone, but doing what?" asked Tristan. There was a pause. Kate moved to the edge of the water. It was now dark, and the lights from the power station were shining off the inky-black water as it rushed past, toward the turbines. Kate turned it over in her mind for a moment, but kept coming back to the same thought.

"The most logical conclusion, right now, is that Geraint was involved. Geraint and Simon had a fight, they ended up in the water, and Simon was trying to get away. If he went into the water here, he would really have to fight against the current," she said, confused. "If Simon was badly hurt, he would have been sucked toward the turbines. You see how the water is being drawn into the sluice gates here."

Tristan nodded.

"Surely, Simon would have swum across the reservoir to the other side; even if he lost his bearings at first, you would swim across to the nearest point of land," said Tristan, indicating the trees directly ahead of them, on the opposite bank of the reservoir.

"But he swam over a mile in the other direction, away from the power station. The adrenaline could have kept him going for a bit. He swims away from something. Logically, a boat. A boat ran him over . . . I'm still having trouble imagining Geraint attacking him. We need to talk to that drifter again. He said he saw a van, but there could be a boat involved too. He might have seen Simon and Geraint on the night Simon died," said Kate.

25

The rain stopped as Kate and Tristan walked to the campsite. They came back to the toilet block and went inside, but the last cubicle was empty. The drifter was gone.

"How long were we down there?" said Kate. "I thought he looked bedded in for the night."

"He left the chocolate bar wrapper, but all his stuff's gone," said Tristan, shining the flashlight in the cubicle.

"Where would he go? We're miles from anything. We need to find him," said Kate.

From outside came the rattling sound of a car engine, and through the gap in the boarded-up window, car headlights lit up the inside of the tiny toilet. A vehicle came to a stop outside, but the engine continued running.

Kate looked at Tristan. A deafening gunshot reverberated through the tiny space, and she grabbed hold of Tristan's arm.

"What the hell!" she said. Her ears were ringing. They jumped again as another shot was fired.

"All right! Come out of there, right now!" shouted a man's voice with a thick Cornish accent.

"Who are you?" Kate shouted back.

"Come out! You're trespassing on private property," said the voice. It had an authority and certainty, which made her think it was police.

"Out! Don't make me come in there!"

Kate moved to the door and announced who they were.

"We are lecturers from the university. We're not drug addicts or homeless people! We know our rights with regards to firearms . . ." Her fear was that they could be shot accidentally.

There was silence, and then they heard the click of a gun magazine being opened and the chink of the spent bullets popping out.

Kate nodded at Tristan, and they cautiously came out of the toilet and into the glare of car headlights.

Kate held up her hand against the light. It was an older-looking man, rather short and dressed in shooting gear, with a long wax jacket. His face was jowly, indicating he was in his sixties, but his hair was dyed jet black and slicked over in a side parting. He was braced on both feet, with the gun lying open on the crook of his arm. Behind him was a large, ancient Land Rover, mud splattered with the engine still running.

"What are you doing trespassing?" he said, looking them up and down.

"This is public land," said Kate. Tristan had his hands in the air. She shot him a look, and he dropped them to his sides.

"The campsite is, but we got a call from the plant saying there were two people on the banks near the sluice gates. That's private property, and very dangerous. You could've fallen in."

Kate went to say something, but he carried on.

"I don't give a fuck about your safety, but if you fell in and ended up in the turbines, we'd have a right mess on our hands and have to shut down."

"Do you work at the power plant?" asked Kate. "Can I see some ID?"

The back door of the Land Rover opened, and an elderly lady got out. She was surprisingly tall, the same height as Tristan. She was wearing a pleated tartan skirt, Barbour wellies, and a wax jacket. She wore a head scarf over her head, but her sharp-featured face was heavily made up.

"Who are you? You were trespassing. There's a two-thousand-pound fine for trespassing. Have you got two thousand pounds to spare?" she said, jabbing a finger with red nail polish at the reservoir and then Kate and Tristan.

"There's an old man sleeping rough in here," said Kate.

"What?" said the woman, her eyes narrowing.

"He said he was hungry and he wanted to sleep," said Tristan. "We gave him some chocolate."

"What are your names?"

"This is public land. We don't need to tell you our names," said Kate. She was always taken aback by the arrogance from some of the well off and privileged.

"You were trespassing on my land and government land. The power station provides a vital function as a public utility. Now get the fuck off before we shoot you and then bill your relatives the fine."

"I'm a private investigator. My name is Kate Marshall, and this is my associate, Tristan Harper. We're investigating the death of Simon Kendal. His body was found in the reservoir in August."

This seemed to have an effect on the woman.

"Yes. A very sad business, but the police are dealing with it."

"We're also investigating the disappearance of another woman, a professor. She went missing close to the reservoir. Can I ask you, have the police conducted a search of the reservoir?"

"Who are you again?" said the woman, advancing on her.

"Kate Marshall."

The woman took the gun from the man.

"Listen to me," she said, carefully. The man fumbled in his pocket and handed a shotgun cartridge to her, which she slipped into the barrel. "This is your last warning. If you trespass again, we will call the police, and you will be prosecuted." He handed her a second cartridge, and she loaded it into the gun and closed the barrel. "Have I made myself clear?" She handed the gun back to the man. She went to the car door and got into the passenger seat, closing the door.

"Is that your car?" the man said, tipping his head toward Kate's Ford.

"Yes."

"Get in it. Go." He pointed the gun at them.

"Pointing a firearm at us is technically an assault," said Kate.

"You better hop to it, then, before I technically pull the trigger," he said. Tristan glanced at Kate, trying not to look scared. They walked over to her car and got in. She saw the man drop the barrel of the gun, but he carried on watching as she started the car and then pulled away.

"Jesus Christ," said Tristan, holding out his trembling hands. "Can they do that?"

"No, but it's our word against theirs." She looked in her rearview mirror as the Land Rover was obscured by trees. "I'd like to know why they showed up. Isn't there a proper security firm who would come and check it out? You okay?"

"Yeah. I've never heard a real gun being fired before," he said.

There was a roar, and suddenly the Land Rover appeared on the track behind them, only slowing at the last minute, with its bonnet against their bumper. She could see the grim-set, jowly face of the driver and the old woman's outline in the shadows of the passenger seat.

Tristan glanced back nervously.

"Let them overtake, Kate."

They got to the main road, and Kate kept calm and pulled out of the junction. She expected the Land Rover to pass, but it stayed very close, almost touching their bumper.

"What's he doing?" said Tristan, as Kate slowed and he matched their speed. The Land Rover's headlights were on full beam, and Kate winced against the glare.

"Intimidating us," she said. They crawled through the winding roads for a few minutes. Kate's heart was thudding in her chest. Then just as they passed a large set of gates to the right, the Land Rover turned abruptly into the driveway, and they were plunged into darkness.

"Where did they go?" asked Tristan. Kate slowed, did a U-turn and doubled back to the gates, and stopped outside. "Careful," he said.

Far up ahead, she could see the rear lights of the Land Rover as it got to the top of a steep hill. Perched on top they could just make out the outline of a large house.

"Can you see what it says on the gate?" asked Kate.

"*Allways Manor House*," said Tristan, peering at the sign.

26

"Do you think we can enhance the photo?" asked Kate, holding up Tristan's iPhone. It was the picture he'd taken of the penknife in the campsite toilet. Tristan was embarrassed and annoyed that the light had glinted off the metal, making the engraved inscription a blur.

"I enhanced it already," said Tristan as he chopped vegetables for a stir-fry. They were back at Kate's house, and he'd offered to prepare dinner as a thank-you for letting him stay. "Sorry I screwed up."

"It's not your fault," said Kate, putting his iPhone down and grabbing hers. "I'm going to check this with Lyn Kendal." She dialed the number and put the phone under her chin. She opened the fridge, and Tristan saw it was rather bare inside. There was a huge jug of iced tea on the top shelf, a saucer with slices of lemon, and a few pieces of cheese. "It's her voice mail."

Kate hung up the phone and filled a tumbler with ice from a bag in the freezer. Tristan set to work on chopping a red pepper and watched as she concentrated on filling the tumbler before garnishing it with a slice of lemon. She took a deep drink, closed her eyes, and sighed. She opened her eyes, and he looked away.

"Sorry, my manners. Would you like a drink?"

"Have you got a Coke?" he asked, as he slid the sliced red peppers off the chopping board and into the pan. There was a pleasant hiss, followed by a delicious smell, and he gave it a stir. His stomach rumbled.

"Yes, I do. Jake seems to bathe in the stuff, so I've still got plenty here," she said, opening the fridge again and finding one in the bottom of the drawer.

"How come you didn't leave a message with Lyn?" he asked, opening the can.

"Messages can be ignored or anticipated. I want to ask her and hear what she says. It's habit. I learned in the police, it's best to talk to people . . ."

Kate's phone rang again.

"Ah, this is Jake, excuse me," she said. She took her drink through to the living room and sat down in one of the chairs by the window. After their weird, long day, it was odd to come back to the same house. Tristan knew he would have to go back and face Sarah. Kate was great, but they already spent a lot of time together, and he didn't want to be in her way. He carried on cooking and heard snatches of her conversation with Jake.

"I thought it was definite that you were coming for half term. It's next week, love. I'd like to know so I can get ready and go shopping," said Kate.

Tristan quickly sliced some mushrooms and slid them into the pan, where the food was cooking nicely. Kate was still on the phone, and he wanted to know if she had any noodles. He was reluctant to go poking through her cupboards.

He turned down the gas under the pan and put the lid on. Then he opened his laptop and logged on to the UK Missing Persons Unit. He opened his notebook and checked what he'd noted down and typed "Ulrich Mazur" into the search box. The result came right back with a photo. Ulrich was handsome. He had short strawberry blond hair, blue-gray eyes, and a wide, round face with high Slavic cheekbones. It was an ID photo, but he was smiling—a broad, warm smile with perfect white teeth. He wore a dark T-shirt, and he was very thin. The missing person report had his stats written underneath. He was six feet tall and weighed seventy kilograms.

Tristan could hear Kate on the phone, now talking to someone else. The conversation was getting a little heated, and she kept saying, *I know, Mum. It wasn't my fault, do you hear?*

Kate's kitchen opened right out into the living room. He debated taking the computer and going upstairs, but there was the food. He turned his attention back to the second name Rachel at the Wild Oak had given them. He typed in "Sally-Ann Cobbs." An ID photo, which looked almost as if it had been taken under duress, appeared on-screen. Sally-Ann seemed very tiny in the photo and was grimacing. She had mousy hair, a ratty face, and acne over her cheeks. She was seventeen years old when she went missing. He thought back to what Rachel said, about Sally-Ann reaching sixteen and having to leave the children's home and go out into the world. It made him think of him and Sarah. When their mother died, he was fifteen, and Sarah was eighteen. If it had happened a couple of years earlier, they'd have both been taken into a home. The food hissing on the stove broke him out of his thoughts, and he got up and stirred the pan.

Kate had finished her call, and she came back into the kitchen. She sighed, went to the fridge, and filled up her glass. Tristan wondered if he was getting in her way.

"Listen, I can get out of your hair tomorrow. I need to go home; I'm running low on clean clothes," he said.

"No, you can stay. I've got two spare rooms, although I'm not sure if Jake is coming for half term . . . He's started to see a counselor. One of the teachers at school heard about us finding Simon Kendal's body in the reservoir. And now the school thinks he should be talking to someone," said Kate.

"That's good, isn't it?"

"It's good, yes. But this counselor, apparently, is now insisting that Jake goes to sessions regularly, which are on Wednesdays. That scuppers him coming here for a week. And Jake has made friends, who he has plans with." Kate put her drink down and rubbed her eyes. "Who knows? They might be using the counselor as an excuse for him not to come and visit . . ."

Tristan saw there was a great deal of emotion going on under the surface with Kate and her relationship with Jake. His own mother had been absent for a lot of his childhood because of drink and drugs. From what he'd heard, Kate got clean when Jake was very young, but her mother had refused to give her back custody of Jake. It was a complicated situation, and he didn't know everything, but Kate was a good woman who had sorted herself out. She deserved to see her son.

"The food's ready," said Tristan.

"It smells wonderful," said Kate, seeming grateful that he'd changed the subject.

"I found Ulrich and Sally-Ann," said Tristan, indicating his laptop as he dished the stir-fry out into bowls. Kate studied the photos.

"It really gets me, the photos they use for missing people," said Kate. "They never think the police will use it for an appeal or in memoriam . . ." She stared at the photos on the screen for a moment. "I was sure Rachel was telling the truth, but here they are, officially."

They sat down to eat at the table.

"Do you still want to talk to that woman, Kirstie?" asked Tristan.

"Yeah. I'm going to try and call her again after dinner. It would be interesting to get her to open up and see what other details she comes out with, presuming she's not lying . . . I know tomorrow is a half day, and then we're on reading week. Do you want to do some digging around about Shadow Sands reservoir and Hedley House nightclub online? I also want to see if there are more stories of missing people. And I want to find out who that woman is with the shotgun-toting driver."

27

Magdalena had drifted in and out of consciousness on the floor of the concrete tiled room. Her nose and head throbbed with pain intermittently, but she was able to sleep for a time.

Time was reduced to her heartbeats. She would get to twenty and the hunger and exhaustion would cause her to lose count. A time later, the pain became more acute in her head, and she couldn't breathe through her nose. She sat up, leaning on the edge of the concrete bed. Her feet and legs were numb, and it took a few painful minutes of shifting and moving, panicking that she was paralyzed, before the feeling came back into her legs.

The sensation of pins and needles as a dead limb comes back to life always made her feel sick, but for once she was glad of it. She got to her feet and washed in the sink, gently swishing water over her face and unblocking one of her nostrils. She also drank and drank, the delicious cold water sharpening her mind. When she turned off the tap, the room was silent again. She strained to hear any noise from above her. Trying to hear past the thud of her heart beating and the sound of her breathing through her mouth.

A couple of times a breeze seemed to waft over her wet face, and she flinched and reached out, imagining that he was still there in the room with her.

Magdalena groped around the room, clawing at the air in front of her, beside her, but felt nothing. She went back out into the corridor, feeling the walls and the space around, checking the small toilet, and then she came back out to the lift doors. They were cold to the touch, and she put her ear to them and listened.

Nothing.

She pushed her fingernails into the gap between the doors and pulled and prized so hard that one of her nails tore off, far down into the quick.

She squealed in pain and put the finger into her mouth. The nail was half hanging off; the sharp edge curled away from the nail bed and was starting to bleed.

Magdalena started to cry. What she wouldn't give for a nail file. She chewed at the nail and managed to bite half of it away, but she was still left with a hangnail. She slid down the steel doors and sat on the concrete floor.

A horrible story came back to her, told by her friend Gabriela from university. Gabriela had been attacked one night on the way home from the library. She'd been walking through a pleasant, leafy neighborhood, when an older man dressed in running gear had stopped to ask directions. He'd been polite and ordinary, quite handsome, but when he gained her attention, he'd pounced and bundled her down a thin alley between houses.

Magdalena had never understood why Gabriela hadn't fought back, and if she was honest, she'd judged her friend for saying that she went limp and let the man rape her.

Let him. Let. Him. Those two words had been so chilling to Magdalena. Now she was in a terrifying situation, one she knew she wouldn't survive. If this man was going to take her life, would she let him do whatever he wanted before he killed her? Would he hurt her less?

Magdalena and her sister had always been told by their father to defend themselves if they were ever in a fight. But her father had been brought up with brothers. He was thinking like a man. Her father had always wished for a son to complete the family. Boys are taught to fight, but should girls be taught to play dead? Magdalena had always been a fighter, but this terrible, terrifying situation she found herself in was making her think differently. How could she have judged Gabriela when all she did was try to survive?

The adrenaline had been surging through her veins, and suddenly it seemed to drop away, and she was exhausted. She had never felt so tired. She lay back against the wall, tucking herself into the part where it met the floor.

Don't sleep! You mustn't sleep! cried an urgent voice in her head, but she breathed in and out, and a warm feeling washed over her.

———

She woke cold and alert. Swallowing and feeling drool in the side of her mouth. A faint sound made her stop breathing. It was coming from inside the room. She put her hands out. She was lying on the bed . . . How had she got to the bed?

There was a scuffing sound of a shoe on the floor. A small intake of breath. The sound of someone swallowing. Did she just swallow? No. It was someone. Was he standing over her? Or was he farther away, watching her from the corner of the room?

In her mind, she saw her father's face. The darkness was so absolute that she was able to see things in her mind when her eyes were open. Her eyes flapped uselessly in the dark.

Never tuck your thumb into your first when you punch someone! he said.

Then she saw Gabriela, lying limp in the alleyway, as she'd often imagined it. The man on top of her. Her eyes wide open and a pool of blood spreading underneath her as he thrusted.

Magdalena closed her useless flapping eyes and braced herself on the bed to fight. She didn't feel him come close to her, and she smelled that faint chemical smell again.

"Do you want to touch the stars?" said a voice right beside her ear. As she gasped in shock, she breathed in the chemical and felt the bottle under her nose. The bed seemed to swallow her whole, and she was gone.

28

After the morning's lectures, Kate and Tristan took some lunch up to her office, and they started to research the Shadow Sands reservoir online. They discovered it was part of a larger estate of land and buildings owned by the aristocratic Baker family. When the family got into debt in the 1940s, their solution was to dam the River Fowey, which ran through the estate, and build a hydroelectric dam. In 1953, six villages and the surrounding farmland were flooded to build the dam and the power plant.

They also discovered that the woman who'd rocked up at the campsite the previous day was Silvia Baker, and at eighty-two she was the oldest living descendant of the Baker family. She owned the Shadow Sands corporation with her nephews Thomas, fifty-one, and Stephen, forty-two, and her niece, Dana, forty. They hadn't been able to find out the name of the man who had the shotgun.

They had googled "Ulrich Mazur" and "Sally-Ann Cobbs" with "Shadow Sands reservoir," but nothing came up to link them with the reservoir. But Kate had found a lot of stuff online about a local protest group called the Right to Roam Alliance, and for the past hour they'd been looking through the search results.

"This alliance seems to have it in for the Baker family," said Kate. "There's loads of stuff, protests and petitions about how the hydroelectric plant damages the environment, and there seems to be a long-running dispute about several public footpaths which run across the estate and beside the reservoir. Two years ago, Silvia Baker apparently let her rottweilers savage a couple of ramblers on the footpath which runs past her house, Allways Manor. She got a fine in court, and the dogs had to be put down."

"Poor dogs," said Tristan. "The Right to Roam Alliance have a YouTube account. There's a news report from 1991 about bodies being found in the water."

Kate came over to sit with him on the sofa. Tristan clicked on a video titled THIRD BODY FOUND IN SHADOW SANDS RESERVOIR 3/3/1991.

It was a local news report. PENNY LAYTON, REPORTING was written at the top of the screen, and a young journalist wearing a blue waterproof coat stood in the grass of the campsite next to the reservoir. To her left was the toilet block, looking much newer and cleaner in 1991. Clouds hung low, and a little way out on the water, a forensics recovery team in a boat was winching a body bag out of the water.

"The body of a young woman was discovered during a routine patrol by one of the maintenance men who regularly check the reservoir," said Penny. "The Shadow Sands corporation has been under pressure for some months to fence off the north side of the reservoir. This is the third body found in as many years—a young woman was found two years ago, and last summer nine-year-old boy Peter Fishwick drowned while camping here with his family."

"Look. This is before they put the fence up by the water," said Kate.

The camera then cut to Penny Layton outside a country pub as she hurried toward a younger-looking Silvia Baker getting into a Land Rover. Silvia wore a burgundy coat with a matching fur trim. Her chestnut-brown hair was pulled into a sleek bun. The door was being held open for her by the same beefy-looking man who had threatened Kate and Tristan with the shotgun.

Silvia looked uncomfortable as Penny pushed a microphone under her nose.

"Silvia Baker, can you comment on the body found in the reservoir?"

"I extend my deep regret that this young woman drowned," she said.

"The police haven't yet confirmed cause of death," said Penny.

"Yes. Of course, but I can only imagine . . ."

"This is the third body found in the reservoir in three years . . ."

"We are cooperating, where appropriate, with the authorities on every level. I'm not at liberty to say any more."

"The Right to Roam Alliance have lobbied repeatedly for the north side of the reservoir to be fenced off. Will the corporation take responsibility for this girl's death if it's ruled as a drowning?"

Silvia's nostrils flared.

"We have fought for many years to have the campsite moved to a safer locale, but it is a public right of way which the public seem to insist on using. If they will insist on using it, then they have to take responsibility for their own safety. There is very clear signage stating that the water should not be entered . . ."

"She's losing her temper there," said Tristan.

"People must take responsibility for their own safety!" cried Silvia on the video.

"So, what you're saying is it's their fault? It's Peter Fishwick's fault he drowned? He was nine years old."

The driver with the dyed-black hair guided Silvia into the back of the car and then put his hand over the camera lens.

The video abruptly ended.

"Hang on," said Kate, grabbing her computer and googling. "Here we go, Peter Fishwick . . . His death *was* subsequently ruled as accidental drowning. Poor little thing."

"There's another video here dated two years later," said Tristan, indicating it in the YouTube search results. It was called SHADOW SANDS RESERVOIR COURT CASE—6/7/1993. Kate clicked on the link.

The video started from outside Exeter magistrates' court. Silvia Baker was emerging from the court and stomping down the steps to her car. The same man with the dyed-black hair opened the door for her. The camera caught up with her as she sat in the back of the car. She reached out, pushed the lens away, and slammed the door.

The driver then hurried inside, and the car drove away with a squeal of rubber, and past a smattering of protesters holding homemade signs saying: **MAKE SHADOW SANDS SAFE! PROTECT OUR RIGHT OF WAY! RIGHT TO ROAM!**

Penny Layton was pictured outside the courthouse in front of the protesters.

"After a lengthy court case, the Shadow Sands corporation lost its final appeal and was ordered to erect a two-mile fence around the north side of the reservoir," she said. "Legal and construction costs are expected to be in the region of three million pounds. BBC *Spotlight* was today given access to the project, to see the heavy-duty fencing being put up along the north side of the reservoir. The Baker siblings were even pitching in today with the fence building!"

The camera cut to Penny Layton standing with two men and a woman. They looked in their twenties and all wore jeans, heavy boots, and suspiciously clean-looking high-visibility jackets.

"Lord Baker, if I can start with you," said Penny Layton to the first young man. He was tall and thin with dark hair parted to the side.

"Please, call me Thomas," he said awkwardly. He was very well spoken.

"Thomas. In the past five years, three people have drowned in the reservoir. Why has it taken so long to put this fence up?"

"We've long been campaigning for this side of the reservoir to be closed off to the public," said Thomas. "It's rarely used, but there are a small number of people who insist that it remain open as a right of way . . . ," he said. He was a serious young man, who looked down at the ground, awkward in the gaze of the camera.

"Penny. If I can interject . . . ," said the young man standing next to him. Penny moved the microphone over to him. He was very handsome with blond, foppish hair. "I'm the younger Baker, Stephen. Spare to the heir, so to speak . . . We have the strongest fencing going up to make this area safe to the public. The Right to Roam Alliance have really behaved terribly. Our family has been the target of hateful threats and all kinds of nasty stuff. I thought walkers and ramblers were nice people, but they're as bad as terrorists!"

"We should concentrate on the positive," said Dana Baker, leaning over to the microphone to stop her brother from saying more. She was small and blonde, with a pixie haircut. "We're deeply troubled that the Right to Roam Alliance have tied this case up in court for so long. These accidents could have been avoided, but today is a positive step toward a safer place for the public to enjoy."

The news report cut to a series of clips showing various protesters with Right to Roam Alliance banners and T-shirts. In the first, the protesters were screaming and shouting at the horses on a local hunt. The second showed them protesting outside Exeter Crown Court, and in the final clip, a group of protesters was at the campsite, launching a huge wooden raft into the water, piled high with some kind of material. They whooped and cheered as they lit the material and the burning raft was pulled by the current toward the hydroelectric turbine, vanishing into the sluice gate.

"We contacted the Right to Roam Alliance, but they were unavailable for comment," said Penny Layton.

Kate and Tristan were quiet for a moment.

"We need to find out the names of the two women whose bodies were found in the reservoir," said Kate. "The first woman would have been found in 1989, the boy drowned in the summer of 1990, and from the video it looks like the body of the woman was pulled out of the reservoir on the third of March, 1991."

"So, we have Magdalena, who has gone missing close to the reservoir," said Tristan. "That was a quarter of a mile from the water, so not directly linked to the reservoir. Then Simon Kendal was found by you last August, Ulrich Mazur goes missing on his way home from Hedley House nightclub in October 2008, Sally-Ann Cobbs in November 2009."

"Seven people, with four bodies, or three. I have a feeling the nine-year-old's death is something different. An accidental drowning. We need to find out," said Kate.

"Are they linked? Or are we wanting there to be a link?" asked Tristan.

"Statistically, there could be accidents around a reservoir, especially if there's fog," agreed Kate. "People walking along the road could stray off and fall in and drown, but if the reservoir regularly has maintenance boats running, why wouldn't they find the bodies? Unless it's weighted down, a body will float . . ." Her phone began to ring on the desk, and she reached over and saw the screen. She looked up at Tristan. "It's Kirstie, the girl from the bar who said she was abducted."

29

Kate had arranged to meet Kirstie Newett on Friday evening at a Starbucks in Frome Crawford, a town on the outskirts of Exeter. When Kate arrived, Kirstie was already there, at a quiet table in the corner. She stood out from the students working at their laptops. Kate knew from talking to Rachel at the Wild Oak that Kirstie was in her midtwenties, but she looked older. She wore black leggings, grubby white trainers, and a pale-blue fleece with a fur-lined hood. Her blonde hair was scraped back from a large, high, shiny forehead and had a few inches of black roots.

"Thank you for meeting with me," said Kate when they were settled with their drinks. "What made you decide to talk to me?"

"Rachel from the Wild Oak rung me. She told me what's been going on . . . ," said Kirstie. "And I looked you up. I saw the stuff about you online. How everyone turned against you when you found out your boss in the police was that serial killer. You've had it rough."

"I'm still better off than most people," said Kate.

"No one believed what happened to me. I thought if I talked to you, it might make me feel like I'm not crazy."

Kate nodded.

"Are you like a proper private detective?"

"I do this on the side. Do you mind if I take notes?"

"No; I mean no, I don't mind . . . ," said Kirstie. She kept making eye contact and then looking away. She was also jiggling her leg nervously. Kate wondered if she was on any drugs, but Kirstie's pupils were dilated, and she couldn't smell alcohol. She was giving off a musty smell of stale body odor and cigarettes.

"Can we start with the date it happened, if you can remember?" asked Kate.

"I'd been out for a night at Hedley House. It was late September in 2009," said Kirstie. "I was working at the Wild Oak and doing nails on the side, you know, from home. I'd done shit jobs for a few years, and I saved up enough to get my nail kit. You need a UV lamp and all the nail polish costs, plus accessories. It was a lot. I was on unemployment at the same time, thinking I could do nails on the side and build up clients, but some bitch shopped me to the Jobseeker's. They cut my benefits. It was right when that happened that I went up to Hedley. It was the end of the night, and I was drunk."

"Were you there with anyone?"

Kirstie shook her head.

"The girls from work said they were going, and I thought I'd see them there, which I did . . . But at the end of the night, everyone was getting off with blokes or had already gone home. I had a fiver in my pocket, and I needed cigarettes. I was living in Ashdean then, and I decided to walk home."

"Had you done it before?"

"Once or twice; loads of people used to do it in the summer when it was hot. It was quite fun cos there was always a crowd going back to Ashdean, but it was really cold for September. I was walking back on the road; quite a few cars passed, but no one stopped. Then this fog came down. I'd been walking on the road so the incoming traffic could see me, like you're supposed to, but I had to get up on the shoulder because the fog got so thick and the cars were crawling past. Then one of the cars stopped."

"Where?"

"I don't know. Some lay-by."

"Had you gone past the Shadow Sands reservoir?"

"I think so. I was slaughtered, and it was now, like, so foggy. I'd fallen down a couple of times, almost ended up in a ditch. And then there was this car, parked up by the side of the road."

"What kind of car was it?"

"It was a pale-colored hatchback. The lights were on inside, and there was an old man in the driver's seat. He rolled down the window, and he seemed very nice. He was local, had a proper local accent, and he asked if I was mad, walking! I was frozen—all I had on was a skimpy skirt and top. No coat. I remember how warm his car was when he wound down the window—the hot air flowed over me."

"What exactly did he look like?"

"He had on a flat cap, with lots of gray hair coming out from under it, like his hair was getting long and he was due for a cut. He also had a big nose, like a gnome. A bushy beard and mustache. Thick glasses which made his eyes look big. His eyes were an odd color, a blue purple . . ."

She shifted her chair and looked down at the table, fiddling with her paper coffee cup.

"Are you okay? Do you need to stop?" asked Kate. Kirstie looked around at the Starbucks. The people were thinning out; a smattering of students remained, working on their laptops, plugged into their earphones.

"No. I'm okay."

"What happened next?"

"He asked where I was going and if I wanted a lift. He seemed doddery and old and nice. I gave him a fake address, thinking I was so smart and that I'd get him to drop me a few roads from my flat, and I got in beside him, closed the door. He locked the doors. He was quiet for half a minute or so. And I'll always remember that he turned to me, his voice changed, and he said, '*Do you want to touch the stars?*'

"He suddenly leaned across and came at me and pushed this bottle up under my nose. Held the back of my head, made me smell it."

"What do you think it was? Poppers?"

"No. Something stronger. PCP, angel dust. I was already drunk, and this just made me feel like I was flying. Everything went whoosh, and I must have passed out. I woke up later in a room."

"Where?"

"I don't know . . . It was pitch black . . . ," she said, her leg now jogging fast and her hands shaking.

"It's okay," said Kate, taking her hands in hers. Kirstie pulled them away. One of her sleeves rode up, and Kate saw scars crisscrossing her wrist. Kirstie pulled her sleeve back down.

"Have you ever been in a place so dark that it's the same when you open and close your eyes? Just pitch black. Nothing."

Kate thought back to a school trip to France when they had visited a cave and the tour guide switched off the lights for a few seconds. She recalled the fear of that short time in the pitch blackness.

"Yes."

"There was a room with a bed, and then there was a sink in the corner, and I found it had water. I drank from the tap. There was a corridor, and some other rooms, I think. I never saw. I just felt my way around."

"How long were you there?"

"I don't know. Days. There was a lift at the end of the corridor."

"How did you know it was a lift?"

"I could hear it, that noise a lift makes, and then one day I was feeling my way around and the lift started to come down, and then the doors opened . . ."

Kirstie had to stop for a moment and take a breath.

"A man came out of the lift in the dark," she said.

"Are you sure it was a man?"

"He smelled like a man."

"A bad smell?" asked Kate.

Kirstie nodded.

"Sweaty, stale sweat."

"Did he hurt you?"

"Not at first. I ran. I fell and hurt myself, and then . . . he hunted me."

"Hunted you?"

"He watched me, followed me. A few times I felt him touch me . . . I let him touch me . . . I thought that might stop him hurting me."

"How long did it last?"

"It felt like hours. Then he made me smell the drugs again, the chemical, and when I woke up, he was gone."

"How many times did he do it?"

"I don't know, three, four."

"Was this over the space of several days, or hours?" asked Kate, thinking that this guy kept his victims for a few days.

"I don't know, it felt like days."

"How did you escape?"

"I didn't. I got really ill with fever and hallucinations, and it was then that he strangled me. I don't remember all of it, but he trapped me in a corner, and grabbed me by the throat and squeezed, and I passed out. I don't know if he thought I was dead, but I woke up later inside a car. It was nighttime, and the car was all steamed up inside, and I was wrapped in a sheet. I managed to get out of the car. I remember there was a sign for Shadow Sands campsite. There was this roaring sound from the power plant. He was outside, and he chased me into the water . . ."

"What did the man look like?"

"I don't know. My throat was so swollen. I'd burst blood vessels in my eyes. It was a blur. He was a shape, not tall, not short. I just ran into the water, and then I started to swim."

"Did you go from the car to the water? Were there any trees between you and the water?"

"There was a fence, and there was a hole in it."

"Did he follow you to the water?"

"Yes, but I kept on swimming far out, and then I heard the sound of a boat motor. The water was really cold, but the air was warm, and it made this steam or fog come off the surface of the water. It was really beautiful . . . It sounds stupid, but it made me want to live. It made me want to see the sun come up and feel the sun on my face again, so I kept swimming to the other side. I kept hearing the boat coming closer, but this fog got thicker and hid me.

"I was surprised when I reached the bank on the other side of the reservoir. There was a place where the tree branches hung low and touched the water. I grabbed hold of one and stayed there. I don't know how long I lay there. I kept hearing the motorboat circling back and forward, and then it was quiet. I got out of the water and walked through the woods, and when I reached the road, I flagged down a car . . . That was a mistake. Almost as bad as getting into the car in the fog."

"Why?"

"The driver was a policeman. He was off duty."

"Can you remember his name?" asked Kate.

"Yeah. Arron Ko."

Kate froze with her coffee cup in her hand.

"Are you sure that's what his name was?"

"Yeah. He was Asian. I remember the odd name. He flashed his ID card when we got to the hospital, and the doctors seemed to know who he was. He found a doctor who saw to me straightaway. I was shocked when I saw myself in the mirror. I had these terrible bruises around my neck. My eyes were almost red because I'd burst blood vessels in my eyes. I had a kidney infection. The doctor listened to me, and he was gentle and did some tests, and then I was taken up to a ward and given a bed, and I just fell asleep."

At this point Kirstie started to cry, and she wiped her eyes with a couple of napkins.

"I don't know how long I was asleep, but when I woke up the next day, I was taken for a wash and given clean clothes by this nurse, and then they put me in an ambulance and told me I was being sectioned. I'd been diagnosed by the doctor as delusional . . . I tried to get away, and I screamed and shouted as best I could. My throat was all fucked up. Then they put me in restraints, and they gave me an injection."

"Did you see the policeman again?"

"No. I woke up in a mental hospital. A secure unit near Birmingham. They pumped me full of drugs, and I lost the plot."

"How long were you in the secure unit?"

"Almost four months. When I got back, I'd lost my flat, and I was put in a bed-and-breakfast until they could find me council accommodation."

Kate didn't know what to say for a moment. She was shocked Kirstie had named Arron Ko.

"Was there ever an official police report filed with your allegations?"

"I don't know."

"Did you go back to the police and make a complaint?"

Kirstie sat back.

"Have you listened to what I just told you? A man locked me up, drugged me, and then no one believed me. A fucking bent copper did this to me. I lost everything. You think I'm gonna go trotting back to the police station and make a fucking complaint?"

"I'm sorry, that was a stupid question," said Kate.

Kirstie shook her head and looked at the table.

"Do you believe me?" she said, looking up at Kate, challenging her.

"Yes, I do."

Kirstie nodded.

"Good. Cos it's all true . . . That girl, Magdalena. She went missing five days ago, didn't she?"

"Yes."

"When the policeman took me to the hospital, I found out that ten days had gone by since the man drugged me in the fog. He kept me for ten days. Are you looking for her?"

Kate was unprepared for the conversation to move so quickly over to her.

"I didn't know that you had been kept prisoner for so long."

Kirstie reached out and took Kate's hand.

"Promise me you'll find this Magdalena. I've been let down by so many men, the police, the social services, doctors . . . I've thought of ending it all so many times. Maybe I haven't yet cos I was meant to talk to you and tell you my story."

Kate nodded.

"So, do you promise?" asked Kirstie.

"I promise," said Kate. Hoping that she could keep that promise.

30

After Kate left the office to meet Kirstie, Tristan got a text message from Sarah:

I'M STAYING AT GARY'S FLAT UNTIL THE WEDDING.

There was no hello or goodbye and no smiley face emojis. It concerned him that they hadn't made things up, but they could both do with a bit of space. He left the office and went back to the flat, changed into his running gear, and went for a run along the seafront, past the amusement arcade and out past the other side of Ashdean.

The run cleared his head, and he came home and took a shower. He got dressed and made spaghetti on toast and then came through to the living room and enjoyed the silence as he ate. He then took out his laptop and started to work on finding the names of the two young women who had been found floating in the reservoir in 1989 and 1991. He dug around, and he found them both: Fiona Harvey and Becky Chard. Both girls were from poor backgrounds; Fiona was described in the newspaper as unemployed, and she grew up in a children's home. Becky was also unemployed at the time of her disappearance, and she was from a single-parent home.

He then made a list of all the victims, both missing and found, starting with Magdalena and working backward.

He was still working on the list when Kate called to say that she had finished her meeting with Kirstie and she was on her way back to Ashdean in the car. He asked if she wanted to come over for something to eat, adding that Sarah wouldn't be there.

When Kate arrived at Tristan's flat, he made her some tea and toast.

"What's with the boxes?" she asked when she sat on the sofa with her plate.

"It's the duty-free booze for Sarah's wedding . . . Oh. Shit. Does it bother you?"

Tristan saw how Kate looked at the boxes of Smirnoff vodka and Teacher's whisky, almost with longing.

"Do you have any iced tea?" she asked.

"I think I've got a bottle of Lipton iced tea," he said. He hurried to the kitchen and found a juice tumbler, a little ice, and he filled up the glass. He topped it off with a slice of lemon, just the way he'd seen her do it at home. She looked relieved and grateful when he presented her with the glass.

"You are a lifesaver," she said, taking a big gulp. Kate ate some of her toast, and in between mouthfuls she recounted Kirstie's story.

"Arron Ko? Jesus," said Tristan. "Do you think she made a mistake?"

"How many senior Asian police officers are there in Devon and Cornwall? There might be more now, but this was a few years back," said Kate.

"This means that we can't trust Henry Ko?"

"No."

"And this bloke kept Kirstie for ten days in the dark?" said Tristan. Kate nodded and drank more iced tea.

"It's five days since Magdalena went missing," she said.

"Do you think she's telling the truth?"

"I've interviewed a lot of criminals and a lot of victims of crime. If she was lying, she's a good liar."

"But remember what Rachel from the pub said: she *is* a good liar."

"But this is different from lying about having a new car . . . Is there any more iced tea?" asked Kate. Tristan took her glass and topped it up. When he came back into the living room, she was looking at the list he'd made.

Magdalena Rossi—(professor) went missing 14/10/2012

Simon Kendal—(student) body found in reservoir 30/08/2012

Sally-Ann Cobbs—(cleaner) went missing late November 2009

Ulrich Mazur—(odd-job man) went missing between 20–31 October 2008

Fiona Harvey—(unemployed) body found in the reservoir 3/3/1991

Peter Fishwick—(9 y/old) drowned in reservoir, during day, dad tried to revive August 1990

Becky Chard—(unemployed) body found in the reservoir 11/11/1989

She took the glass of iced tea from him and gulped half of it down and closed her eyes for a moment, then took a deep breath. Her hands were shaking.

"Everything okay?" he asked. Kate opened her eyes.

"Yeah. I think I'm just tired and run-down . . ." She looked at the list again. "Peter Fishwick should be discounted. His death was a terrible accident. He drowned in front of his parents . . ." Tristan crossed Peter Fishwick off the list. "Simon's death was too quick for whoever is doing this, abducting, if that's what's happening. I found his body two days after he'd gone missing. He'd only been dead for a day or more, so it's not following the same pattern."

"What's the pattern?"

Kate clutched her glass in both hands and took a deep breath.

"Low-income, unemployed people with little or no family. No one to miss them . . ."

"But that pattern doesn't work for Magdalena. She's a lecturer, well off. And if whoever is doing this is going for a certain type of person, then he would need to get to know them first. Magdalena is new to Ashdean and the UK . . . I thought about the farmer, Barry Lewis, the one who posted the paw print on Facebook. I looked him up, and he's only been in the UK for eighteen months. He had a farm in Auckland."

Kate nodded. She went to take another sip of her drink, but the glass was empty.

"Sit down," said Tristan, "I'll get you a top-up."

He took her glass and went through to the kitchen. He didn't want to make a fuss of Kate getting the shakes, but it concerned him. Was she experiencing some kind of withdrawal? Had she fallen off the wagon? He made her another drink and took it back through.

"I've run out of ice, I'm afraid," he said. Kate was sitting on the sofa with her head tipped back, rubbing at her eyes.

"I think I'm just tired, low blood sugar," she said. "It would have been a fluke if it was the farmer. We could have solved the case, found Magdalena, and . . . I don't know . . . moved on."

Moved on to where? thought Tristan. When she spoke to Kirstie, it had given them a breakthrough. She'd named Arron Ko and implicated a senior police officer mixed up with it all.

"I did a bit more research when you were with Kirstie," he ventured.

"Good, what did you find?" asked Kate, taking another big gulp of her iced tea.

"I looked into the Right to Roam Alliance, and as far as I can see, they've disbanded. However, the guy who ran it, Ted Clough, *also* worked at the Shadow Sands reservoir, running the maintenance boats. He got fired a few years ago. He tried to sue the company for wrongful termination, and he lost the case. I think we should try and talk to him. He may have seen something during his time working the reservoir."

Kate nodded and rubbed her eyes. Tristan thought she looked so pale. "I can message him. He's on Facebook," he said.

"Yeah. It's worth a shot," she said. She put down her glass and gathered up her things.

"Kate. Are you okay?"

"Yeah. I think I just need some sleep," she said. "Go ahead and message this guy, and I'll call you early tomorrow. I'll be back on form after a kip. Good work," she said, and she left.

———

Kate left Tristan's house and drove along the seafront. The wind was blowing hard off the sea, and she had to put the windscreen wipers on to combat the spray.

To get home, she would normally carry along the seafront promenade, which then turned into the main road out of town. When she reached the end of the promenade, she found herself signaling right. The road turned back around into the high street, and she slowed as she drove past the student bars and clubs. It was Friday night, and the clubs and bars were lit up, the colored lights reflecting in the sea spray on the edges of her windscreen. The thump of the music drifted into the car, and she saw groups of laughing students moving up and down the high street, dressed up for a fun night out.

The list of names had set her off or triggered something in Kate. It made her wonder what the hell she was doing. Kate thought back to the promise she'd made to Kirstie, that she would find Magdalena. Why had she made that promise? Was she growing soft in the head? As a police officer she would *never* have made such a promise.

Kate reached a set of traffic lights, and they were green, but a group of young girls was waiting to cross. She stopped and watched as they skipped over the crossing in front of the car, tottering on high heels. One of the girls had long dark hair, parted in the center. Another had short blonde hair, and another, red hair. Kate envied how carefree they were.

The dark-haired girl turned to look at Kate as they crossed, and she waved her thanks. Kate nodded and smiled.

A car behind her honked, and she set off again. She shouldn't have stopped at Tristan's house. She had been exhausted after talking to Kirstie. The list and all those crates of alcohol had triggered her.

Who do you think you are? a voice said in her head. *You're past it. You're not a police officer. You didn't have the guts to make a go of it as a private detective two years ago when the time was right . . . Jake is grown up. You missed that boat. A senior police officer has just been named by a victim. You remember how that turned out, the last time you tried to bring in a bent copper . . .*

It's half term.

You don't have to get up in the morning, Kate. Or the next morning, or the next.

Go on, have a real drink. You deserve some pleasure in your life.

You tried to be a good mother. You tried to work hard and be successful, but it didn't work out.

At least you tried.

Go on, just have a bloody drink.

And before she knew it, Kate was turning into the small car park next to the Oak Cask, one of the older pubs at the top of the high street.

There was an inner door of cracked safety glass through the main entrance. The bar inside was fairly grotty with a sticky carpet and faded wooden tables. It was half-full, mainly locals and serious drinkers, and Kate went to the bar. It was as if her body were on autopilot. The Oak Cask wasn't popular with students, so there was space at the bar. She took a seat.

"What can I get you?" asked the barmaid, a young woman with a pierced nose and a short scrub of green hair. Kate opened her mouth and took a deep breath. "I said, what can I get you?" she repeated, now impatient. An older man at the other end of the bar was whistling and holding up a ten-pound note.

"Jack Daniel's neat. A double, please, with lots of ice and a slice of lime," Kate heard herself saying.

The small tumbler of caramel liquid was in front of her on the bar before she could think about it. The ice clinked. The old man whistled again.

"Come on, love, get your tits in gear," he said to the barmaid.

Kate let out a long breath, put her hands around the tumbler full of whiskey, and picked it up.

31

Magdalena slept. It felt as if she were deep underwater, where it was warm and she was tucked away, while the storm, the reality of her captivity, raged above her on the surface.

She dreamed of home in Italy, the small village near Lake Como, where her tight-knit family lived. What were her mother and father doing? Her younger sister.

She kept reliving the last night before she came to England and the argument between her mother and grandmother over her open suitcase. Her nonna was insisting that she pack in her suitcase a heavy wooden rolling pin and a wooden frame for drying pasta. The best Italian cooks didn't use a pasta machine; they used a rolling pin.

Magdalena watched the memory play out again, like it was on a screen in front of her.

Her mother kept taking the rolling pin out, saying that Magdalena had only a certain amount of space and a weight limit for her suitcase. Nonna kept putting it back in. Magdalena didn't want to say that she bought dried pasta when she was in England.

Her things were laid out on the bedspread with the cornflower pattern, next to the suitcase and ready to pack: her clothes, Wellington boots for walking on the beach, her books, computer, packets of her favorite Baci chocolates. They were similar in shape to Hershey's Kisses—*baci* meant *kisses* in Italian—but the chocolate was better, soft centered with hazelnuts, and in each blue-and-silver foil-wrapped choc-olate there was always a little piece of paper with a "love note" printed by the chocolate company.

As she watched the memories on the screen, Magdalena felt the throbbing pain in her head from where she'd hit the side of the bed. It had sliced open her forehead at the hairline. She also heard the sound of breathing. The throbbing pain and the breathing were separate from the memories playing out in her dream. The throbbing was like a ham-mer being used to tap in a nail, but she stayed deep under the surface, watching her mother and Nonna bickering over the suitcase, gesturing and waving their hands. The rolling pin kept going back in the suitcase and coming out again. Magdalena's little sister, Chiara, sat next to her on the end of the bed, her small legs dangling with white sandals on her feet. Chiara was six years old, and her bright-yellow sundress was beau-tiful against her olive skin. As the rolling pin battle continued, Chiara smiled and walked her small fingers across the bedspread to the pack of Baci chocolates and pulled it back toward her. She slid off the end of the bed to the carpet, out of sight. Magdalena moved to the end of the bed and looked down at Chiara sitting on the carpet, tugging at the wrap-per. The bag suddenly split, scattering the chocolates all over the floor.

Their mother and Nonna saw the mess and started to pick up the chocolates. There was no sound; Magdalena couldn't hear their voices, just the sound of the heavy breathing.

Chiara was sitting on the carpet. She peeled the foil off one of the Baci chocolates, and she held it out to Magdalena. She could see the small strip of paper nestling in the foil under the small chocolate. She plucked it out. In small, black letters was written:

DO YOU WANT TO TOUCH THE STARS?

Magdalena was pulled out of the dream, back to consciousness. She heard herself take a deep breath, as if coming up for air. She was back in the cold darkness, lying on the bed. Her head was in pain. The scrape of a foot made her stop breathing. She could feel a presence in the darkness.

There was a ragged breath above her. He was in the room, standing over her.

She squeezed her eyes shut. Closed her legs and hunched her shoulders. Trying to close herself off.

He carried on breathing.

"Please don't hurt me," she said. Her voice sounded so weak and feeble.

The breathing came closer down to her level on the bed.

"Do you want to touch the stars?" came the voice. It was educated, smooth. Oily. Her head was gripped from the back.

"No, no," she said and tried to roll herself in a ball, but a strong chemical smell was under her nose, and the glass of a small bottle. It took only a small inhale and she felt the drug hit her. It was more terrifying in the darkness than it had been when the man had put the bottle up under her nose by his car.

It was as if her body started to travel at high speed, and she was unable to move. She felt him climb on top of her, and as her head spun and the blood roared in her ears, a pair of cold, clammy hands started to unbutton her jeans.

32

Kate's phone rang in her bag, just as the glass of whiskey was about to touch her lips. The sound of it startled her out of her trance. She put the glass down and fished her phone from her bag.

It was Tristan.

"Can you talk?" he asked.

"Yes," she said, still staring at the whiskey glass.

"That old guy, Ted Clough, messaged me back on Facebook. He says he can talk to us . . ."

"Yes?"

"He wants to meet now. He said he's ill and he's a night owl. I know it's late, but he says he has some pretty damning information about the Baker family."

Kate took a deep breath and pushed the whiskey glass away.

"Do you want to meet him now?" she said.

"I'm stuck in an empty flat, and my mind is running away with me, so yes, but I know you're tired."

"No. I could do with a distraction too," said Kate. "I'll come and pick you up."

She left the pub, frightened at how close she'd come to falling off the wagon.

———

Ted Clough lived a short distance from Ashdean, along the coastal road west, out in the countryside on a small farm. Thick fog began to descend as Kate and Tristan drew close, and the country lane was lined with impenetrable woodland.

As they rounded a sharp turn, Kate had to slam on the brakes when the whirling fog parted and the figure of a wild-haired old man was standing on the grass shoulder. He wore a long coat and a flat cap and was holding an oxygen canister, and an oxygen pipe was wrapped around his face and under his nose. Kate wound down her window.

"Hello? Are you Mr. Clough?"

"Yes; please, call me Ted," he said with shallow breaths.

"Hi. I was the one who messaged on Facebook," said Tristan, leaning over. Ted rolled his tongue over yellowing teeth, and he wheezed breathlessly. Kate couldn't work out how old he was, perhaps in his sixties.

"Go through the gate," he said, pointing. "I've got my car. Follow me up."

"Thanks," said Kate. The car lurched and bumped as they left the road and went through the gate onto a densely wooded track around where mist hung in pockets. The gate made an ominous keening sound as it was closed behind them.

"He looks on his last legs," said Tristan, peering through the window as Ted walked slowly with his canister to a small, red, mud-splattered car and got in.

He set off, and they followed him up the long, winding track until a small house with a light on in the downstairs window came into view. They parked next to the back door, which led into a boot room and a small, cluttered kitchen, lit by a dim overhead light. There were cats on every surface—the fridge, kitchen table, chairs—and several half-finished bowls of graying cat food dotted around the floor.

"Would you like a cuppa?" asked Ted.

"Please," said Kate. She still craved a proper drink, but the craving was receding.

Ted placed his oxygen canister on the floor. The pipe was long enough to let him move between the fridge and the kettle. Tristan gave Kate a look when he opened the fridge and they saw it contained nothing but milk and cans of cat food.

"Thank you for meeting us at such an odd time," said Kate.

"I can't sleep at night. Time is everything and nothing to me," he said, stopping to catch his breath as he took a bottle of milk from the fridge.

"Are you sure we can't help?" asked Kate.

"I'm very particular about my tea, and if I've only got a little time left, I want every cup to be just right," he said. He saw them looking at him. "Lung cancer. I've been given a month, maybe less."

"Sorry," said Kate.

Tristan nodded. "Sorry."

"I don't want your pity. I need to tell you things," he said. Kate wanted to press him further, but they let him make the tea.

When it was made, they followed Ted down a cramped, book-lined corridor. Clocks ticked in the silence. It was damp, and everything seemed to be covered in a layer of dust. There were more bookshelves and filing cabinets in his study. Ted lifted a cat off an armchair by the desk. He clicked his fingers at the sofa, where two other mangy cats jumped down, leaving copious amounts of hair behind. Kate and Tristan sat down.

"Where do you want me to start?" he said when he'd caught his breath.

"We found you online because you were part of the Right to Roam Alliance?" asked Kate.

"Yes. I'm a local lad. The reservoir project, back in the 1950s, was controversial. Six villages were flooded, villages that had been there for hundreds of years. The Baker family had people forcibly removed from their homes. Public rights of way vanished overnight, and around the reservoir they had to be redrawn. I got involved years later, when the Bakers tried to ban people walking within half a mile of the reservoir. That's ancient moorland that people have enjoyed for centuries. It was a land grab, pure and simple. We'd already lost so much to the reservoir, so we had to fight it."

"But you also worked for the Bakers at the power plant? Wasn't that a conflict of interest?" asked Kate.

"Not when the Right to Roam Alliance was a peaceful campaign. It was only in the last few years it turned nasty, and that's when I resigned."

"You were sacked from your job at the reservoir?"

Ted sat back and took a gulp of his tea and caught his breath.

"Yes." He looked between Kate and Tristan, and for the first time he seemed uneasy.

"What was your job?"

"Waterway maintenance. We'd go out in a boat and make sure the water was free of obstacles. Large trees, dead sheep and cows."

"Dead bodies?"

He took a shallow breath and coughed.

"I was sacked after I refused to lie about a dead body we found in the water."

"Who asked you to lie?"

"The manager, Robbie Huber. He's now dead . . ."

"Old age?"

"No. Car accident. But I'll come back to that in a minute. I was out in the boat one morning, early in March, when we found the body of a young woman. It was a beautiful day. One of those mornings when all is still and you can see the reflection of the daffodils at the edge of the reservoir in the water. We narrowly missed running her over. She was blown up huge with gases. I've never seen anything so shocking. Have you seen how large a human body can blow up with decay? I thought it was an animal. The body was naked. The legs were partially wrapped in bits of a sheet, fabric. The arms were tied with rope, and the legs were too. We could just about make out the cuts. There were cuts and slashes all over the face, belly, and the breasts."

Kate and Tristan exchanged a glance.

"Did you run over the body in the boat?"

"No. It was there, floating in front of us, like a balloon poking up out of the water."

"You said early March 1991?" asked Tristan.

"Yeah. I was working the maintenance crew with another bloke, Ivan Coomes, who's since died."

"Died?"

"Old age. Heart attack. Ivan was in charge of me. We were both leant on to report that we found this body at the mouth of the reservoir, two miles up. Where the River Fowey flows into the reservoir. There's a sluice gate, which can be opened and closed. We were told to say we found the body up there."

"Who told you to say that?" asked Kate.

"A man called . . . Dylan Robertson," said Ted, shifting uncomfortably in his seat at the mention of the name.

"What's his job at the reservoir?" asked Tristan.

"He's everywhere and does everything he's asked to by Silvia Baker. He also works as her driver."

"We've already had a run-in with him," said Kate. She quickly explained how he threatened them with a shotgun.

"He would have used that shotgun on you, I've no doubt," said Ted.

"Dylan asked you to say this body was found by the sluice gate. Where did you find it?"

"A few hundred meters from the sluice gates. Silvia Baker is the head of the family. She pulls the strings. Dylan is her eyes everywhere. He said we had to lie because the reservoir was having problems. The Bakers were in talks with a foreign investor about a buyout. A suspicious dead body in the water, that close to the turbines, would have closed everything down and ruined a deal. If we said it was by the sluice gates, that puts it in the River Fowey, and it meant the body could have been carried downriver. The River Fowey goes all the way up into the Cotswolds. We towed the body up the reservoir and pushed it to the other side of the sluice gates. It was disgusting. The body was so badly decayed, and the way it was tied up . . . The death was ruled as accidental . . . misadventure. Drowning."

"Did they identify the body?"

"Yes. It took a few weeks for them to identify her, through dental records. I only saw it by chance, a tiny piece in the local paper where they named her . . . I've got it here."

He went to a drawer and pulled out an old exercise book, having to pause to catch his breath. He searched through it and found a tiny piece of cut-out newspaper, dated May 16, 1991. He handed it to Kate.

> A body found two months ago in the Shadow Sands reservoir, close to Ashdean, has been identified as Fiona Harvey, a young woman from the local area.
>
> Police said her death was being treated as unexplained, but there were not believed to be any suspicious circumstances.

"Seeing the lie in print shook me up," said Ted. "It made me question the world. No one at work wanted to talk about it. I tried to bring it up with Dylan, but he told me to keep quiet or I'd lose my job and he'd kill me . . . I kept quiet, to my guilt."

"Do you remember the police officer who worked on the case?" asked Kate.

"Arron Ko."

Tristan and Kate exchanged a look.

"Arron Ko. As in chief constable?" said Kate. She scrabbled around in her bag, found her phone, and called up the article about Arron Ko retiring. She held up the photo.

"Yeah. That's him."

"His son, Henry, is now a DCI. He's been investigating the death of Simon Kendal. The body I found in August."

Ted started to laugh, and it turned into a cough.

"You two be careful. You can see how this has worked over the years. The Baker family keep it in the family," said Ted.

"You think Arron Ko was corrupted by the family?"

"Course! He's good friends with Silvia Baker. Known each other for years."

"Oh Jesus," said Kate. "What about the second *unofficial* body that was found?"

"I only heard about it when we found the young girl in 1991. In 1989, the boat was out checking the reservoir, and they thought it snagged some old fishing line. It felt like they were dragging a huge weight. It was the body of another young woman. Wrapped up in a shroud, it looked like."

"Where did it snag?" asked Tristan.

"Robbie, the lad who was out on the boat, said that it snagged in the middle of the reservoir, but they had insisted that he say it must have snagged up by the sluice gates. They identified the body a few months later by dental records."

Tristan got out the piece of paper with his list.

"Becky Chard, found 11 November 1989?"

Ted nodded.

"When the bodies were found, did the police search the reservoir? Did they send divers down or use scanning technology?" asked Kate.

"No. I would have known . . . Robbie was told the same thing we had been told. Keep quiet, and tell the police the body was found by the sluice gates. Don't mention it was in a shroud. Robbie went along with it the first time, but when word got around that the second body we found was also tied up, he freaked out. He said he didn't want to be accused of lying. He went to the police. He told them everything. He said that they listened and they asked him to come back a few days later to make an official statement. We all thought the cards were going to fall for Dylan. And I was ready to talk to the police too . . ." He leaned forward and adjusted the oxygen canister. He took a deep breath. "Two days later, Robbie was involved in a smash in his car. He lost control and drove into a tree. Killed instantly."

"Jesus," said Kate.

"His brakes failed . . . It scared the shit out of us all at work. And we were all worried about our livelihoods. We had kids and bills to pay. The whole thing was buried."

"Why were you fired?"

"It wasn't for anything noble, like telling the truth. My knee got crushed between two of the maintenance boats. I was encouraged by a doctor to get compensation. I wasn't asking for a lot, but the Bakers didn't like that, so they fired me."

"When was this?"

"Twelve years ago, just before the millennium."

"Why are you talking to us now?"

"My lungs are shot to shit. I don't have much time left. My wife is dead. My two sons live in Australia, and maybe I need to off-load this guilt. I've got no proof beyond what I'm telling you, what I saw with me own eyes."

"Does the whole family run the power plant?" asked Kate.

"They don't do the grunt work, but they're all in charge. Dana, Silvia's niece, runs the art gallery in the visitors' center. She seems the most normal and amiable. Thomas is the current Lord Baker, although he doesn't use the title in his work life. He lives on the estate near Silvia in Carlton Manor. The original Shadow Sands manor house was demolished in the 1950s to avoid inheritance tax. He's got a wife, no children.

Stephen Baker is the black sheep. He's broken away from the family. He went to live in America a few years back and met and married an American girl who Silvia didn't approve of. They have loads of kids. He runs a posh cookware shop in Frome Crawford. Before he fell out with the family, he ran Hedley House."

"Hedley House?" said Kate.

"Yes. It's an old manor house on the Shadow Sands Estate. It was converted into a club for a few years, then got too expensive to run. The family said, a few years back, they want to develop it into flats."

Kate and Tristan then outlined their side of the story and their theory about how the deaths and disappearances, Kirstie's story, and Magdalena all fit together.

"It makes me glad I'm not long destined for this world," said Ted, holding the list of probable victims. He looked exhausted and very scared. He was coughing almost nonstop. Kate checked her watch, and it was coming up to one a.m.

"The Baker family all live close by?" she asked.

"Yes. All of them have big houses. Dana lives in Exeter. Silvia and Dylan both live in Allways Manor—he has his own quarters . . . Thomas and his wife live on the same estate. Stephen and his family live above their shop in Frome Crawford."

He studied the list for a long moment, his hands shaking. He had been pale when they arrived, but now his face was like chalk. He shook his head.

"Have you shown . . . this . . . around . . . to many people?" he asked, starting to cough.

"No," said Kate. "You're the only one."

Ted launched into a painful coughing fit, and they waited awkwardly until he'd finished. "Please . . . That's enough. I need to get some sleep," he said.

When Kate and Tristan left Ted's drive and pulled onto the coast road, there was a full moon, giving them a beautiful view across the sea. They stopped for a moment to take in the moonlight glittering on the calm water.

"Do you think it's one of the Baker family who's doing this?" asked Tristan.

"I know the Hedley House connection has really put me on high alert. And the fact that Arron Ko could have been in on it, which in turn means Henry Ko could be mixed up in it too," said Kate.

"Whoever it is would need a basement or a cellar, and those big old houses could have that," said Tristan.

"Do you think Ted changed when we showed him the list?"

"He seemed scared, but he's a dying man with secrets. I'd be scared too."

"Scared of what?" asked Kate.

"He's been scared of repercussions for years; that's the reason he said he didn't talk until now. The Baker family is powerful. The chief of police is mixed up in it. There's nothing more terrifying than when the police have been corrupted and are working against you."

"I want to talk to him again," said Kate. "Let's phone him tomorrow."

Tristan nodded, and they pulled out and started back to Ashdean.

———

After Kate and Tristan left Ted's house, he had to hurry upstairs to the bathroom, where he had a long, painful coughing fit, which ended up with him hanging over the toilet and bringing up blood.

He sat back on the bathroom floor when it had subsided. His favorite cat, a gray Siamese cross called Liberty, appeared in the doorway and wound her way between his legs and purred. Ted looked down at Liberty's bright green eyes. She seemed to be able to look into his soul and comfort him. There was a warm sound of purring as four more of his cats climbed the stairs and came into the bathroom, winding their way around his legs, nuzzling their noses into the palm of his hand to comfort him, pressing their warm, furry flanks against him. Ted knew that he was going to die alone, but he was suddenly gripped with fear for his cats. He knew how ruthless the Baker family could be, and he had left directions in his will for his cats to be rehomed, but what if those bastards took out their revenge on his cats? They were the only companions he had left in the world.

"Why did I talk to them? Why did I do it? I'm sorry, I'm so sorry. They're not going to hurt you. I won't let anyone hurt you," Ted whimpered, burying his face in the cat's smooth neck. He heaved himself up off the bathroom floor and went to the phone in the hallway.

With leaden, shaking hands, he picked it up and dialed a number. The voice that answered hadn't lost its ability to make him cold with fear.

"I'm just telling you, want to tell you . . . I had a visit tonight from a couple of private investigators . . ." He coughed and wheezed. "They were asking me about the drownings in the reservoir. I tried to throw them off the scent, but I think they're close to working out who it is . . . ," he said.

33

Kate managed to sleep for a few hours and woke just after eight. She went down to the beach and took a long swim. As she came back into the kitchen, the front doorbell rang. It was Tristan, with fried egg baps from the greasy spoon near his house.

"Sorry, am I too early?" he said.

"No, come in," she said. He came through to the kitchen.

"You okay?" he said, seeing her concerned face. He sat down at the kitchen table, and she handed him plates.

"If Ted Clough and Kirstie Newett are to be believed, and I think I do believe them, then this investigation is getting dangerous," she said, switching on the gas hob and filling the kettle.

"It also means we're getting closer," said Tristan, peeling the greasy paper off a floury white fried egg bap and biting into it.

"Tris, I don't expect you to follow me into the fire. You're young, you have your whole life ahead of you, and I don't know what we're doing. I'm not a policewoman anymore. We're not detectives, we're not working with anyone . . ."

"You forget that someone from our university is missing. And we could find her."

"Yes, but if Arron Ko and other police officers are involved in this, corrupt police, well, you know what happened to me the last time I discovered a police officer was also a criminal . . ." Kate pulled up her sweater to show the long, ugly purple scar across her belly. "Peter Conway did this. A policeman desperate to keep his secret . . ."

Tristan had stopped chewing. He swallowed with difficulty. Kate pulled her sweater back down.

"I'm sorry to be so graphic, but it's relevant. Arron Ko is a high-ranking retired officer . . . It scares the hell out of me that he might be involved in this."

"Kate. I've come this far. I'm not going to wimp out. And isn't it the right thing to do, especially if the police investigating this don't really want things solved? What if we can find out what happened to Magdalena? And think of all those teenagers who didn't have families to mourn them or look for them."

"We can't go and knock on the doors of the Baker family . . . And we can't barge into the police station and demand to see Henry Ko's computer files. I don't know . . ."

"What about Varia Campbell?" said Tristan. "She was a DCI in this borough for fifteen years. Now she's moved to London. She might be willing to talk to us."

Kate paused with her hand on the kettle.

Detective Chief Inspector Varia Campbell was the investigating officer on the Nine Elms copycat case, and she had been grateful to Kate and Tristan when they solved the case. At the time, Varia had said that she owed them, and if they ever needed help, they were to call her.

"When Varia said to call her if we needed help, she was probably thinking if we got a parking ticket or something like that," said Kate.

"She got promoted to superintendent when she moved to the Met. Surely that gives her access to stuff," said Tristan. "She might be able to tell us something about Arron Ko. She might like the opportunity to solve a high-profile case."

Kate liked his enthusiasm. It was infectious.

"She might not even take my call," she said.

"If she doesn't, I'll phone her. And at the end of the day, it's just a call. We've got nothing to lose," said Tristan. "And we're not crackpots; we solved that case when she couldn't. That's got to count for something."

They finished their breakfast, and Kate took a quick shower. When she came back downstairs, they put the phone on speaker and made the call. Varia was in her office when she answered.

"To what do I owe the pleasure?" she said.

"Do you have a few minutes? We have a story to tell," said Kate, cutting to the chase, knowing that Varia's time had its limits.

They told the whole story as concisely and quickly as they could. There was a long silence when they finished.

"This is all very disturbing, but as you know, I'm now a Met police officer. Devon and Cornwall are no longer my borough," said Varia.

"Do you mind us asking why you left Devon and Cornwall?" said Kate.

"Chief Constable Arron Ko retired. He resisted, but he'd reached the maximum age for a serving officer. At the same time, I was offered a generous relocation package, promotion to superintendent. I knew I had earned it, regardless of the reason Arron had for pulling a few strings . . ."

"His son, Henry, took on your role as DCI?"

"Yes. But I will say again, I had earned a promotion, and as a woman of color, these opportunities are rare."

"How well did you know Arron Ko?"

"He was our big boss. I'd spoken to him a few times. I'd never had any direct dealings with him, but he had a lot of influence, as a chief constable does."

"Why do you think he picked you?" asked Kate.

"I don't know. I wasn't the only DCI working out of Exeter, but I was the best."

"He didn't want you showing up his son."

"Uh-huh, and if I'm being cynical, he got to promote a woman of color, which can't have hurt him in the eyes of top brass," said Varia.

"Okay, so what do you know about the Shadow Sands reservoir?" asked Kate.

"I was aware that the Baker family, who are major shareholders in the project, are divisive. But there's a lot of money down in Devon and Cornwall. A lot of divisive rich people. As you know, the borough covers a huge area. There is a vast swath of coastline, which throws up its own problems. Drug smuggling occupied a lot of my time."

"Were you ever warned off searching the reservoir at Shadow Sands?" asked Tristan.

"No. And I had no reason to. I worked there from 1998 to 2012. There were no reports of any homicide victims found in the reservoir."

"We have the dates of the bodies that were found in the reservoir in 1989 and 1991, both confirmed by our witness, Ted Clough. He contradicts the official reports saying the deaths were accidents. What if we got him on record?" asked Kate.

"Then the police would be required to act, Kate. You know this, as an ex–police officer. If you can get Ted Clough on record, all he would need to do is give a signed statement to a police officer from your borough. That would then be enough for the police to investigate the death," said Varia.

"Would it be enough for the police to search the reservoir?" asked Tristan.

"You listed the inconsistencies with the missing people in the area. But the reservoir is a government project, a power plant. You would need compelling evidence to open a case."

"Do you think Henry Ko was parachuted in to do Arron Ko's dirty work?" asked Tristan.

"I can't prove that, Tristan. Nepotism is alive in every walk of life. Henry Ko was promoted to the rank of detective straight out of Hendon. He was sent to North London, but he clashed with his DCI.

He then came here to West End Central and was promoted to the DI rank for a few years."

"Is there anything on his record?" asked Kate.

"I would have to look, but officers I spoke to thought he was a rather uninspiring officer. A bit *meh*, to use the phrase. He then came down to Devon and Cornwall and into my old job. You remember what it's like, Kate. You have to resist corruption, but there are ways to grease the wheels. You have to work with the rich and powerful without compromising yourself. Perhaps that's what happened with Shadow Sands reservoir. The project is worth a great deal, both to the family and the government, who own a large stake."

"If we get Ted Clough on record about the cause of death for these two young women being incorrect, then that could lead to other aspects of our investigation being explored. If we do that, can you help?" asked Kate.

"I'm not an officer in your borough."

"You can have a word, though. If we go to uniform with a statement from Ted Clough and there is a bent copper trying to cover this up, it'll go nowhere."

There was a pause on the other end of the phone.

"Okay, come back to me when you have the statement. I will nudge things so it goes higher, but I'm only promising to nudge, Kate. That's all."

34

Kate phoned Ted Clough straight after the call with Varia and asked if he would be willing to go on record with his story. There was a long, wheezing silence, and for a moment, Kate thought he had hung up the phone.

"Today's rather busy," he said.

"Ted. I know it's a big thing to ask this," said Kate. "But if you go on record and say that the bodies of Fiona Harvey and Becky Chard were found in the center of the water, and tied up, the police will have to reopen their cases. They would have grounds to question Dylan, Silvia Baker's driver, and search the reservoir."

There was another pause, Ted wheezed, and there was the sound of a dog barking in the background.

"Today I have my hospital appointments," he said. "I can't miss them."

"Okay. What about afterward?" said Kate. "Ted. I think Magdalena Rossi is being held captive somewhere. It's six days since she went missing. When I spoke to Kirstie Newett, she told me she was held captive for ten days before he tried to kill her . . . Ted, please. Do the right thing . . ." There was another wheezing pause. Kate looked over at Tristan, who was sitting next to her on the sofa. She was trying to keep calm, but his hesitation was maddening to her. Hadn't he said he would be dead in a month? He could do so much good if he used the last part of his life to speak the truth.

"The police are involved in covering this up," Ted finally said. "What good is talking to them?"

"I have a contact at the Met Police in London who was a Detective Chief Inspector in Devon and Cornwall police. She's clean and uncorrupted, and she's going to make sure that your statement goes right to the top so it has to be investigated," said Kate. Tristan glanced over at her with a concerned look on his face. This wasn't strictly true, but time was ticking. "Ted, please. There are four young women and two young men who either went missing or died a brutal death, and Kirstie Newett has been left traumatized by her ordeal. If we don't stop this person, it will go on and on. More death, more victims."

"Yes! Yes, okay . . . ," he said, lapsing into another coughing fit so loud that Kate had to hold the phone away from her head. "This evening . . . ," he said when he'd recovered. "Six. I'll do six o'clock this evening."

He hung up.

"He sounds very scared, but he's going to do it," said Kate.

"We need to make sure that the officer who takes this statement isn't part of Henry and Arron Ko's crowd," said Tristan.

Kate phoned Varia again and explained that Ted was willing to go on record.

"She's going to get a colleague, DCI Della Street, to come to Ted's house tonight. She works mainly with the marine police unit," said Kate when she came off the phone again. "I've asked if we can be there, too, and she says that's fine."

"Do think he'll want us there?"

"I don't care if he does or doesn't. He's making that bloody statement, even if I have to stand over him."

"He's dying," said Tristan.

"All the more reason to do it," she said. Kate got up and looked at her watch. It was only ten a.m. "We've got eight hours. We can't waste them," she said, thinking about Magdalena. "I'm going to have another crack and call Alan Hexham. It would be useful to get the postmortem files for Fiona Harvey and Becky Chard. If they were both held captive, like Kirstie, and then dumped in the reservoir, their bodies would have shown evidence of malnutrition."

"Do you want to go to Exeter morgue and see if you can talk to him?" asked Tristan.

"No. It's a better use of time if I phone him. I also want to check out Dana Baker and Stephen Baker. Dana runs the visitors' center at the reservoir, and Stephen has a cookware shop, which means we can get to them quite easily," said Kate. "Dana spends her working day looking at the bloody reservoir, and God knows what else she's involved in as a shareholder."

"What about Stephen?"

"If he's the black sheep of the family, he could be willing to spill a few beans. I also want to find out more about Silvia Baker's driver, if that's what he is. According to Ted, he was more . . . But he has a shotgun and isn't afraid to use it, so I think we need to tread a bit more carefully."

"What about Thomas Baker?"

"I don't know yet. We need to find out more about his movements."

"Aren't we just going to be like stalkers?"

"Not when Dana and Stephen both work in public spaces. When I was a police officer, I liked to use the element of surprise. We don't have any leverage to make them talk to us or answer any of our questions, but if we go in there and make them uncomfortable, it could be interesting to see how they react," said Kate.

35

"It looks like a giant ship moored up on the edge of the water," said Tristan as they pulled into the car park of the Shadow Sands visitors' center. The huge glass-and-steel building was built in the shape of a boat, four stories high with curved bows. It was surrounded by manicured lawns, and several statues were dotted around, some garishly modern and others fashioned from bronze. The rest of the land around the reservoir seemed desolate and unkempt, almost sinister, but this felt busy and welcoming.

The car park was half-full. There were six coaches parked up at the back, and a group of Japanese tourists were filing off the coach next to the main entrance. When Kate and Tristan got out of the car, there was a low roar from the turbines. They went to the opposite wall of the car park and could see the bridge and the precipitous drop down to the water rushing out from under the wall of the dam.

A faint spray floated up from the churning waters, casting a rainbow in the air. They could see where the river carried on toward the hills before disappearing beside a tor.

Kate and Tristan joined a queue of bewildered-looking Japanese ladies, all wearing straw croupier hats, paid the entrance fee, and went through the turnstile. The gallery opened out into a large, airy space filled with sculptures, prints, and an exhibit of glass and crystal. At intervals along the wall there were large round windows looking out over the reservoir, which gave more of a feeling that they were on a boat. The water looked completely different, peaceful.

Kate asked a steward where they could find Dana Baker, and they were directed to go through the gallery and coffee shop to her office at the back. The coffee shop had a long window taking in a view of the water and a large white boathouse opposite, where a boat was just pulling out.

They reached the office, and Kate was about to knock on the door, when they heard shouting coming from inside. Tristan raised an eyebrow, and they leaned closer.

"You can't just keep doing freebies cos he's your brother," said a male voice with an overenunciated cockney accent. "He's minted. If he wants us to host an event, he can pay. We're not a fucking charity!"

"Technically we *are* a charity," said a woman, with a more refined voice.

"Don't be smart, Dana."

"One of us needs to be. It's a family obligation. I do it every year, and they are the kind of guests who donate a lot. It's happening whether you like it or not!"

"Family. You lot are like the mafia. You always close ranks."

The door suddenly opened, and Kate and Tristan stepped back. A handsome man in his fifties with short-cropped gray hair and glasses and a smart suit pushed past them and stalked out toward the coffee shop.

The office inside was small, and the front narrowed to a point where they were at the bow of the ship-shaped building. Light flooded in through a window on each side. A woman fiddled nervously at her desk, dressed in what Kate saw as high fashion: a baggy black pinafore-style dress with thick-soled clogs. Her plum-colored hair was styled in an immaculate, shiny bob. She wore glasses with thick white frames, and lots of chunky jewelry. It was Dana Baker, completely different from the scruffy, blonde, freckle-faced young woman in the video on YouTube.

"Hello, please come in," she said, recovering her composure.

Kate was about to launch into a prepared spiel about investigating Simon Kendal's death when Dana added, "Can I get you both a coffee, after your long journey?"

Kate realized Dana thought they were someone else, someone she was expecting. She gave Tristan a subtle look to play along.

"Coffee would be lovely," said Kate.

"Yeah. Milk and sugar, please," said Tristan, closing the door behind them.

"Please. Sit down," said Dana, indicating a large hot-pink-colored sofa under the window facing the road. Tristan glanced at Kate, as if to say, *Are we going to tell her who we are?* Kate nodded to Tristan. Dana made a call requesting coffee.

"We couldn't help overhearing. You got quite an earful," said Kate when Dana came off the phone.

"Yes. The perils of mixing business and pleasure. Working with your boyfriend. I thought you'd spoken to Harrison . . . About the funding package?" She narrowed her eyes. "You're Callie Prince?" she said, looking at her diary. "From the Arts Council?"

There was a long pause. Kate knew they would have to come clean.

"No. I'm Kate Marshall, a private investigator. This is my associate, Tristan Harper. We're investigating the death of Simon Kendal." She saw Dana stiffen.

"I wasn't told the police were coming. You usually call in advance."

"We work as private investigators . . . Why would the police call you in advance?"

Dana sat down at her desk, now stony faced.

"Rather dishonest of you to pretend that you were from the Arts Council," she said, ignoring the question.

"You assumed, and I didn't correct you," said Kate.

"I have nothing to say."

"I haven't asked you anything; well, I did ask you why the police would call you in advance of them coming?" Kate raised an eyebrow.

"We know several senior police officers socially, my family does," she said. "Now, I must ask you to leave, I'm expecting . . ."

"You have a prime view of the reservoir," said Kate, indicating the huge window looking out over the water. "You must see a lot."

"A lot of what?"

"The recovery of Simon Kendal's body after he drowned? The police in the aftermath?"

"The young lad was camping, wasn't he?"

"Yes."

"And the police suspect his friend?"

"Yes," said Kate.

"What do you think?" asked Dana. Her question seemed genuine.

"We have our concerns—we're questioning how Simon ended up in the water, and he was such a strong swimmer."

"Oh Lord, you're not here from that dreadful right-of-way group?"

"No. Dylan, your aunt's associate. What's his role within the company?"

Dana seemed surprised at the change in the conversation.

"Dylan's been with my aunt Silvia for many years. He's her driver. He protects her. He's had to over the years from those loonies at the Alliance. One of the disputed rights of way runs next to her house. Did you know, one of them broke in and threatened her with a knife?"

"Was she hurt?"

"No. Dylan shot him."

"He killed the intruder?" asked Tristan.

"Yes, in self-defense, which is legal. This man would have killed my aunt if Dylan hadn't defended her."

"Dylan threatened us with a shotgun three days ago when we were in the campsite," said Kate.

"As I said, he's very protective over Aunt Silvia. And his shotgun is legally registered."

"It's illegal to threaten someone minding their own business on public land," said Kate.

"Look. If you are here—"

"What about Hedley House?" said Kate, firing questions at her. "Did Dylan work there?"

"At the nightclub? Yes, he was in charge of the door staff."

"He was a bouncer at the nightclub?"

"I think so, yes. There were often problems with the locals."

"Arron Ko is a family friend?"

"Yes, he and my aunt have been friends since they were young. I don't see how these questions are . . ."

"Henry Ko. Is he a family friend too?"

"He's Arron's son, of course. I don't have to answer these questions, and we were away when Simon Kendal drowned."

"We?"

"Myself and Harrison were at my villa," said Dana.

There was a knock on the door, and Harrison opened it. He was standing with a dark-haired woman, who was wearing a thick houndstooth coat.

"Dana, this is Callie Prince . . . We've got a meeting booked."

"I'm very short for time," said Callie.

"These two are just leaving," said Dana. She looked shaken up by the questions.

Kate and Tristan came back out to the car park.

"What did you think?" asked Kate.

"I don't know," said Tristan. "I find posh people hard to read. She seems a bit dim."

"That doesn't mean anything," said Kate. "I wanted to challenge her about the other people who've gone missing, but I don't want to jeopardize Ted's statement. Dylan's become very interesting, though. It seems he's involved in everything to do with protecting the Baker family."

36

Kate and Tristan drove over to the Hubble Cook Shop, owned by Stephen Baker, in a small village called Frome Crawford, a few miles outside Ashdean. It was on a high street of well-heeled shops including an old-fashioned butcher, an artisan baker, and a run-down Boots pharmacy.

They parked in a small pay-and-display car park opposite and then crossed the road. Despite the drizzle and the lengthening shadows, the cookware shop had a display of smart silver pots and pans outside on the street.

The window had a Halloween-themed display with a convincing-looking backdrop of a midwestern prairie farm, complete with a barn and a corn silo. A thin wooden windmill was slowly turning in the background, and there were rows of real corn. Nestled among it were orange Le Creuset dishes, dressed to look like pumpkins, and a tractor made out of kitchen equipment with frying pan wheels and a bread maker engine. A small boy with a white-blond bowl cut appeared in the window, wearing a red pullover and jeans and holding a teddy bear.

"Christ. It looks like a scene from *Children of the Corn*," said Tristan. A woman with long blonde hair came running out the front door.

"Truman? Truman!" she shouted, looking up and down the road. She had an American accent and wore tight yoga workout gear and trainers. Her figure was enviable.

"Is that who you're looking for?" asked Kate, pointing to the gormless little boy staring at them from the window display.

"Yes. Thank God!" she cried and hurried back inside. Kate and Tristan followed her into the cramped and cozy shop. Copper pots and pans, china, and expensive-looking cookware were piled high in brightly colored displays. The small boy had pulled a plastic corn on the cob from the display of maize and was trying to eat it. The woman stepped into the window.

"Truman, honey, don't do that. Come and play with your brother and sister," she said, scooping him up into her arms. Truman turned to face Kate and Tristan, watching them solemnly as the woman carried him down to the front of the shop.

Kate and Tristan followed through the cluttered aisles. The till was at the back, on a wide wooden table surrounded by boxes, piled high.

A man who looked to be in his early forties sat behind the table, reading a copy of the *Guardian* with his bare feet resting on the corner. He had strawberry-blond stubble on his cheeks and shoulder-length blond hair, and he was wearing jeans and a black Metallica T-shirt.

"Can I help you?" he asked, smiling up at them. Kate could see the family resemblance to Dana.

"Hi. Are you Stephen Baker?" asked Kate.

"Yes. That's me," he said, looking between them. The woman took the little boy through a door behind the till. They heard her raise her voice.

"Look at all this mess! I'm talking to you, Banksy!" she said. There was a crash and a scream.

"Are you looking for something in particular?" asked Stephen, seemingly unperturbed by the commotion behind him. Kate went to speak, but another blond boy and girl, who both looked older than the first child, came running out the door, screaming. The woman followed them down to the front of the shop.

"Banksy! Tallulah! Mommy's mad!"

"Don't run!" said Stephen half-heartedly with a smile. "Sorry, what is it you want?" he asked, turning his attention back to them.

"We're private investigators, looking into the death of Simon Kendal at the Shadow Sands reservoir."

His face dropped.

"Yikes. Yeah. I heard about that," said Stephen, pulling back his hair into a ponytail and fastening it with an elastic band. "Poor lad."

"I'm Kate Marshall, and this is my associate, Tristan Harper. Can we talk to you?"

"Why?"

"We know you have shares in the company, and we wanted to ask you about the reservoir."

"It's big and wet, that's about all I know. I left the family business a few years back," he said.

"You also ran Hedley House nightclub, and we think that a few young people who went to the club are now on the missing persons database," said Kate.

Stephen seemed genuinely concerned at this second piece of information. "Missing persons?"

"Yes. A young woman and man who went missing after a night out at Hedley House."

"Look. Do you want a cuppa? My office is out back."

"Thank you," said Kate. There was a huge crash from the front of the shop, and the woman scolded the children again.

"Jassy. I'm just going to the office," said Stephen. "Come this way," he added, leading them through the door at the back.

Stephen's small office was filled with old wooden furniture and a pile of LEGOs in the middle of the floor. He cleared some toys off a sagging sofa and indicated they should sit.

"Tea or coffee?" he asked. "I've got this machine," he added, indicating a capsule coffee machine on the corner of the desk.

"Coffee," said Kate.

"Me too, thanks," said Tristan.

They sat down on the sofa.

"We just spoke to your sister, Dana, at the visitors' center."

"Did you meet the handsome Harrison?" asked Stephen, loading up fresh capsules in the machine.

"Yes."

"Dana loves a bit of rough. She loves a cockney. Ray Winstone visited the gallery once, and she *properly* creamed her drawers."

There was a pause. Kate didn't know what to say to that. He finished making the coffee and handed them each a small cup.

"I found Simon Kendal's body," said Kate.

"Shit," said Stephen, clasping a hand to his chest in overexaggerated remorse. "That must have been awful for you." He perched on the edge of the desk.

"I was diving with my son."

"I don't know why people like diving in the reservoir. It's just muck and gloom."

"The sea was rough that day. And he wanted to see the sunken buildings."

"Did you?"

Kate nodded and took a sip of her coffee. "The church. The water was very low."

"Yes. It was a dry summer . . . Right. Well, shit. What can I help with?"

"Dylan. Your aunt's associate. He's involved with the maintenance boats."

"Is he?" asked Stephen, looking earnestly confused.

"Yes. He was also a bouncer, at Hedley House."

"Oh, shit. You mean the boats on the reservoir . . . I thought you meant maintaining boats. Our family has a yacht and another couple of sailing boats we use on the Norfolk Broads."

"Is Dylan prone to violence? Was he a handful as a bouncer?" asked Kate. She couldn't work out if Stephen was being clueless or slippery.

"No. You know what trashy townie nightclubs are like. I'm going to be honest. Hedley House was a *gold mine*, but it wasn't a great place to work. There was always trouble. We needed a tough old bastard like Dylan to keep order."

"There were two people who went missing after a night out at the club. A guy called Ulrich Mazur in 2008 and a young woman called Sally-Ann Cobbs in 2009. They were both reported to the police. Did the police come to the club?"

"Wow, no. I don't remember that. Missing? Jeez."

"Yes, they left the club on foot at the end of the night to walk home, and they just vanished."

"That's terrible," he said, shaking his head and rubbing at his stubbled chin. "We may have had a request for CCTV, but we only had cameras inside." He checked his watch. "Look, I'm happy to chat, but what does this all have to do with me? I can't leave poor Jassy with three kids and the shop to look after," he said with a nervous laugh.

"One theory is that they left the club drunk and on foot and could have ended up falling into the reservoir," said Kate, improvising. "Have the police ever made a formal request to search the reservoir?"

"I wouldn't know about that. As I say, I don't remember the police coming to talk to us at Hedley House about these missing people. I'm not at all involved with the power plant or the reservoir. My family didn't approve of me marrying Jassy. My brother, Thomas, the lord of the manor, is the man to talk to about that," said Stephen. There was another crash from outside and a scream from one of the children. A phone outside the door began to ring.

"Do you have a number for your brother, Thomas?" asked Kate.

"No. I don't give his number out to strangers. At his request."

Jassy appeared at the door to the office and smiled at Kate and Tristan.

"Sorry to interrupt. Stevie, can you go and watch the kids? I'm on a call with DHL about those boxes," she said.

"Yes, if that's all?" said Stephen. He didn't wait for Kate or Tristan to answer and indicated they should leave. They came out of the office, and Stephen hurried down to the front of the shop, where the children were still being noisy. Jassy was on the phone at the till, arguing that a delivery of boxes had been sent to the wrong address.

"No, not the telephone exchange; it's Hubble on Frome Crawford high street."

She nodded and smiled at them as they passed. Kate and Tristan didn't see Stephen as they left the shop. He was with the children in another aisle. When they came back out onto the high street, the sky was filled with black clouds.

"What did you think of all that?" asked Tristan.

"I don't know. He seemed nervous at times, but we're two people off the street asking questions."

"Is it weird that he gave us the time of day? It's not like we were pretending we were going to buy an expensive saucepan."

Kate smiled. "I don't know."

She checked her watch. It was two p.m.

"Let's get something to eat and then head over to Ted Clough's house."

37

Ted Clough arrived home after a long morning of hospital appointments where medication was doled out and he was told his prognosis had deteriorated. Two weeks. He had two weeks left to live. It hadn't come as a surprise.

Talking to the police had been on his mind in the hospital waiting room. The more he thought about the Baker family, and what they'd done, the angrier he became. He had to talk to the police, put it on record. Tell them everything. He would ask that his name be kept out of things whilst the police investigated. Hopefully, he would be dead and gone by the time the shit hit the fan. He'd spoken to his solicitor and informed him that it wouldn't be long now, and he'd insisted that his cats were the first priority, as per his will. They had to be taken care of.

Ted went upstairs to have a wash and make himself presentable. He had given up taking baths. His knees couldn't get him in and out of the bath anymore, and he didn't want to get stuck. They'd never had a shower put in, so he was using an attachment shower hose, which made for a very weak shower.

This was the only time he took off his oxygen, and he had to keep taking breaks while sitting on a large plastic packing crate in the bath. Even moving his arms caused him shortness of breath and another painful coughing fit. The light was fading outside. From his vantage point on the box in the bath, he could see out the bathroom window and across the back garden to the forest. It was such a remote spot that they'd never bothered to put in frosted glass. Two of his cats were perched on the windowsill—a small white one that lay comfortably and the huge ginger tomcat, who was constantly shifting and shuffling to stay on the slippery tile.

A flock of black crows sat along the power line running across the back of the house. Ted shivered as he waited for the small plastic jug he used in the bath to fill with warm water, and he lifted it with shaky hands and poured it over his head, scrubbing with his free hand to get all the shampoo out. There was the sound of a car door shutting, and the flock of crows flew up off the power line, cawing. A moment later, he heard a noise downstairs.

"Hello?" he called. There was silence, and then he heard the creak of floorboards as someone came to the bottom of the stairs. "Is that you, Arthur?"

The postman sometimes let himself in to check on Ted, but not without knocking first and then yelling through the door to see if it was okay to come in.

He hurriedly dried his hair and stepped out of the bath onto the worn-out carpet. He heard the stairs creaking as someone slowly climbed.

"Who is that?" cried Ted, as he fumbled to fit the loop of the oxygen pipe over his head. He was grappling to fit the small air holes under his nostrils when the bathroom door opened.

"Hello, Ted," said the voice. He looked up at the man and saw he was wearing, along with his winter coat and boots, thick black gloves.

"What are you doing here?" asked Ted. The man moved swiftly and yanked the oxygen pipe. "What? No!" Ted fell forward, tripping over his feet, and he landed on his stomach, winding himself.

"Come on, get up," said the man, grabbing Ted by the hair. He screamed in pain as the man dragged him, naked, out of the bathroom by his hair and onto the landing.

Ted tried to cry out again, but he had no air in his lungs. He felt a leather glove on the bare skin of his leg, and he was lifted.

"We're going to take a little trip," said the man.

———

DCI Della Street had phoned Kate at four thirty and agreed to meet them at Ted Clough's house just before six.

There were two police cars parked by the back door when Kate and Tristan arrived in Kate's car. It was dark, and the kitchen door was wide open. A group of Ted's cats were moving in circles in the light shining out from the kitchen, and they were purring agitatedly.

The kitchen looked the same as before, but when they came through to the hallway, Della Street was crouched next to the body of Ted Clough at the bottom of the stairs. He was naked, lying on his front against the wall. Kate could see his neck was broken so his head was facing the wrong way. He still had the oxygen pipe looped around the twisted skin on his neck.

"Oh Jesus," said Tristan. Kate shooed the large ginger tom away from Ted's body as it started sniffing him.

"What happened?" asked Kate.

"We got here five minutes ago and found him," said Della. A young uniformed officer came down the stairs.

"There's no one here. No sign of a break-in," he said.

"Look at the bruising on the right leg. That's a handprint, and the loose skin on the back of his neck looks torn . . . ," said Kate. "You think someone threw him down?" She glanced at the bloody dent in the plasterwork at the bottom of the stairs. Halfway up the stairs lay a thin, pale bath towel, and a couple of steps down, Ted's oxygen tank.

Kate started up the stairs as Della's radio sounded with a message that officers were on their way. The bathroom was a mess—the medicine cabinet had been pulled off the wall, and its contents were strewn

Shadow Sands

over the floor. She quickly checked over the other rooms, but they were empty.

When Kate came back downstairs, Henry Ko was just arriving with three other officers, including DI Merton with his crumpled suit and equally crumpled face.

"What the hell is she doing at the crime scene?" asked Henry when he saw Kate.

"How did you know this was a crime scene?" asked Kate, looking between Henry and Merton. "Della only got here five minutes ago."

38

Kate and Tristan were taken to a small police support van and told to wait.

It was windowless and cramped inside, with a small seating area and a table.

"Are we being held in here?" asked Tristan. He was sitting on the bench. Kate paced up and down the small space. A police officer was stationed outside the door of the van.

"It feels like it," said Kate. She opened the door. "We need some fresh air," she said to the officer standing outside. The forensics van had arrived, and it was parked outside Ted's house with two more police squad cars.

"We need you to stay in there, just so we can check around the house for any forensic evidence," said the young woman, adding, "Do you fancy a cuppa?"

"I could have a cuppa," said Tristan. The police officer came up the steps, closed the door behind her, and started to make them tea in a tiny kitchenette in the corner.

It was an hour later when Henry Ko came into the support van to talk to them. He asked them to take a seat and sat opposite them in the cramped space.

"Della just told me she was contacted by Superintendent Varia Campbell at the Met Police," he said. "You had arranged for Ted Clough to make an official statement about the two bodies found in the Shadow Sands reservoir in 1989 and 1991 . . . Why didn't I know about this?"

Kate made a decision to be open with Henry and tell him what they had discovered. She said it was true. Ted Clough had damning information about the deaths at the reservoir and a cover-up orchestrated by the Baker family. He was due to go on the record, but when they arrived, they found him dead.

"He didn't fall down those stairs. It wasn't an accident," said Kate. "The way his head hit the wall, it looks like he was thrown down the stairs . . ."

Kate then went on to share the rest of the information they had so far, about Magdalena's disappearance, the murder of Simon Kendal, and the other missing young men and women. Henry listened to all this and seemed genuinely troubled, but he became angry and agitated when Kate got to the part about Kirstie Newett being picked up by Arron Ko.

Henry put his head in his hands.

"Oh Jesus," he said. "Kirstie Newett. She's going to haunt my family forever."

Kate looked at Tristan, who was equally surprised at Henry's reaction.

"You know Kirstie Newett?" asked Kate.

"I don't know her, I know *of* her. Myself and my family."

Henry rubbed at his face and took a deep breath. He went to the door of the support van, where a couple of police officers and the forensics team were now milling about outside, and he closed it.

"I'm going to tell you a few things. They need to remain confidential. I can't have you two running amok, spreading these crazy theories," he said. He sat down in front of them.

"These are not crazy theories . . . ," started Kate.

He put up his hand. "Please, let me talk."

"Okay, talk," she said.

"Firstly, I agree. Ted Clough's death looks very suspicious, and we're treating it that way. He was a collector of rare gold coins. We've been called out twice in the last three months after reports, from him, of intruders on the property. He had almost twenty grand's worth of gold coins in his office, just in drawers. No lock. We've been telling him for ages to put the collection into a bank safety-deposit box . . . We arrived at the scene so quickly because we were in the area and we heard Della on the radio. Since you've been waiting here, we've discovered that all his gold coins are, indeed, missing. We think he scared an intruder or intruders, who killed him."

"He had damaging information he was going to give us."

"And I am certainly going to look into that, Kate," he said. He seemed so genuine, but she wasn't ready to buy his bullshit.

"What about Kirstie Newett? She named your father to me without prompting."

Henry's face clouded over again. He got up and went over to one of the computers in the van.

"I have access to HOLMES in this support van. I'm showing you this only to explain," he said.

He called up a police file, then pressed "Print." There was a silence as he waited for the pages to emerge from the printer. Tristan glanced nervously across at Kate. Henry returned to the table.

"I'm showing you these in strict confidence," he said, handing over several sheets of a police report with KIRSTIE NEWETT written at the top. Kate read them through, her heart sinking.

"Kirstie didn't mention that my father took out a restraining order on her in 2010, shortly after she was released from a secure facility in Birmingham?" he said quietly.

"No," said Kate, reading through the police reports and passing them to Tristan. She read that six times Arron Ko had called in the police when Kirstie had been found in the garden of his house just outside Exeter, and then on two occasions when she had broken into the family home. The most recent being Christmas Day in 2011, when she'd broken a mirror and slashed her wrists in the family's bathroom. Kate thought back to the scars she'd seen on Kirstie's wrist.

"For several years she's been stalking my father. She's since threatened my mother and my brother . . . Have you ever had a stalker, Kate?" asked Henry.

"Yes."

"Then you'll know how terrifying it can be. It was only because of our quick thinking and knowledge of first aid last Christmas that we saved her from bleeding to death in our bathroom. I didn't want her to die in our house and for us to have to live with that," said Henry.

"This doesn't explain how Kirstie's infatuation with your father began," said Tristan. Henry nodded.

"My father was the face of the police, often on news reports and on local *Crimewatch* appeals. He also went into schools for several years. He went into Kirstie's school when she was sixteen. We think that's where she first saw him."

"What about Simon Kendal?" said Kate. "Why did you rush to pronounce his death an accident and then backtrack?"

"I didn't pronounce his death an accident. I was taking my lead from the coroner."

"Why was another coroner brought in? Alan Hexham should have done the postmortem," asked Kate.

"That's correct; Alan Hexham wasn't asked to do the postmortem. The government owns fifty percent of the Shadow Sands reservoir and the hydroelectric dam, and the dam provides electricity for millions of people. It's not unusual for the government to send in someone to look at a suspicious death, someone who perhaps has a higher security clearance."

Kate shook her head.

"That's stretching credibility," she said.

"Is it? What if Simon Kendal had been a terrorist planning to sabotage the power plant?"

"He was a local student."

"We know that *now*," said Henry. "I know it's a long time since you've been a police officer, Kate. But we'd rather have a knee-jerk reaction to something that turns out to be harmless."

"So, now you know Simon Kendal was just a student, don't you think his death was suspicious?"

"Yes," said Henry. "And we have a murder weapon. We found a tent peg in the mud at the side of the reservoir. The tent peg had Geraint Jones's prints on it, and it was used to stab Simon. We know that there are holes in the fence next to the reservoir. With this information, we have a stronger case against Geraint Jones. This gives both Simon and Geraint a clear way to get to the water without having to climb the fence."

Kate sat back on the tiny, lumpy seat in the van. Everything she had investigated so far had been demolished. Were they wasting their time? Playing at being detectives? When police officers like Henry could look up the details of witnesses through police files on the HOLMES network? Kate always prided herself on having all the information. She could see now that they had none.

"What about Magdalena Rossi?" said Kate. "You recovered her scooter from that ditch."

"Yes, and that ditch leads along twenty meters into a storm drain, where we found one of her earrings," said Henry. "She could have conceivably come off the road in the fog whilst driving the scooter and landed in the ditch. The storm drain carries water off the fields and out to sea. If you remember, there was a huge rainstorm that evening. We're working on the theory that her body was carried away by the floodwater. We already have the coastguard alerted to the fact that her body could have been washed out to sea, but as you know, the coastline in this area is volatile, with strong currents and tides. Magdalena's scooter was found lodged in the mouth of the storm drain, which makes us believe that she could have been washed out to sea and we may never recover her body. We're hopeful that we will . . . You both have to understand that I'm sharing this information with you in confidence, the strictest confidence."

Kate's mind was turning it all over, trying to find another question or fact that would disprove what Henry was saying. There were still so many questions about the young men and women who had gone missing—the bodies that Ted had found in the reservoir, tied up, and that he had been forced to lie about.

"I still think that you should search the Shadow Sands reservoir." Kate could hear the quaver in her voice.

"On what grounds?" said Henry.

"On the grounds that bodies were dumped there and passed off as accidents; there could be more bodies at the bottom," said Kate.

"I can't justify closing down a major power plant and diverting the resources of our marine unit on the hunch of a . . ." His voice trailed off.

"On the hunch of who?"

"On the hunch of an amateur detective, who, if I can be frank, has had her own troubles in the past."

"Now you're being rude," said Tristan.

"No. I'm being plain. I'm being direct," said Henry. "And I think you need me to be direct with you, before you find yourself looking foolish."

There was a knock at the door of the police van, and DI Merton came up the steps. "Sorry, guv. Forensics are almost done. It looks like a back window was where the intruder got in. We've got broken glass, a partial thumb, and footprints outside . . . You also have a, er, visitor."

Kate and Tristan followed Henry out of the van.

A tall, thin man who looked to be in his early fifties was talking to one of the uniformed officers at the police tape cordon at the back door of the house. He was dressed in an expensive pin-striped suit, a long black coat, and polished black shoes. He was very pale with graying hair and a blue-tinged five-o'clock shadow on his face.

"Yes, Lord Baker, but I can't let anyone in until forensics are finished," said the police officer.

"Of course, I quite understand," he said. "Ah, Henry," he added when he saw him with Kate and Tristan.

"Thomas," said Henry.

"I just heard from the Estate Office," said Thomas, eyeing Kate and Tristan.

"Yes. We're trying to piece it all together. It looks like a burglary," said Henry. Kate was confused as to why Thomas Baker was there, and she must have been glowering at him, because he turned to her and Tristan.

"Have we met?" he asked. "I'm Thomas Baker."

"Why are you here?" she said, ignoring his outstretched hand. His eyes narrowed.

"Perhaps you could introduce yourself?" he said.

"Kate Marshall. This is my associate, Tristan Harper."

"Associate of what?" he asked imperiously.

"I'm a private detective, and we've been investigating the death of Simon Kendal in the reservoir . . ."

"Kate isn't affiliated with me or the police," added Henry. Kate could see they had the attention of the other uniformed officers.

"Why are you here at this crime scene?" repeated Kate. Thomas shifted uncomfortably. He stared at her for a long moment. He seemed to be weighing up his answer.

"Ted Clough's house is part of the Shadow Sands estate. He was my tenant," he replied icily. "As the owner of the estate, I am party to any crimes committed on my land and the welfare of my tenants. Is that enough of an explanation for you, Miss Marshall?"

Kate felt her cheeks flushing red under the gaze of everyone around. There was something about the way he spoke, and the way everyone else was reacting, that reminded her of being told off by a schoolteacher.

"You don't like being questioned, do you?" she said, standing her ground and forcing herself to look him in the eye. Thomas looked to Henry, and his face broke into a lopsided, nasty smile.

"Not by an amateur detective and her, what was it, sidekick?" he said, chuckling.

Henry and the other police officers around laughed along awkwardly.

"Ted Clough was about to go on the record and say that when he was employed at the reservoir, he was given direct orders to lie about two bodies found in the water . . ."

Thomas stopped chuckling.

"In 1989 and 1991 the bodies of two women were found with their arms and legs bound. He was told to withhold this information, and he was told to lie about the location where the bodies were found . . ."

Thomas put his hand up and moved closer to Kate, lowering his voice.

"One of my elderly tenants has been viciously attacked just a few paces from us, and here you are shouting at the top of your voice about serious, and if true, highly sensitive matters. I'd like you to moderate the way you are talking. And I suggest you make a formal statement to Henry, DCI Ko, here . . ."

"She's already given me the information," said Henry.

"Good. Then I can leave that with you, Henry. I trust that you will investigate these allegations robustly, and of course, if I can be of any help, I will cooperate with you on every concern," said Thomas. A man from the forensics team appeared at the back door and told Thomas Baker that he could come into the house.

"If you'll excuse me," he said, ducking under the police tape and disappearing into the house. Henry followed.

"Make sure they're escorted off the premises," he said to DI Merton.

———

Kate and Tristan drove back down to the main road, followed closely by DI Merton in his car. He stopped behind them at the gate and watched until Kate had pulled out onto the main road.

There was a horrible silence in the car.

"Are you angry with me?" Kate said finally.

"No. I'm just confused. Pissed off with the way he spoke to you . . . I wish I'd opened my gob and said something," said Tristan. "Stuck-up twat."

"Thank you," said Kate.

"Henry's made me question everything so far . . . Kirstie . . . Geraint . . . The other victims," said Tristan.

"What about Ted? Why didn't he tell us his house was on the bloody Shadow Sands estate and that he rented from the Baker family?"

"We'll never know. He's dead . . . ," said Tristan.

"A burglary is logical. It's also bloody convenient . . . And Magdalena? Do you *really* think she came off the road and fell into a storm drain?"

Tristan rubbed at his eyes.

"She was a crazy driver, Kate . . . I saw the way she used to take corners on that scooter. There's always stories of cars coming off the road and ending up in ditches . . ."

"Fuck!" said Kate, slamming her hand into the steering wheel. "We hung our whole theory on what Kirstie told me."

"Do you think Henry could have falsified the police reports?" asked Tristan.

Kate shook her head. "I watched him log into HOLMES, the central police database. Those records could have been falsified, but it's a huge risk . . . And I saw. There were multiple report entries in the file, by several officers on different dates, all reporting on stalking incidents concerning Kirstie. Any cover-up would involve a huge number of officers from different ranks and locations."

"What the hell do we do now?" asked Tristan.

"I don't know," said Kate. She didn't know what or who to believe anymore.

39

Magdalena had woken from being drugged, feeling sore and bruised. When she felt his disgusting stickiness between her legs, something had snapped in her head.

No. This won't happen to me again, said a voice in her head.

"He's not going to do this to you again, you hear me?" she said. "You are going to survive."

Magdalena said it in Italian, and then in English, just to be sure. She was going to survive. She had to beat him and survive this.

She hadn't eaten in days, her clothes felt loose, and she kept having to hitch up her jeans, but she had access to clean water. This would keep her alive and lucid. She remembered a documentary she'd watched about the US Navy SEALs. One of them had been interviewed, and he'd said fear was his constant companion on a mission. He said fear creates a huge amount of adrenaline and energy, and you could harness this and turn it around so it works for you. He also said that whenever he was in a dangerous environment, he had to use everything he had, however small and insignificant.

Magdalena got up from the bed and started to explore the dungeon. It was time to fight, not to cower in the dark. She felt her way down the length of the corridor, from the lift doors to the room with the bed and the sink. The bed base was a square of concrete, the mattress was fitted onto it and made of thin foam with a sewn-in sheet. The sink was heavy porcelain, and both it and the tap were screwed down firmly in place. She moved her hands over every inch of her prison, mapping the walls with her hands. She felt for any loose tiles, noticing sticky residue in places, but the tiles were all firmly grouted in. The floor was smooth and cold. It felt like concrete.

When she got to the small room in the corridor with the toilet, she steeled her nerves and felt all around it. The toilet bowl was made of heavy porcelain and had no seat. She felt around the soil pipe behind it, which was firmly plastered into the wall. *Yuck, so sticky.*

A thin pipe led from the bowl up to an old-fashioned cistern, high above the toilet. The long chain that would have been attached to the flush mechanism had been removed.

Magdalena carefully climbed up onto the toilet bowl, balancing her feet on either side, and reached up to the cistern. It had a porcelain lid that was too heavy to lift. As she slid it to one side, it went past its tipping point and fell, landing on the concrete floor with a deafening crash. Magdalena slipped, and her left foot plunged into the bowl, followed by her right.

"Great. Disgusting," she said. She managed to stay standing upright, and gripping the walls, she stepped out of the bowl, shaking off her wet feet, thankful she had flushed the toilet.

Climbing back up on the toilet bowl, she reached up and felt around inside the cistern. The ball cock was firmly attached, and she couldn't feel whether anything else was loose, no other mechanism. The water was very cold and quickly left her hands numb and useless. She climbed down, perched on the edge of the toilet bowl, and dried her hands on her jeans, rubbing some warmth back into them. The hunger pangs had returned. They came in waves, and this time her stomach contracted and she doubled over in pain. She gritted her teeth and waited for them to pass, which they did after a few minutes.

Her bare foot touched the edge of the cistern lid, and she could feel that the thick porcelain had broken into pieces when it hit the floor. She knelt down and carefully felt the pieces. To her excitement, there was a corner piece with a sharp, spiked end. It had a smooth edge, which fit neatly in the palm of her hand.

It was a weapon.

40

"You should get some sleep," said Kate to Tristan, when she dropped him back at his flat. She could see dark circles under his eyes.

"You too. Things will look better in the morning," he said, leaning into the open door. He didn't sound convinced. "Want me to bring breakfast over first thing tomorrow?" he added. "Fried egg and bacon on a floury bap?"

"Yes, something to make me get up tomorrow morning," said Kate.

"Do you want to come in for some food?" asked Tristan.

"I'm fine, thanks."

Kate could see he was worried about her, and for that she was grateful, but she just wanted to go home and have some time alone.

Her house was freezing cold when she opened the front door. She came inside and built a huge fire in the hearth, made herself cheese on toast with an iced tea, and ate it in the dark living room, staring at the flames.

It felt like things were slipping away—her hold on the facts of this case and belief in herself. She wanted to talk to Kirstie. She wanted to believe that Magdalena was washed out to sea. She also knew she should go to her AA meeting later, but she just sat in front of the fire; her legs and face were growing hot from the flames, but she couldn't shake off the chill on her insides.

Her phone pinged with a text message, and she pulled it out of her jeans pocket. It was Jake, asking if she was around to Skype. She texted back that she would be ready in ten minutes. She hurried around the living room tidying up old plates and paperwork and switching on the lights. She went to the bathroom and brushed her hair and splashed cold water on her face, hoping that Jake would be confirming that he was coming to visit for half term next week.

Kate sat down in her favorite armchair by the window with her laptop just as he rang.

When she answered the call, the video screen popped up, and Jake was sitting on the sofa next to Kate's mum, Glenda. They had already eaten dinner, because her mother was still wearing her apron with I ♥ YORK CATHEDRAL written on the front. Jake had on a black T-shirt, and his hair was still shoulder length.

"Hey, Mum," said Jake, raising a hand.

"Hi, love," said Kate.

"Catherine, we're just waiting for your father. Come along, Michael. We're waiting for you," she said, looking past the camera.

"Is everything okay?" asked Kate. Her mother sometimes popped her head in on Skype chats with Jake, but she rarely joined the call unless there was something serious to talk about, and Kate's dad joined in only if it was very serious.

"How is the weather there, Catherine?" trilled her mother.

"Cold. As you'd expect it to be," she said.

Kate's father, with a mop of gray hair and his glasses around his neck on a gold chain, lumbered into the frame and sat down heavily next to Glenda. He was dressed in a bright-red jumper with a yellow diamond pattern.

"Hello, Catherine, love," he said, picking up his glasses on the chain and slipping them on. He peered at the screen. "You're looking well." He always said that. Kate mused that she could be shot in the face at point-blank range and her father would still comment that she was looking well.

"Yes, I'm swimming still, every day," she said.

"I see you've got the fire going!"

"Yes."

"When did you last have the chimney swept?" he asked.

"Um, last year, I think."

He tutted.

"You should get that swept again, Catherine. You don't want a chimney fire; that would be bad news."

"Michael, we're not here to talk about Kate's fireplace," said Glenda. Jake glanced across at Glenda and Michael. Glenda nodded.

"Mum, I need to talk to you about this week, half term," said Jake. *Here we go,* thought Kate. *He's bailing on me.* She took a sip of her iced tea. "I'd like to come over tomorrow, if that's not too short notice, and I'd love to stay for a couple of days."

"Okay, that's fine," said Kate, thinking she'd misread the situation. Although she'd hoped he'd stay the week. Especially now everything was in disarray, a bit of normality would suit her.

"Mum. There's something I want to do. Need to do . . . ," said Jake, clearing his throat. "You know I've been seeing a counselor, after what happened in the summer?"

"Yes."

"He's been great, and he's been helping me with some other stuff."

"What other stuff?" asked Kate, a little sharper than she intended.

"Stuff to do with . . ." Jake seemed very uncomfortable, and he was looking down at the floor. His long hair fell across his face.

"Jake, look at your mother when you talk, and don't hide behind your hair," said Glenda.

"Grandma! I'm trying to talk," he said, tucking his hair behind his ears.

Jake took a deep breath.

"Roland, that's my counselor. He got me to talk about my father in my sessions . . . I know who he is, and I know what he's done, but I'm going to go and see him."

"Go and see who?" asked Kate, confused for a moment.

"My father. Peter Conway," said Jake.

Kate forgot to breathe. The sound of the waves on the beach below roared in her ears. On the screen, Jake carried on talking, but she couldn't hear him, could only see his mouth moving.

Kate took a sudden intake of breath, and Jake's voice came back loud and clear.

"I've really thought about it, and I'm sixteen. I can legally see him if I want to . . ."

The three faces on the sofa looked back at her expectantly.

"He won't want to see you," said Kate, finally. Her voice was quiet, and it was difficult to speak. Her mouth was dry. She cleared her throat. "I've been told he hasn't wanted to see anyone."

"Peter has already agreed to see Jake," said Glenda, smiling awkwardly. "We got in contact with the hospital, where he's, erm . . . er . . ."

Kate felt a sudden surge of anger toward her mother. After everything that their family had been through, she was sugarcoating things.

"Staying? Mum. Is that what you were going to say? He's being held indefinitely, in a secure mental hospital at Her Majesty's pleasure. He's a multiple murderer."

"Kate, please. I'm no more thrilled about this than you are, but Jake has a right to see his father."

"Stop calling him his father!" shouted Kate, standing up. "He's not anything. He's nothing! He's no more than an accidental part of—"

"Mum. MUM!" said Jake. Kate was still fuming; her heart was thumping. "Mum. You need to respect my decision. I need to go and see him. I need to. You have to understand that. I don't want to be best friends with him . . ."

"What do you mean, best friends? You'll barely get close to him being civil. He doesn't care," said Kate. "He's a monster, and I say that as someone who believes in people's ability to reform. He tried to kill me, Jake. Twice. And the second time you were there, and he was pretty violent with you too. He wanted you to watch!"

"I know, Mum."

"What do you mean? Don't you have any loyalty to me?" asked Kate.

"Now, Catherine. I understand how you must feel," said Michael. "But that's enough about loyalty. Jake is only just an adult, and he's done nothing but love you, despite your problems in the past . . . which we're not blaming you for."

"Peter Conway gets a free pass during this discussion, does he? But my problems in the past are still being held against me?"

Michael put his hands up. "Kate. We know you're sorry. We're proud of how you're getting, how you've got your life back on track. The lad just wants to sit down and talk to Conway. Just for an hour. Jake has a right to be curious about his biological father. Jake is under no illusion as to who Peter is, and what he's done . . ."

"*Getting* my life back on track?" said Kate.

"My mistake. Sorry."

"Dad. I've been sober for ten years. I have a respectable career. No debts. But I always have to be sorry, don't I? I will never be forgiven . . . I just have to grovel and apologize until the end of time. And that monster Peter Conway, who has committed untold horrors, gets to dictate the terms of this meeting with Jake. Why are you all kowtowing to him? Talk about male fucking privilege!"

Kate could feel herself starting to lose it. She wanted to throw her computer through the window onto the beach below. She loved Jake, but why did he want to see Peter Conway during the precious time they had together during school half term? She'd spent years trying to make up for being a bad mother when he was tiny, and yet Peter Conway, who had done nothing but cause misery and hurt, was being treated to a visit.

"Mum! You don't need to be sorry, Mum. Never," said Jake, leaning closer to the camera. Kate felt herself begin to cry. She wiped away a tear. "You are my mum and I love you. And I know you love me. I know Peter will never be a real father to me."

Kate sat down.

"I just miss you, Jake. I have all this guilt that I wasn't there for you. I was apart from you so much, and now you're about to be an adult, and you'll go off and have your own life . . . Which you should, but I feel like I never got the chance to be your mother."

There was an awkward silence. They weren't the most demonstrative family at the best of times.

"Mum. I just have to meet him and talk to him," said Jake, almost pleading. "For years, I've heard how people talk about him and whisper behind my back that my dad is this serial killer . . . They've turned him into this legendary bad guy, this celebrity. I've got to go through life with that on my shoulders. I don't want to be afraid of him. If I can just talk to him, and make him real. He's just a person."

There was a long silence. Kate still hated the idea of Jake visiting Peter, but she was impressed by what he'd said. Her bottom lip started to tremble.

"Oh, Catherine," said Glenda. "We all love you. Just know that."

"I have to get a tissue," said Kate, feeling the tears and snot on her face. She hurried and grabbed a wad of kitchen towel, blew her nose, and tried to gather herself back together. She took some deep breaths and heard Jake and her parents talking on the computer.

"Okay. I'm back," she said, sitting down again. "So. What's your plan to see Peter?"

An awkward glance passed between Jake, Glenda, and Michael.

"Mum, I'd like to come over to yours tomorrow, and then the visit with Peter is booked for Monday. It's at Great Barwell Hospital, of course."

"Why are you coming all the way over here when you'll just have to drive back again?" asked Kate.

There was another awkward pause.

"Peter Conway has only agreed to see me, Mum, if you come too."

41

The man got in the lift. It was an old service lift, gray and functional. It was operated by a key, which he pushed into a keyhole on the left-hand wall of the lift and turned to the right. The doors closed, shutting out the light, and the lift started its rumbling descent.

The night vision goggles he wore were small and compact, and he slipped them down over his eyes. They activated with a mechanical whir, and he saw the inside of the lift in black and white with a green hue.

Opening the small revolver in his hand, he checked the bullets nestling in the chamber. He spun it around and clicked it back into place. *Six shots.* He had to use them wisely, and it was easy to panic if they got out of hand. You had to be calm.

He had kept her for a week, and he'd had fun with her, lots of fun, but she was getting weak. He'd kept a couple for longer, and they'd gone completely crazy, harming themselves. One girl had died suddenly, robbing him of any kind of climax. Another girl had gone on dirty protest. Which had disgusted him. It was better that he chose their demise when they were still sane enough to be scared.

His favorite part was at the beginning, when he just watched them, following them in the dark, drinking in their fear. He liked to leave obstacles for them to trip over. He loved their anger at falling, their loss of control. The moment when they started to fall apart mentally but they still had hope. He liked to slap, poke, and prod them in the dark, disorientate them.

He'd abducted a few guys in the past, but they weren't as much fun. They fought back more readily. He'd used a knife for the guys; cutting the tendons in their knees wasn't fatal, but it kept them from moving around too much.

As far as sex was concerned, he preferred it with the girls, but the boys were equally thrilling to violate.

He chose to use a small handgun to end them. A shotgun tore through flesh and caused so much damage. He'd shot one of the boys in the head, but they made such a terrible mess, brains.

The lift moved slowly down the two stories to the basement dungeon. Technically, it was only one level down, but it was two stories deep, buried under layers of soil and completely soundproof from the outside world. Despite the depth, he'd put a tape recorder up on the main level to test the sound the first time he'd fired a gun in the basement. The noise had been deafening, and it bounced around the confined space, but the tape recorder had registered nothing more than a faint crack up top, and he was sure this didn't carry outside the building. It was so well insulated.

The lift came to a juddering stop. He turned the key back to the first position, and the doors opened.

He wasn't prepared to see her standing outside the lift doors, bathed in the green glow picked up by the night vision goggles. In the green-tinged sepia she now looked thin and weak. Her cheeks were hollow, and her long hair was greasy.

"There you are . . . ," she said, looking right at him. He faltered for a moment, flipping up the night vision goggles, momentarily making himself as blind as she was. Was there some light escaping out from somewhere; did she see him? The goggles made an electronic whizzing sound when he flipped them up. It was pitch black.

"I can see you with my ears," she growled. In the darkness he heard her give a yell. He flipped the night vision goggles back down, but she was coming at him with something in her hand. She ran into him, knocking the gun from his hand, and he felt something slice through the flesh on his shoulder.

The gun skittered across the floor, away from the lift. They crashed into the lift together and slid down onto the floor. She stabbed at him, screaming, slicing through his shirt; he felt something sharp slice perilously close to his right nipple.

How the fuck did she do that? he thought. She struck him again in the side of the head.

He yelled, and she caught him again in the ribs before he managed to kick out at her, landing a blow to her belly. The night vision goggles had been knocked to the side of his head, and he adjusted them. He kicked her again, and she rolled outside the lift, groaning.

Panicking, he inserted the key in the lift and turned it to the right. He watched her as the lift doors closed. When it rumbled to life and started back up to the top floor, he leaned against the wall. He was shaking and out of breath. *Jesus.* He checked himself over. His shirt was slashed at the shoulder and twice on his chest, and he was bleeding. How could this have happened? She was half-starved.

He could feel himself crying, which only angered him more. He started to breathe normally again only when he reached the top floor and the doors opened.

He stepped out into the dim light and sat down on the floor, clutching at his wounds. His shoulder would probably need stitches. How the hell was he going to explain that one away?

"Fuck!" he yelled.

Then he realized.

No, no, no. NO!

The gun. He'd dropped the gun.

42

Magdalena felt the gun all over, rolling it between her hands. It was real. She'd never held a gun before, and this gun had a solid heft. It wasn't plastic. She'd heard something skitter to the floor when she ran at him, and she'd imagined a knife. It chilled her to think he'd come down with a gun.

Did he come down here with the safety on or off?

The police at home carried guns, but she'd never even seen an officer pull out his gun. What a sheltered life she'd lived, she thought; well, until now.

Magdalena ran her fingers over the side of the gun, and she found what she thought was the safety catch and clicked it.

She held the gun up and away from herself, and she put a small amount of pressure on the trigger. It didn't move, and she felt resistance like it was locked in place.

He came down here with the safety off; he was going to shoot me.

She rolled that over in her mind. Why was she shocked? He'd raped her, twice that she knew of, and he had been down here, watching her in the dark. A few times when he'd come close, she'd heard him inhaling her.

She shuddered. He was done with her, and he was going to kill her. Would he have done it quickly? She doubted it, and it depended on how many bullets he'd loaded into the gun.

It took a few tries, but she got the chamber open. Keeping the gun tipped forward, she felt around inside. There were six bullets slotted inside the circular chamber.

Her mind was turning fast. He would come back, and he would try to get the gun or kill her before she could use the gun on him. It was driving her insane that she couldn't see anything.

A few months back she'd been to watch a play at the university about life in the trenches during World War I. The actors had used a real gun, with blanks, but when it was fired, it had been so loud, and the flash of the gunfire in the dark theatre had made the audience yell out in fright.

If she fired the gun down here in the dark, there could be a flash of light, which would show her surroundings.

Shit, now that's an idea, she thought. Was it enough time to see her surroundings, in the blink of a gunshot? *I have six bullets.* It felt so awesome to have some power, after endless hours and days in the dark feeling powerless. She almost didn't want to give up those six bullets. She couldn't see them, but in her mind they were silver. Six silver bullets. Six silver chances to protect herself.

The walls were made of plaster, and the lift door at the end of the corridor was made of heavy steel. Her best option was to fire the gun down the corridor to the left into the plaster wall; the bullet wouldn't bounce back at her off the plaster.

With a shaking hand, she lifted the gun, aiming to the left. She slipped off the safety, opened her eyes wide, and pulled the trigger.

BANG.

It was terrifyingly loud, and the kickback was powerful, but she made herself keep her eyes open. In that split-second bright flash, she saw the hallway, lit up. She'd been in the dark for so long that the image was temporarily burned onto her retinas. She kept blinking her eyes, trying to catch as much information as possible before it faded. It was an empty corridor. The door of the small toilet was on the right side, and it was painted a horrible pea-green color. The wall to the right was splattered with what looked like a large bloodstain. *Oh God.* She shuddered to think that she'd felt so much of that wall with her fingers and put her ear to it. There had been other victims, who had died down here.

There wasn't time to be scared. She'd seen something else in that split-second flash, in the ceiling above the lift doors. There was a hatch in the ceiling above the lift.

She had five bullets. Magdalena pivoted on the spot, and she fired a bullet against the back wall of the room with the bed and sink.

BANG.

In the flash of the charge, she saw the outline of the room, and she felt repulsed. The tiles were pale and grimy with blood spatter, and the mattress was stained with huge spots of blood, blooming out in a tie-dye pattern. The room, in her mind, had been white. She'd also seen the bed, in her mind, as being clean. Did this mean she was an optimist? She'd always thought of herself as a pessimist, a glass-half-empty girl. *Perhaps being trapped in a dungeon by a crazed rapist helped you to see everything else in a positive light*, she thought, darkly.

There was no hatch in the ceiling or hidden door.

She coughed as she breathed in the dust from the exploded tiles. She put the safety back on the gun, tucked it into the waistband of her jeans, and felt her way back down the corridor toward the lift doors.

He would come back; she didn't know how soon, but he would realize she had the gun. She hoped she'd cut him badly enough for him to need stitches. It could buy her time.

She found the lift at the end of the corridor, and put her arms up. They didn't reach the ceiling, and from the gun flash she'd seen that the ceiling in the corridor was quite high.

How was she going to reach the hatch?

43

He froze when he heard the loud crack of the first gunshot echo up the lift shaft. He was ready with his hand on the key, about to go back down. His hand hovered over the key. She'd found the gun already, and she'd fired it. What if she'd killed herself? No. She was too feisty to blow her head off.

He removed the key, came out of the lift, and went to the toolbox he kept by the main door. He took out a length of rope, the bottle of angel dust, and a crowbar. He inspected the sharp, curved end of the crowbar. He smiled.

"You fucking bitch. You'll pay for this," he said.

He went back into the lift and inserted the key. He should go right back down there. She was still in the dark. He could still overcome her if he was prepared. He would hit the bitch over the head and give her a fatal dose of angel dust. No, he would stab her in the spine. Paralyze her and treat her to a slow and painful death. He looked down at the key. It was spotted with blood.

"Shit, shit, shit," he hissed. Blood was running down his arm from under his sleeve. He tucked the crowbar down the back of his jeans and went to his bag and rummaged inside for tissues.

He fumbled with a pack of tissues and blotted at his wounds. He tore at the sleeve of his shirt, managing to pull it off where she'd slashed at him, and he used the bottom half of the material to bandage the wound.

The front of his shirt was soaked with blood, and he opened the buttons. The two slashes on his chest were less deep, but he would have to get them seen to.

He wiped his shaking hands and adjusted the night vision goggles on top of his head.

Crack.

He jumped, again, at the sound of another gunshot, and the crowbar fell with a clatter.

Four bullets. What was she doing? Was she trying to bust the lift open?

An image flashed in his head from that movie *The Ring*, when the scary, gaunt girl with the long, wet, greasy hair climbed out of the well, her elbows and legs all twisted and angular. Was she going to climb up the empty lift shaft?

"Fucking snap out of it!" he shouted to himself. He leaned down to pick up the crowbar, and more of his blood dripped onto the floor. The front of his shirt was now saturated with two spreading stains of blood. He felt faint.

He hesitated, then pulled the key out of the lift wall, stepped out of the lift, and inserted the key in the keyhole on the wall outside. He turned it, and the lift doors locked.

Now she couldn't get out, even if she climbed up the shaft. And if she got into the lift shaft and started climbing, he would set the lift running back down and crush her freaky, angular body.

He looked down at his blood-stained hands. They were still shaking.

"Stop! Stop!" he said to his hands.

He would have to work out what to do next.

He had to calm down. He had to see a doctor. He would let her sweat, let her get weaker, and he would return with a shotgun. He would blast at her the second he came out of that lift, and screw the mess.

He would only feel safe when her brains were all over the walls.

44

Kate and Jake arrived at Great Barwell Psychiatric Hospital at nine a.m. on Monday morning and reported to the front gate. The hospital was a huge sprawl of Victorian redbrick buildings, dwarfed by a huge expanse of manicured grounds. It was built next to a road of residential houses. One side of the road looked like any other suburban street, but on the other side, the pavement was lined with a twenty-foot-high fence, topped with razor wire.

For so many years, Peter Conway had defined Kate's life. He had been her boss in the Met Police, and he had taken her under his wing, promoted her, and encouraged her career. They had briefly been lovers—she'd known at the time it was a terrible mistake, even when she just thought he was a police officer—and then she'd made the shocking discovery that he was the Nine Elms Cannibal.

Kate's greatest triumph, catching Peter, had also been her greatest failure. The story wrote itself in the tabloids. Rookie police officer sleeps with the boss, outs same boss as a serial killer, and then as a juicy conclusion, gives birth to his child.

He was the person she blamed for everything: her downfall, the end of her career in the police force, her alcoholism, and her troubled relationship with her son. She held so much anger and fear and hatred toward him, and those emotions had built Peter Conway, a.k.a. the

Nine Elms Cannibal, into an almost mythical creature. A monster crouching in the dark to torment her forevermore.

At the gatehouse, a stone-faced woman sat behind a bank of television monitors, studying grainy images of the road and perimeter fence. As Kate opened her mouth, a wailing siren started up. The woman, who had just taken a large bite out of a pasty, waved a gloved finger.

"SIREN TEST!" she shouted, swallowing her mouthful of pasty. "Have you got any ID?"

Kate and Jake took out their passports and pushed them through the hatch. The woman took their passports and flicked them open, thumbing through with what Kate thought were rather greasy fingers, until she located their photo pages. Jake's passport was due to expire in a month, and in the photo, he was a skinny, gawky eleven-year-old, grinning into the camera with his front teeth missing. The woman cracked a smile. The siren fell to a low wail and ceased.

"You've grown into a handsome young man," she said.

"The siren sounds when someone escapes?" asked Jake.

"We test it on Monday mornings at nine a.m.," said the woman.

"We're here to see Peter Conway," said Kate. The penny dropped, and the woman's attitude changed toward Jake, and she went back to being stony faced as she printed off their visitors' passes.

"The last time it went off was when your father escaped. He killed a doctor here too," she said, slipping the passes across the counter. "Go down to the main gate there, and someone will be waiting for you."

They walked up to the main entrance in silence. The hospital housed some of the most dangerous criminals in the United Kingdom, but the grounds were beautifully kept, ordered and peaceful. The only giveaways were the high fence and the viewing towers dotted around at intervals, where armed guards sat in crow's nests, watching.

"The doctor he killed. He sliced open her throat with a homemade shank, didn't he?" said Jake, breaking the silence.

"Yes. Her name was Meredith. She had a husband and a little boy," said Kate. It was always better to tell the truth, she thought.

"Mum, I'm a bit scared," said Jake.

"A bit?" said Kate. "I'd be worried if you weren't scared . . . He's going to be behind a thick piece of glass. He can't touch you."

This all seemed crazy. How would seeing this monster help Jake to explore his past? They carried on walking in silence and reached the main entrance.

Peter Conway had struck a deal: Kate would go in first and visit him for one hour. Then he would meet Jake. Kate had driven to her parents' house in Whitstable the day before, where they'd talked and talked about the past and the implications of Jake meeting Peter. Glenda had said something that stuck in Kate's mind.

"You have to demystify Peter Conway, Catherine, for your own sanity, and Jake's too. He's many things—a monster, Jake's father, the reason our family was blown apart—but he's also just a person. He's held all of us in his grip for too long."

There was a lengthy process for Kate and Jake to go through security: two sets of X-ray scanners, a body search, and then more locked doors until they arrived in a reception area, which was large, airy, and painted white.

A glass partition ran down the middle of the space, meeting a perpendicular glass wall. The glass continued through it, marking off a visitors' room. On each side of the outside partition were security guards, sitting at desks with monitors. The screens had images of the visitors' room and the corridors outside. Kate and Jake were met by a man who introduced himself as Dr. Grove. He was dressed informally and put them at ease.

"The law prevents us from recording your visits. You will need to leave all mobile devices, computers, tablets, and laptops with the security guards before you go in," he said.

Kate and Jake took their phones out and handed them to the officer at the desk.

"If you wish to terminate the interview, please signal, and one of the officers here will let you out. Jake, I'll take you to the cafeteria whilst your mother meets with Peter."

"Good luck, Mum," said Jake, and he went off with the doctor. One of the security guards went to the glass door and keyed a number into a pad. The door clicked and buzzed open.

"Remember, signal if you need me," he said with a smile.

Kate went through the door, and it closed behind her with a click and a buzz. All background noise ceased. The officer outside went back to his desk, talking to his colleague. His mouth was moving, but there was no sound. Kate turned back and looked around the room. It was starkly lit and painted light green. Three of the walls were windowless, and the fourth was a floor-to-ceiling thick glass partition that looked into an identical room. A square plastic table and chair were bolted to the floor, and this was mirrored on the other side of the glass.

There was movement outside, and a man with a stooped gait was being escorted with his hands behind his back. It took her a moment to realize it was Peter Conway. When they had worked together, all those years ago, he had been an athletic man, six feet tall, and even until recently, in a rare picture of him in his cell, he had seemed like a caged animal. His large frame constrained in the small space.

The man approaching the glass partition looked almost elderly. He was rail thin. His shoulders were curved and hunched over. His face and mouth were sucked, and he had deep lines around his face. His thinning gray hair was tied back in a ponytail. He wore thick reading glasses, jeans, and a pale-green pullover. His hands were cuffed behind his back, and the two orderlies with him were armed with batons, Mace, and Tasers in their belts. He wasn't wearing a mesh "spit hood." Kate had read that Peter had to wear it at all times in communal areas. He'd bitten several orderlies and patients over the years.

Kate couldn't hear what the guards were saying since the sound system was muted. They got him seated opposite her. Peter didn't look up. He was asking the officers something. It was then that she saw he had no teeth. Just gums, and this was what made him look so old.

Suddenly, the sound activated and his voice came over the speaker implanted in the glass of the partition.

"I want them now."

"You'll get them when we leave," said one of the orderlies. He slipped off Peter's handcuffs. The other orderly stood to the side, ready with a Taser in his hand.

"Remain seated until we leave, Peter," said the orderly, pocketing the cuffs. He placed a small plastic box on the table, and they then both retreated backward toward the door. It buzzed and opened, and they left, closing it behind them. When the door buzzed and locked, Peter reached for the box on the table and picked it up. He turned away, and when he looked back, he was more the man she remembered.

"Hello, Kate," he said, smiling with a row of perfect, white false teeth. "You've put on weight."

45

Kate and Peter sat in silence, looking at each other from each side of the thick glass partition.

Her mother had asked her what she was planning to wear for the visit. Glenda seemed concerned that she should look her best for the occasion, and it struck Kate as rather warped, that she should dress up for the man who had tried to kill her. Twice. In the end Kate had decided to wear what she would wear for a normal day at work: smart blue jeans and a green woolen jumper. The irony wasn't lost on her that, today, she and Peter were wearing similar outfits.

Kate thought she would feel afraid when she saw Peter, but now, she didn't know what to feel.

"What happened to your teeth?" she asked, breaking the silence. He smiled. It was a creepy Hollywood smile.

"You've heard the phrase, *I'll kick your teeth so far down your throat, you'll need to stick a toothbrush up your arse to clean them*?"

"Yes."

"The inmate who threatened me was true to his word. By the time he finished, I was only left with my back molars intact," he said. "He also broke my nose and my left cheekbone."

"You'll have to point him out to me. I'd like to shake his hand," said Kate.

"You wouldn't want to touch his hand after you know where it's been," said Peter, still smiling. "He's a nasty, violent pedophile."

Kate didn't let him see her revulsion. They sat in silence for a full minute, refusing to break eye contact. She suddenly sighed and sat back.

"So. What are we going to talk about for the next . . ." She checked her watch. "Fifty-seven minutes?"

"Have you been anywhere nice on holiday?" he asked.

"No. Have you?"

"No, but I hear solitary confinement is very nice this time of year."

This was a flash of the man she once knew. For a moment he seemed normal, making a stupid joke. Acknowledging their shared discomfort. She wanted to smile but stopped herself. This was surreal. After all he'd done to her, he'd almost made her laugh. It reminded her how dangerous he was.

"Why do you want to see Jake?" asked Kate. "You've never been bothered you have a son."

"Jake wanted to see me. That pisses you off, doesn't it?"

"What are you going to say to him?" she said, her voice hard. Peter put up his hand, waving her away. She saw how his fingers were bent and misshapen with arthritis.

"I'm happy just to look at him and hear his voice."

"He doesn't look like you," said Kate, more stridently than she wanted.

"That's a shame. I was a handsome bastard. *Wasn't I?*" Kate raised an eyebrow. "Yes. I was, whether you like it or not. I got into your knickers, and my, you were wet when I got in there."

Kate got up.

"You're just a sad, dirty old man who has to put his teeth in a cup by his bed. I've got better things to do with my time," she said. She went to and knocked on the glass door, feeling her face flush with embarrassment.

"Kate, Kate . . ." He stood up. "I'm sorry . . . Come back. Let's start again. For Jake. That's the deal, isn't it? You see me, I see him?"

There was desperation in his voice, and Kate, despite every fiber of her being wanting to leave, knew Jake had to see his father. If only to see he was a pathetic old man. She took a deep breath and came back to her chair. They both sat down. There was another long silence. Peter took off his glasses and polished them on his pullover.

"You said you had better things to do than visit me," he said, slipping the glasses back on. "Like what?"

"I have a life, Peter. It's none of your business," she said, but she didn't sound convincing.

"It was Jake's counselor who suggested that he meet me. He's having counseling because *you* found a dead body when he stayed with you in the summer," said Peter, leaning closer to the glass and pointing to emphasize the *you*. "Jake saw the body, too, didn't he?"

"Yes. We were diving in a reservoir," she said.

"What did the body look like?"

"It was a young lad, only a few years older than Jake," she said.

"Was he badly beaten?"

"His body was covered in lacerations. The police thought at first he'd drowned and been run over by one of the maintenance boats that patrol the reservoir."

"What do the police think now?"

Kate hesitated. "They think it was his friend."

Peter sat back.

"Hmm. But *you* think different, don't you?"

"It doesn't add up as a crime of passion."

"Were they lovers?"

"No. I mean passion as in a flash of anger, violence."

Kate went on to describe the circumstances of Simon's death and Kirstie Newett's story of her abduction, and then she found herself telling him about the whole case, the other missing people, and Magdalena. Kate could feel herself unloading the burden of the case onto Peter, and he listened intently.

"Simple Simon saw something on his midnight walk by the reservoir."

"Yes," said Kate.

Peter closed his eyes and recited, *"Simple Simon met a pieman, going to the fair . . . Said Simple Simon to the pieman, let me taste your ware."* He opened his eyes and stared at her. "Do you think Simon was closeted? Gay?"

"No."

"He wasn't cruising for sex at night by this reservoir? There was no pieman whose wares he tasted, and then things turned nasty?" Kate looked at him skeptically. "I'm not teasing you. You have to take a step back and think about these things."

"No. Simon saw someone by the water," said Kate.

"Why don't you think it was Geraint?"

"Geraint didn't have access to a boat; I think Simon was pursued by someone in a boat after he was stabbed."

"Could Geraint have seen Simon being pursued by this person in a boat?"

"He could have done, but he would have said something. He was on probation when it happened. Wouldn't he have jumped at the chance to blame someone else?"

"What about the old man, the drifter? The one who has Simon's knife," asked Peter.

"He found the knife in the mud by the water. I don't think he saw anything . . . I don't know . . ." Kate rubbed at her eyes, feeling the confusion of all the conflicting information.

"Where is this drifter now?"

"I don't know."

"Simon had no enemies that you know of. He wasn't rich. His friend had no designs or motive to kill him. So, logically, Simon was killed because he saw something."

"How can you be so sure?" asked Kate.

"I have nothing to lose. I can look at it objectively. Throw into the mix a rich, influential family, it's quite a case."

"What about Magdalena?"

"She's probably dead already. What is it? Eight days since she went missing? You need to focus on finding her body. He'll need to get rid of it. That's the point where the two strands of the case will collide."

Kate looked down at her hands, feeling bleak. Bleak for her personal life, her connection to this monster in front of her, and bleak that she didn't have the power to solve the case and save Magdalena.

"You were a good police officer," said Peter.

"That's an odd thing for you to say."

"You were."

"So were you, Peter," she said, looking up at him. "Think of all the good you could have done."

He rolled his eyes.

"You always were an idealist, Kate. You thought that as a police officer you could *do good*. The bad is already out there. A police officer can't spread goodness any more than the tooth fairy. All they can do is stop people from doing more 'bad' things . . ." His bent fingers lifted up to put the word *bad* in air quotes.

"Why were you a police officer?" she asked. "It's a genuine question, if we're talking about 'good' and 'bad.'"

He clicked at his dentures with his tongue.

"I like to solve puzzles. I didn't care about the nature of the perceived crimes. It didn't give me any great rush when I got the bad guy and arrested him. I just wanted to outwit them. Solve the puzzle."

"A murder case being a puzzle," said Kate.

"Yes. It's a superior feeling when you work it out. And of course, for me, the reverse was exciting, getting away with it."

"Is that why you hate me? Because I caught you? I got to feel superior?" asked Kate.

"I don't hate you, Kate. You were the only one who solved the puzzle, and for that, you had to go."

It chilled Kate to hear him talking so matter-of-factly. She had a flashback to the rainy night in her flat, when she solved the puzzle and knew he was the Nine Elms Cannibal. He'd known. He'd shown up at her door and forced his way inside.

Peter had cornered her in the bedroom of her small flat, and he was on top of her, pushing a knife into her abdomen . . . His face crazed, blood pouring from the gash in his head, lips curled back over pink-stained teeth.

She had carried on fighting as the blood pooled on her belly. She'd thrown him off and hit him hard over the head with a lava lamp.

She'd limped to the phone to call the police, all the time looking at the knife sticking out of her belly. The pain had been so bad, but she'd known if she pulled it out, she would have bled to death.

How close had he stabbed to the tiny embryo growing inside her? How close had the knife come to killing Jake?

There was a buzzing sound, and Kate looked up. Their meeting had come to an end. The scar on her belly tingled.

"It sounds like a fascinating case. I would say that I hope you catch him, but part of me hopes you don't. You will let me know when you find Magdalena's body?" said Peter. The spell had been broken, and the old Peter, the police officer she'd known, had vanished.

Kate went to answer, but the sound was cut between them. She wanted to give him a parting shot, but he couldn't hear her. Kate looked up and saw Jake was waiting at the door to come in and see his father.

46

It was a long journey back from Great Barwell Hospital to Ashdean, and Jake was quiet in the car for the first part of the journey. It wasn't until they pulled over on the motorway services that Kate asked him what he had talked about with Peter. They ordered coffee and found a corner with empty seats.

"He seemed really nervous," said Jake. "Did you see when I went in, he was fiddling with his mouth?"

"He's got false teeth," said Kate.

"Okay. I thought they looked really white."

Kate smiled and took Jake's hand. "Did he scare you?"

"No."

"Did he talk about anything horrible?"

"Mum, stop it," he said, embarrassed, pulling his hand away. There was a pretty teenage girl on the other side of the café who was looking over. He stirred his coffee and looked at the table.

"What did he say to you?"

"I dunno. We just chatted. He wanted to know all about my iPhone."

"Your iPhone?"

"Yeah. He said that when he'd been arrested, he didn't have a phone; he had a car phone, and mobile phones were still new . . ." Kate recalled the bricklike handset with an antenna that she'd had in 1995. "I told him about, you know, iPhones, the App Store, and how I use it for stuff. I went back and asked the security guys at the front desk outside the room if I could have my iPhone back and show Peter my photos and stuff, but they wouldn't let me . . ."

"What else?"

"He asked me what music I liked, cos as part of the whole iPhone conversation I told him that I get all my music on iTunes. He said I was lucky, he used to have to go and buy records, and his mum only played the records that she liked. He had to ask her permission to buy a record. Even if he had the money. He said that a couple of times he'd come home with a record she hadn't heard, and she'd only give it half a minute of a listen, and if she didn't like it, she would snap the record in half."

"That's harsh," said Kate.

"Yeah. He loved the idea of the iTunes store. He wants to send me an iTunes voucher for Christmas . . . I said I'd ask you and Grandma if that was okay." Kate nodded, trying not to let her discomfort show. "He loves David Bowie."

"What?" said Kate.

"Peter. He loves David Bowie. He's the guy from that film *Labyrinth*, the one we used to watch when I came to stay. The one who has two different colors in his eyes, like me."

"Yes, I know who David Bowie is. And he doesn't have different-colored eyes. The pupil is permanently dilated in one of his eyes, which makes it look like it's a different color."

"Oh," said Jake. He seemed disappointed that his eyes weren't the same. Kate thought it was odd that after all these years she hadn't known Peter Conway liked David Bowie. She knew so many intimate details of his childhood and the disturbing relationship he'd had with his mother, Enid. Knowing his favorite music had never been at the top of her list. "Peter told me to check out an album, *The Rise of Ziggy Starburst* . . . Or something."

"*The Rise and Fall of Ziggy Stardust and the Spiders from Mars,*" said Kate. "I think I've got it at home."

Jake already had his iPhone out, and he was tapping at the screen.

"There, I've got it downloading," he said.

"That is fast," said Kate. She didn't know what she'd expected from their visit. She'd secretly hoped that Jake would have been disgusted by his monster of a father. She'd never expected Peter to start recommending stuff for Jake to buy on iTunes.

"What did you and him talk about?" asked Jake, sucking cappuccino froth off his spoon and looking over at her quizzically.

"Our visit was more difficult . . . We didn't talk about music. But we settled on talking about our old police days," said Kate, wondering if it was screwed up that they hadn't talked more about Jake . . . but then again, she didn't want Peter to have a relationship with Jake.

"I know what he did to you, Mum . . . I remember how cruel he was to both of us."

"Did he say sorry? Show remorse?"

"No. We didn't talk about it," said Jake. "But I haven't forgotten. I know what he did to you, and all those women . . . I read that Ted Bundy was, apparently, a good dad. His girlfriend had a completely different experience of him. She saw a side of him that no one else saw. Maybe I was lucky today, and I just got to meet the part of him that's still good."

Kate was taken aback by his maturity and insight.

"Do you want to see him again?"

Jake shrugged and stirred his cappuccino.

"He wants me to come again. I said we should write to each other maybe first?"

"It's up to you, Jake. You know that until you were sixteen, he wasn't allowed to contact you, but if you want to write to him, they can give him your address, or you can set up a post office box."

Jake nodded. "What about his mother, Enid? She's my grandmother, isn't she?"

"Yes. She's due to be released from prison next year," said Kate. She was happy they were having such a sensible conversation, and she bit back the urge to say, *Never call that sick bitch your grandmother.* Enid Conway had a disturbing relationship with Peter. There had been rumors of a sexual relationship between them. She had also been involved in the plan to help Peter escape from the hospital, and for this she'd received a three-year sentence.

"If Peter had managed to escape and they'd gone to live abroad, they would have been out there in the world . . ." Jake shuddered. "I think I prefer it when he's behind thick glass, surrounded by guards."

Kate nodded and smiled.

"We should Skype Gran and let her know how it went," said Kate. "Are you okay?"

Jake nodded. She went to squeeze his hand again, but mindful of the attractive blonde girl across the cafeteria, she gave him a smile.

They finished their coffee and then resumed the journey home. They drove back listening to *The Rise and Fall of Ziggy Stardust and the Spiders from Mars*, and Jake fell asleep in the passenger seat, snoring lightly.

Kate thought back to her discussion with Peter, about the mindset of a serial killer, and her mind came back to Magdalena.

She had that niggling feeling in her gut. She had to talk to Kirstie Newett again. Even if she had become obsessed with Arron Ko, that didn't mean her story wasn't true. There were too many other things that didn't sit right with Kate.

If there was someone abducting women, how did he do it? Women these days, she hoped, were savvy. Why would someone as smart as Magdalena stop and get into a stranger's car? If it was someone dressed as an old man, then she might have been more inclined to stop.

Kate looked up and saw they would be home in a couple of hours. She would get Jake settled, and then she wanted to speak to Tristan.

47

Magdalena's arms and hands were almost numb with exhaustion as she scraped at the concrete floor around the pedestal of the toilet. It seemed so smooth and solid, and impossible to break.

She was using pieces of the broken cistern lid to scrape away at the concrete and plaster fixing the toilet to the floor. If she could pull the toilet bowl away and drag it out into the corridor, then she could use it to stand on and reach the hatch.

Magdalena didn't know how much time had passed since she had fought off the man and found the gun. She was feeling dangerously weak. She had water, but she hadn't eaten in so long. The stomach cramps were coming in ever-increasing waves, making her double over in pain. It took all her strength to pull up the reserves of energy and keep scraping away at the floor around the toilet. She kept listening out for the lift, with the gun by her side, tucked into the waistband of her jeans with the safety on.

She wanted to sleep, but she was scared to fall asleep in case he came back in the darkness, found her, and took the gun. When she started to hear the voice of her nonna Maria, she knew she was close to the edge of her sanity.

Come on, you are a strong girl, Magdalena. The strongest girl I have ever known. You need to keep going. We're all waiting for you outside, above the soil . . . And when we're all back together, I'm going to make you your favorite gnocchi, with mushrooms picked from the garden. Just promise me you won't go to sleep, that you will keep going.

The voice lulled her and made her forget about her numb arms and hands. Magdalena felt herself begin to drift off, and she pressed her head against the cold porcelain. The vile smell jolted her awake again.

Keep going, keep going. You are so close, my darling, so close.

48

After an intense few days working on the case, Tristan felt strange, waking up on Sunday and Kate being away. She had called to say she had to take Jake to meet Peter Conway. They'd spoken briefly and she'd, understandably, been distracted.

Despite everything Henry Ko had told them at the Ted Clough crime scene, Tristan still felt uneasy. He didn't want to give up on Magdalena. He spent Sunday and Monday online, looking at the land registry website, researching buildings on the Shadow Sands estate. There were several commercial premises, shops and offices, and lots of tenants, like Ted, who rented properties on the estate. There were also three large manor houses—Thomas and Silvia lived in two of them, and the third was the derelict Hedley House nightclub. Tristan had been out clubbing to Hedley House a couple of times as a teenager. He remembered it was like a huge ballroom inside, a cavernous space with a bar, cloakroom, toilets, and very little else. He tried to find plans or blueprints online but didn't have any luck.

It was beginning to get dark on Monday afternoon, and Tristan was working at the desk in his bedroom when he heard a floorboard creak downstairs.

"Hello?" he said. There was no answer. There was another creak, and he heard footsteps. He got up and grabbed the large empty bottle of champagne from his eighteenth birthday that he used as a doorstop.

Holding it up like a baseball bat, he went out onto the landing. He checked the bathroom and Sarah's bedroom, but they were empty.

There was another creak from downstairs and a rustling sound. The image of Ted Clough's body came back to him. He saw him crumpled at the bottom of the stairs, his neck broken. It had looked like such a violent death, and it had caused him sleepless nights.

Tristan clutched the champagne bottle, and he crept down the stairs. The living room door was ajar, and he could hear more creaks and rustling sounds coming from inside.

He kicked the door open, advancing into the room with the champagne bottle above his head.

"Christ! Tristan!" cried Sarah, clutching her chest and dropping a pen and notepad she was holding. She was crouching next to an open wine box by the kitchen door.

"Jesus! I thought you were an intruder," said Tristan. His heart thudding in his chest, he put the bottle down on the dining room table and rubbed at his big toe where he'd hurt it on the door. "Didn't you hear me?"

"No."

"I was upstairs, and I called out 'hello,' and you didn't answer."

"If you were talking to me from upstairs, then I wouldn't have heard you," she said.

"What are you doing here, Sarah?"

"What do you mean what am I doing here? I live here."

"You said you were staying with Gary until the wedding. You could have given me a heads-up."

"I've already been back twice to get clean clothes. I thought you'd be at work," she said.

"It's reading week at uni . . . Half term."

"Oh."

She picked up the notepad. Tristan saw she'd written down a long list of figures.

"What's that?" he asked.

"The wedding venue phoned me. They've decided they're going to charge us corkage. *A quid* a bottle, which is going to add up with all this," she said, indicating the boxes piled high.

"That's not good."

"Can you give me a hand to pull this pile of boxes out? I can't remember if there are six or eight bottles in a box. It's written on the side facing the wall."

Tristan went to the pile of boxes near the kitchen door and carefully maneuvered them away from the wall.

"Eight," said Tristan.

"Eight times sixteen is a hundred and twenty-eight; bloody hell, that's a hundred and twenty-eight quid corkage just for the white," said Sarah. "The cost of this wedding is getting out of hand. Donna-Louise has gone up two dress sizes since they put her on the carvery at the Brewers Fayre, and I'm having to fork out for extra fittings. Ugh! I'm sick of talking about the bloody wedding!" She put her notepad down and wiped her eyes. Despite everything, Tristan felt sorry for her.

"Fancy a beer?" he said.

"Yes, thank you."

He went and fetched two cold beers from the kitchen and handed her one of the bottles. Sarah took a long gulp.

"Thanks. That's good," she said, wiping her mouth with the back of her hand.

"Cheers. Nothing like a cold beer," he said. They tapped bottles and drank again.

There was an awkward silence. It had started to rain, and Tristan could hear it clinking on the gutter pipes outside. Sarah put her beer down on the table.

"Tristan. I think we should deal with the elephant in the room," she said.

"I thought you didn't want to talk about Donna-Louise and her bridesmaid's dress?"

Sarah burst out laughing. Her whole face lit up, and she looked completely different. Happy and carefree. Tristan was pleased to see her laugh. It happened so rarely.

"That's not funny," she said, laughing again, despite herself. "I'm talking about you, what you told me. You being gay. I'm sorry if my reaction was harsh, but it goes both ways. You can't expect us to just carry on as normal."

"Why not?"

"It's lots to take in . . ."

"Yes, you heard something. I'm the one who has to live it."

Sarah sighed and sipped at her beer.

"The police phoned. They said you went and gave a statement. You told them that me and Gary didn't know you'd gone out that night. Thank you."

"No problem. Why didn't Gary come with you today? You two are usually joined at the hip."

There was an awkward pause.

"He was going to, but he's never met a gay person before. He was nervous."

"What do you mean he's never met a gay person?"

"He hasn't, Tris."

"*I'm* a gay person. I've known Gary for a year. I went with you both to France, to get all this wedding booze—four times! He's saying he doesn't know me?"

"Of course he *knows* you, Tris. He just doesn't know you as gay."

"It's me, Sarah. Nothing's changed!"

"I know, I know. Like I said, it's all new to us too . . . ," said Sarah. There was another awkward pause. "Is that girl, Magdalena, still missing?"

"The police think she came off the road driving her scooter, fell into one of the ditches on the A1328, and was washed out to sea, but me and Kate think differently . . ." He didn't want to mention finding Ted Clough's body. Sarah would only be worried and concerned and go off on one. He could already see she was pursing her lips at the mention of Kate. Tristan drained the last of his beer. It was becoming impossible to talk to Sarah about anything in his life without it being awkward.

"Do you need help to move the boxes of booze?" he said, changing the subject.

"No. Thank you. Gary's friend Sammo has offered to help. He's a driver for Harry Stott, the lorry delivery firm. He's going to do it on the side, as a favor. Make a space in one of the lorries on a Sunday and pick it up when he comes past."

"That's a bit naughty."

"I can't afford to hire a large van, and Harry Stott lorries are constantly going past Ashdean to Exeter. Sundays are their busiest days," said Sarah.

Tristan put his beer down, his mind suddenly racing.

"The Harry Stott lorries, they go from where to Exeter?"

"I think they use the motorway from Portsmouth and Bournemouth. They go past Ashdean to Exeter. Sammo should be able to swing by here without getting into trouble. The firm has GPS on their lorries."

"So, they use the A1328 as their main route through to Exeter?" asked Tristan.

"The A1328?"

"The main road that runs from Ashdean past the Shadow Sands reservoir and Hedley House club to Exeter?" said Tristan, getting impatient with Sarah.

"Yes. Sammo says Harry Stott runs a distribution lorry through there every hour on Sunday, so there should be room for our boxes."

"Can you give me Sammo's number?"

"He's got a wife. He's married."

"I don't want his number in *that way*," snapped Tristan, impatient at her stupidity. "I want to ask if he was driving past Shadow Sands reservoir last Sunday."

49

Kate and Jake had been home for only a short while when there was a knock at the front door. When she opened it, Tristan was outside.

"Kate. Sorry to barge in. I might have a lead from someone who saw Magdalena on the A1328 before she was abducted," he said, breathlessly. He peered through the hallway to the living room. "Sorry. Is this a bad time?"

Kate could see Tristan was very excited.

"No. Jake's up in the shower. What? Who? . . . Let's go outside," she said, grabbing her coat.

They came out the front door and walked round the house to the sand dunes at the top of the cliff. There were a couple of deck chairs set up next to a sand dune, which was shelter from the wind, but neither of them sat down.

Tristan quickly explained about Sarah's wedding alcohol and Gary's friend who worked for Harry Stott.

"Sarah gave me Sammo's number, and I talked to him. He wasn't driving the A1328 route last Sunday when Magdalena went missing, but he's asking around, hopefully right now, to see if any of the other drivers saw anything . . ." He pulled out his phone and checked the screen. "I've got full bars so hopefully he'll call soon. I also had a look at all the properties and buildings on the Shadow Sands estate. I've made a list." He took out a folded piece of paper from his pocket, and then his phone rang.

"Who is it?" asked Kate.

"Unknown number," he said, showing her his phone screen.

"Put it on speakerphone. And let's sit down, it's not as windy . . ." They sat on the deck chairs, and Kate scooted hers closer to Tristan. "And don't ask him any leading questions, if he knows something."

Tristan nodded and answered the phone.

"Hey, Tristan? I'm Dennis. Sammo says you wanted to talk to me?" said the voice on the other end of the phone. He sounded older, with a trace of a Devon accent. Tristan thanked him for phoning, and he explained why they wanted to talk to him, being careful not to lead him in any way. "I'm here with Kate. She's my boss," added Tristan.

"Hi," said Kate.

"Yeah, hi. Sammo told me about the missing woman. I saw a young woman with long dark hair on a yellow scooter. She stopped to help this old geezer who was parked up on the side of the road," he said.

"Can you remember when this was?" asked Tristan.

"A week ago, last Sunday. Sunday the fourteenth," he said. "I don't know, around mid to late afternoon."

Kate put her head in her hands for a moment and then looked up in shock at Tristan. He grabbed her hand.

"Where exactly was this where you saw her?" asked Kate, trying to keep her voice calm.

"A few miles outside Ashdean, just before the reservoir . . . I remember it because the old geezer let a spare tire roll in front of my lorry. I nearly ran him over."

Tristan gripped Kate's hand harder.

"Did you see what the old man looked like?" asked Kate.

"He was dressed like so many old duffers round here. Old trousers, a tweed jacket. You know, like he got a suit from a charity shop years ago. He wore a flat cap, glasses. He had a big, bushy gray beard and hair coming out from under his cap . . ."

When they came off the phone with Dennis, Kate started to pace up and down on the sand.

"It matches what Kirstie Newett told me," she said. "Kirstie described an old man with gray hair who abducted her, in a pale-colored, old car. She said his eyes were a weird blue color, almost purple, as if he was wearing contact lenses."

"It could be a disguise," said Tristan. "Just changing the color of your eyes isn't going to make much of a difference. It could be that he's wearing a wig, or he grows a beard, then shaves it off again."

Kate was now shaking with excitement as well as shock. To think that she'd nearly been swayed by Henry Ko. She'd allowed him to debunk their whole theory.

"This means that Kirstie Newett was telling the truth—she was abducted. And Magdalena was abducted. She didn't get washed away in the ditch during a rainstorm," said Kate.

"What should we do now?" asked Tristan.

Kate stopped pacing.

"It's been eight days since Magdalena went missing, and the police don't even have that on their radar. No one is looking for her." She checked her watch. It was just after seven p.m. "I've been thinking about Hedley House. Ulrich Mazur and Sally-Ann Cobbs left Hedley House and were abducted on their way back to Ashdean. If the Baker family is somehow involved in all this, then it's logical that they could have been held somewhere in Hedley House, and that's where Magdalena is being held. I don't know if it has a basement, but I think we should check it out."

"When?" asked Tristan.

"Tonight. Now," said Kate.

50

After what felt like hours and hours of rubbing and grinding at the floor, Magdalena felt the concrete at the base of the toilet bowl crack, and the toilet started to come loose from the floor.

She got up and rubbed her hands to get some feeling back into them. She allowed herself only a few minutes' rest and a drink of water, and then she started to shift the toilet bowl from side to side. It came loose pretty quickly, and with a sudden crack it came away from where it was stuck to the floor. The pipe connecting the cistern up on the wall came away easily. Her heart gave a little zing of excitement, and she didn't notice that the water had spilled out over her jeans. She was dripping with sweat from the exertion.

Magdalena dragged the toilet bowl out of the small room, across the corridor, and there was a soft clanging sound when the porcelain touched the metal doors of the lift.

She climbed up onto it and was overjoyed that she could touch the ceiling and feel the rough plasterwork. She was a little off to the left and found she had to lean over to reach the hatch. She repositioned the bowl and climbed back up. As she ran her hands over the hatch in the ceiling, she could feel it sat flush with the outer bracket and the ceiling. There was a small slot, where a key or a coin could be inserted and turned so that the hatch opened.

"Shit," she whispered. Her shoulders sagged. Would this ever end? Would anything ever be easy? She climbed back off the toilet bowl down onto the floor, feeling dizzy at the effort.

Broken tiles. They broke when I fired the second bullet, she thought.

She hurried back to the room with the bed, feeling her way along the walls with her hands, touching the walls and doorframes and trying not to think about the blood spatters she'd seen in those brief moments of gunfire. She found the bed, and underfoot were the pieces of broken tile.

Squatting down, she moved her hands carefully, sifting through the shards. There was a long, thick piece of tile with a flat corner ending in a sharp, thin spike that would make a good weapon to add to her arsenal. She tucked it into the waistband of her jeans with the gun. Then she found a flat sliver of tile that had the thickness and width of a coin. She hurried back out to the hallway, found the toilet bowl, and climbed up. She slotted the piece of tile into the opening mechanism of the hatch. It fitted perfectly. She was able to turn it to the right, and she had to duck out of the way as the heavy hatch fell open.

She immediately felt a draft, but her eyes were dazzled by the light. She felt the sting as her pupils retracted, and she had to keep her eyes half-closed for a few minutes. She stood enjoying the draft as her eyes got used to seeing again. The hallway was filled with a dim, gray light— barely bright at all, but after days of darkness it was just enough.

She could see that, next to the lift doors, there was a small keyhole in the wall. Her hands must have missed it in the dark. She stepped down and went to it. It was a small, gold keyhole. *That must be how he opens the lift doors from down here.*

All sorts of crazy thoughts went through her head: Why hadn't she thought of this? Why hadn't she searched more for the keyhole? Could she have let him come closer to her in the dark and tried to search him for the key? No, that was ridiculous. She ran her fingers over the hole, wishing she had a bobby pin. She didn't know how to pick a lock, but she could at least try.

She looked back down the corridor; now that she had light, maybe there was something, anything that had been forgotten about . . . She peered up into the hatchway.

A dim light shone out from high above, and she could see that the hatch led into the lift shaft. There was another lift door around ten meters above. Her arms were still weak and shaky, and it took all her energy to pull herself up off the toilet bowl and climb through the hatch.

There was a small platform to the side of the lift shaft, and she lay for a moment panting, trying to get her breath back. Far above her hung the lift, loose cables looping down underneath.

She stood up and tried to find a foothold in the walls of the lift shaft, to climb upward, but the walls were smooth. There was nothing she could use to climb.

"No, no, no," she said, hammering her fist on the side of the wall. She sat back on her haunches, feeling exhaustion wash over her again.

He was going to come back, and he was going to make sure to kill her.

She had to lie in wait for him. Use the hatch to surprise him, and kill him before he killed her.

51

Kate asked Myra to stay with Jake, and she and Tristan set off in her car for Hedley House.

They had to double back toward Ashdean to get onto the A1328. A thin mist started to roll off the coast as they drove toward the Shadow Sands reservoir, and it made Kate uneasy. The visibility was poor enough on this lonely road with no streetlights. She switched on the high beams. There were no other cars, and as the road curved away from the cliff, a thicket of trees sprang up on either side, and the fog grew thicker.

"I don't like this," said Tristan, gripping the dashboard as wispy pockets of fog hit the windscreen, obscuring their view for a few seconds. Kate slowed a little, but she was desperate for them to get to Hedley House. What if Magdalena had been there the whole time? They had driven past it on several occasions, and it was so close. Was Kate losing her touch? Had it been staring them in the face?

"Kate, slow down," said Tristan as they came to a bend in the road and the fog pockets grew thicker. The car skidded as she took the bend in fourth gear, and they hit the shoulder, making the car jolt and shudder.

"Sorry," she said, braking and slowing the car for the next bend. They emerged into a clear section, and visibility was better, but up ahead, the fog was pushing its way through the trees. When they reached it, the car was completely enveloped in white, and Kate could see only a few feet in front. The headlights bounced off the fog, making it seem like a white wall was in front of them. They burst out of the fog patch into a clear part of the road, but standing in front of them was a deer. Kate had no time to react, and instinctively she swerved to avoid the beautiful creature. The car came off the road and mounted the shoulder, and they bumped down a steep bank, through thick trees for a few meters, and then collided with a tree.

Kate didn't know how long they'd sat there when she opened her eyes and saw the deflated airbags. Tristan was sitting beside her, also dazed.

"Are you okay?" she asked, checking herself over. Her face and neck were sore, but she wasn't badly hurt.

"Yeah," he said, checking himself over. He put his hand to his face. "I thought airbags were meant to be a good thing. I feel like I've been slapped in the face."

"Me too," said Kate. She tried to open the door and saw that it was right up against a tree trunk. "I can't get out of my side." Tristan managed to get his door open and climbed out. Kate clambered over the gear stick and followed.

The car didn't look badly damaged. They'd come off the road and driven down a ten-meter-long slope, ending in a huge oak tree with knots bulging out of the trunk. The front bumper had saved the car. It was pinned to a bulge in the tree and hanging off with the two front wheels suspended in midair. The driver's door was crushed, but the rest of the car looked okay.

"Do you think we can reverse the car back up?" asked Tristan. Kate followed his gaze back up the slope, then looked back at the front wheels suspended off the ground.

"Let's see if we can push it off the tree," she said. They both moved to the front of the car and leaned against the bumper.

"Is the hand brake off?" asked Tristan.

"Yes," said Kate as they pushed. "It's no good, it's stuck."

"Where's my phone?" she added, patting at her jacket pocket and jeans. She reached back into the passenger side and picked up her phone from the footwell on the driver's side. There was no signal.

"I haven't got a signal either," said Tristan, holding up his phone. They clambered up the soft earth of the slope, grabbing trees and bushes to help them up. When they reached the road, it was quiet with no cars.

The deer was gone from the spot where they'd swerved off the road, and the pockets of fog were starting to disperse. They both stepped out into the road to get away from the trees and try to find a phone signal. Nothing.

Kate turned the other way and walked a little farther along the road with her phone in the air. It curved sharply to the right, and stretching away was the long, straight expanse of road running past the reservoir, and at the end, against the clear night's sky, was Hedley House, perched on top of a hill.

There was a light glowing in one of the windows.

52

It was eerily quiet as Kate and Tristan walked toward Hedley House. When they'd seen the light glowing in the window, they'd set off toward it, with no questions or hesitation.

The River Fowey appeared through the trees on the left, and for twenty meters or so, it rushed past noisily. It was a happy sound among the darkness and fog and the trepidation Kate felt.

As the reservoir came into view, the river was suddenly silent. It met the sluice gate and was swallowed up into the still, black expanse of water.

Kate thought back to her dive with Jake, when they'd found Simon Kendal, floating deep down by the church spire that was covered in freshwater crustaceans.

Kate stopped and looked back at the sluice gate where the river met the reservoir.

"What?" asked Tristan, stopping.

"Dylan Robertson told Ted and the other maintenance workers to lie about the bodies they found in the water, to say they were found on the other side of the sluice gate . . . Kirstie Newett was left for dead and was about to be dumped, too, until she woke up . . . Ted Clough was about to give us a statement and put it on record, and he's found dead. And it all comes back to the Baker family. Please, God, don't let Magdalena already be down there, under the water . . ."

Kate could hear her voice crack with emotion. She was exhausted, but adrenaline was coursing through her veins.

"Come on," said Tristan, pulling her forward. Kate nodded, and they picked up the pace even more toward Hedley House.

The car park was large and overgrown, dotted with weeds at waist and shoulder height. They came off the road and walked through the weeds, which rustled as they brushed against Kate's shoulders.

She put her hand on the Mace in her bag, keeping an eye on the building, which seemed to grow huge when they came close. It was deceptively far from the road when you drove past it, and now, as they stood in front of it, the building towered above them.

A car approached on the road. They ducked back into the weeds so they were hidden from the road. The car slowed, its headlights projecting long, misshapen shadows from the weeds onto the building, and it turned into the car park.

Kate felt like they were out in the open, masked by only a few thin, tall weeds. She put her hand out for Tristan to stay put. It could just be someone using the car park as a lay-by for a pee.

Two people got out of the car. A tall and a short man. When they both moved to the boot of the car, Kate saw their faces. It was Thomas Baker, his long, tall frame and bony, long face looking haggard in the dim light, and with him was Dylan Robertson, Silvia Baker's driver. He was hunched down wearing a thick winter coat with the collar pulled up. They opened the boot and took out two large spades and a pile of sheets. Thomas carried them over to the front entrance of Hedley House, and Dylan took a shotgun from the back of the car, opened it to check it was loaded, and clicked it shut. He slammed the boot of the car and followed Thomas to the main entrance.

Thomas was working on a padlock, and he got what looked like a temporary steel door open. They disappeared inside.

"What's inside the club?" asked Kate.

"What do you mean? It's a nightclub," said Tristan.

"No. What's the layout inside, can you remember?"

"It's mainly a huge old ballroom, which takes up most of the space. There was a bar at one end, with toilets. There was also a manager's office. I remember a girl at school saying that she got taken to the office by one of the bouncers for a shag. I think there was a kitchen at the other end, but I can't be sure," said Tristan.

"When we follow them inside, we'll come out into a huge ballroom and they'll be able to see us?" said Kate.

"No, there was a cloakroom through the doors with toilets, and another set of doors to go through to the main ballroom and bar . . . What do you mean, when we follow them inside?" said Tristan.

"Come on," said Kate. She made sure the small can of Mace was the right way around in her hand, and then she started toward the main entrance, through the shoulder-high weeds. The scuff of their feet on the gravel and the rustle as they parted the reeds seemed so loud in the darkness.

Kate slowed when they came close to the front door; it had been pulled closed, but the padlock was unlocked. They stopped and listened. Kate couldn't hear anything. Then she saw there was another vehicle, parked against the side of the building in the shadows.

They moved to get a closer look. It was a mud-splattered Land Rover. Kate turned back to Tristan.

"What should we do?" she asked. She could see he was scared.

"We've come this far. Magdalena could be in there. I don't know why all these cars are here. There could be something nasty going on with her . . . We can't just leave. We should take a look inside, and then we should call the police," he whispered. Kate nodded.

They moved back to the front door. Kate put out her hand. The door opened easily, and they went inside.

53

The light from the lift shaft gave Magdalena new energy. She could now see, instead of having to stumble through the darkness.

She sat and thought about her next move. It came down to two things. The lift wouldn't operate without the key. She either needed to find something she could fashion as a key, or she had to get the key when the man returned.

She quickly scoured the corridor, toilet, and room with the bed and sink, hoping that she might find a piece of metal or even a bobby pin that she could use to MacGyver a key. In the dim light, as she searched, she tried to block out the bloodstains and blood spatter that covered the walls and the patches that had saturated the concrete floors. There was nothing. It would have been a dream if she could have made her own key and just let herself out of this prison.

Magdalena would be quite happy just to escape and slink away in the night, find her way home, pack her bags, and go back to Italy. She remembered the ordeal Gabriela had gone through after the rape, the endless questions she was subjected to by the police, and then the court case. At one low point, Gabriela confided in Magdalena that she wished she hadn't said anything to anyone.

At the time, Magdalena had thought that was crazy—the man had to pay for what he did. But now she understood. Magdalena wanted to live, and if she did, she never wanted to talk about this experience to anyone.

She came back to the lift, stood beside the toilet bowl in front of the doors, and looked up at the hatch. If she could lie in wait for him above, he wouldn't be expecting that. She didn't have much strength left, but from that vantage point, she could shoot him the moment he stepped out of the lift. She would aim for the top of his head and blow his brains out. Then she would get the key for the lift and escape.

The only problem was the toilet bowl. She looked down at it. It was large and heavy, and if it was there when he stepped out of the lift, sitting below the hatch, he would be alerted to her presence. He would know she was up in the hatch.

Magdalena perched on the edge of the toilet bowl. It was made of porcelain and weighed a lot. It had taken all her effort to drag it out of the bathroom and into the hallway. She saw something and sat up in excitement. The seat had been removed, but there were two holes that had been made in the porcelain where the seat had been attached.

She got up and hurried through to the room with the bed. She didn't want to call it the bedroom—that made it sound like a place she was staying—but she needed to look at the bed. In the dim light from the hallway, she could see the mattress lay on top of the concrete base. It was thin and completely filthy, with a fitted sheet sewn onto the foam.

Magdalena took out the sharp piece of porcelain tile and started to tear the sheet into long strips.

54

When Kate and Tristan entered the club, it was dimly lit, and there was a stench of mold. Kate could feel that the carpet under their feet was damp. To their left was a long wooden counter, which was covered in bird droppings and dust, and in the shadows behind were rows and rows of coat hooks; some were broken and hanging off the wall. To the right were the ladies' and gents' toilets. The doors had been removed from both. They were in the cloakroom.

Kate and Tristan ducked inside the female and male toilets respectively.

"Nothing but old, stinking toilets and dirt," whispered Tristan when he emerged. Kate nodded. She had seen the same in the women's toilets. At the end of the cloakroom were three sets of double doors with round glass windows. They were closed, but a light glowed through the glass. Kate went to the middle door and peered through the glass. A bright lamp on a stand was lit, and it sat in the middle of the enormous, empty ballroom. It was a mess of rubbish, dead birds, and bird droppings.

Kate could see that the light didn't reach the edges of the ballroom. She opened the door, which creaked slightly, and they crept into the huge space.

It had once been ornate and elegant, and large chunks of the original crown molding were intact, but there were large craters in the plaster ceiling and holes in the roof, where they could see up and out to the night sky.

The ballroom floor was made of wood, covered in a layer of filth and dirt, and it was wet underfoot. Running along the back were the dark shutters of a long-neglected bar.

Tristan pointed to the right; at the end of the long ballroom was a set of double doors, where light spilled out. They couldn't see what was inside the room, but they heard the murmur of voices. *Were there more than two voices?* thought Kate. It was difficult to tell. She looked around the ballroom; to their left was another set of double doors, and she could see a small sign: **BASEMENT**.

Kate was mindful of the fact that they'd seen Dylan come into the ballroom with a shotgun. Thomas had also brought in two large, heavy shovels. There could also be more people in the back offices who were armed or willing to fight. It didn't make sense, though, for so many people to be involved, did it? But there was a lot at stake with the cover-up of the disappearances of Magdalena and the others.

Kate pointed at the door. Tristan was very pale, but he nodded. They hurried across the ballroom and through the doorway into a small, dingy corridor. To the right the corridor led down to a huge kitchen, which sat empty and cavernous. Grimy squares on the walls showed where the kitchen equipment had been ripped out. In the center of the floor were the remnants of several fires. They came back out and hurried along the corridor in the other direction, and at the end were the metal doors of a large lift. Kate didn't expect anything to happen when she pressed the button beside it, but the small window in the door lit up from the inside.

Tristan's eyebrows shot up in alarm. Kate pulled the handle, and the door opened smoothly.

"Hang on, what are we doing?" said Tristan, in a low voice.

"Magdalena could be down there," said Kate. "We saw Dylan and Thomas come in, so they must be in another part of the building. We need to go down and help her. I have this can of Mace. If I activate and press it, it'll spray in a huge arc."

Tristan looked at the small can in her hand.

"I wish we had a gun," he said.

"We don't."

"Okay, let's go down," he said. They got in the lift. There was only one button, and underneath it: BASEMENT.

Kate pressed it. There was a lurch and a loud clanking as the lift jolted to life. The corridor through the small window in the door rose up and out of sight as the lift started to slowly descend. It was very loud, with the whir of the gears and the whine of the motor.

A minute later, the lift came to a stop with a jolt.

"I can't see anything on the other side," said Tristan, peering through the window in the lift door.

The door creaked as they opened it, and Kate and Tristan stepped out into darkness.

They activated the lights on their mobile phones.

It was a huge, empty space with a concrete floor and black walls where water was dripping down into pools. Kate swung her light wide around the space, and so did Tristan. It was completely empty apart from a pile of old bricks and cement in one dark corner. Shafts of light came from a small window in the ceiling on the right-hand side, and when Kate approached it, she could see it was a ventilation shaft, looking up to the car park high above.

Kate looked at Tristan. She had been certain that Magdalena was being kept in the basement at Hedley House. They searched the space with their flashlights once more to be sure, and then they went back to the lift and got inside.

"What are we going to do?" asked Tristan.

"We need to get out of here without being seen," said Kate. She reached out to press the button, but before she did, the doors closed. The lift lurched into life and started to climb back up again.

Kate pulled her hand away.

"I didn't touch the button, and it's taking us back up," said Kate, hearing the fear in her voice. She took a deep breath and found the Mace in her pocket. "Keep behind me. I'll yell out if I spray this, and if I do, close your eyes and cover your nose."

Tristan moved with his back to the wall, and he look terrified. The lift seemed to move so slowly, and yet there was nothing they could do but wait. There was no other button on the wall, not even an emergency stop.

The lift came to a juddering stop, and the door was yanked open.

Waiting outside the lift were Thomas Baker, Dana Baker, Stephen Baker, and Silvia Baker. Next to Silvia was Dylan Robertson, who had his shotgun trained on Kate and Tristan inside the lift. To his right side stood Henry Ko with his father, Arron Ko. It was a shock to see them all, and it was the first time that Kate had seen Arron Ko. He looked much the same as he did in the newspaper photo, but this evening he was dressed casually in old jeans and a fleece coat. Kate was relieved to see Henry Ko, though there was something uncontrolled and gleeful about the way they were all peering into the lift. As if they had been lying in wait for a rodent, and now that they had it cornered, they were going to flush it out.

"Get out of the fucking lift," said Dylan, peering at them down the barrel of the gun.

55

Kate winced, and she put her hand up to cover the glare of a flashlight.

"Didn't you hear him?" shrilled Silvia Baker, aiming the flashlight into the service lift. "Come on. Out! You're trespassing!"

Silvia was dressed like the queen on a day off: sensible Wellingtons, a pleated kilt, a padded Barbour jacket, and a head scarf.

"Hang on, hang on, this isn't kids trespassing again," said Thomas.

"They look a bit old to be kids who've broken in to light another fire," said Stephen. He was also dressed casually and wearing a thick fleece. "Hey, I know you," he said, as if they were old friends meeting in a gentlemen's club. "They came to see me in the shop."

Kate and Tristan inched forward out of the lift.

"You can put the gun down," she said to Dylan, who was glowering at them and shifting on his heels. She was emboldened by the presence of Henry and Arron Ko. She looked to Henry, but he seemed nervous. "Detective Chief Inspector Ko," said Kate. "Perhaps you could ask him to put the shotgun down?"

Henry didn't look happy, and it was Arron who leaned forward and put his hand on the gun.

"Come on now, Dylan, that's enough," he said, and he pushed the muzzle of the shotgun down until Dylan loosened his grip.

"I'm legally within my rights to shoot trespassers," growled Dylan.

"Doesn't mean you have to, Dylan," said Arron.

"But you are trespassing," said Henry. There was another silence as they looked expectantly at Kate and Tristan. "What the hell are you two doing here?"

"We were talking to a lorry driver," said Tristan, speaking up. "He saw Magdalena Rossi with an old man by the side of the road on the day she went missing. His description of the old man matches the description provided by Kirstie Newett, which means her story of being abducted could be true."

There was a moment of silence. Kate scanned the faces of the Bakers and the Kos. They all looked nonplussed. Dylan looked annoyed, as if he'd been denied the opportunity to fire his gun.

"Henry. Who are they? Who are you?" asked Silvia, not waiting for his answer. She hadn't recognized either of them.

"I'm Kate Marshall. I'm a lecturer at Ashdean University, and this is my research associate, Tristan Harper," said Kate. Silvia seemed to warm a little to the news that they were academics.

"But why are you here? Is it to do with the university?"

Are you stupid or just playing the fool? thought Kate.

"No. We thought that Magdalena Rossi was being kept captive here in the basement. This building is derelict and out of the way, and it has a basement," said Kate. Now, when they were staring at the whole Baker family, it sounded stupid.

"Is this what you were talking about when you came to the shop?" asked Stephen.

"Yes. They came and talked to me, too, harassed me at work about this missing young woman," said Dana, speaking for the first time. She was standing behind her aunt. She wore a long blue trench coat and red high heels.

"Why are you all here so late at night?" asked Kate.

"We have no obligation to explain ourselves to trespassers," said Thomas. He looked down at Kate and Tristan as if they were two rather naughty schoolchildren. "We're planning to develop Hedley House into residential apartments. We're all joint shareholders of what will be this new project, apart from Henry here, but, er, Arron is."

Arron Ko nodded.

"I'm not in the best of health . . . Not very well at all; Henry is my heir," he said, taking a step forward. Kate noticed that he was limping badly and walking with a cane.

"Arron, don't, please. You don't have to tell them . . . ," said Silvia, her voice trailing off. She sounded genuinely distressed at what he was saying. "Who is this Magdalena?" asked Silvia. "Thomas?"

"Yes, Thomas. I still don't understand why you arrived so quickly the other day when we found Ted Clough's body," said Kate. She knew she was making a leap and throwing this accusation out, but she had nothing to lose.

Thomas opened his mouth to protest, but Henry stepped in, placing his hand on Thomas's arm.

"I've already spoken to Ms. Marshall and Mr. Harper about this," he said. "I've told them that they need to drop this ridiculous theory that the Baker family and my father have something to do with the disappearance of Magdalena Rossi."

Arron Ko looked genuinely surprised at the accusation.

"What? Look at me; I'm hardly in fighting shape to go abducting anyone," he said, holding up his walking stick.

"How do you explain what happened to Kirstie Newett?" asked Kate.

Arron Ko closed his eyes and leaned on his stick. From the rest of the family's faces, Kate could see that they all knew about Kirstie.

"Bloody hell. That young woman, she won't leave us alone!" said Arron. "It's true, I found Kirstie on the side of the road late one night when I was coming back from work. I took her to the hospital. I was aware of who she was when I picked her up. She'd been brought into the police station several times for soliciting. She also had a drug problem, and for a time she hung around with a rather nasty bunch of drug dealers."

"You didn't believe her when she told you that she'd been abducted?" asked Tristan.

"I believed that someone could have abducted her," he said. "But you have to realize, Kirstie had previously lied to the police. My first thought was that she needed help. She was in a terrible state, beaten up and wet through. I took her to the hospital and transferred her to the care of a psychiatrist."

"Why are you a shareholder in the corporation?" asked Tristan. "Isn't that a conflict of interest?"

"Arron, don't answer that!" snapped Silvia. "The impertinence of this young man. This is ridiculous. We don't have to justify ourselves to any old idiots who break in to our property. *We* should be the ones asking the questions here!" Arron reached out and touched her shoulder, rubbing her arm.

"It's okay," he said. "Myself and Silvia go back many years. We have known each other since we were young, and she kindly gave me the opportunity to invest in the company, albeit modestly," he said.

"Arron, enough," said Silvia, her face softening a little.

"I still don't think it's right, Thomas, for a senior police officer like Arron, and now Henry, to be so intimately involved with your family business," said Kate.

"As a civilian, Arron has the right to do business and be a shareholder," said Thomas. "But remember, the Shadow Sands estate is very large, with a community of tenants, and the hydroelectric dam is a massive infrastructure project, part owned by the government. I would be concerned if the local police *weren't* involved in protecting the community and the dam . . ."

Kate could see a vein was pulsing in his neck. He didn't like being questioned.

"I understand that when you retired, Arron, you had DCI Varia Campbell promoted, without her applying for a promotion, and Henry was brought in to take her place as a DCI in the Devon and Cornwall borough."

"Oh, you're being frightfully common," said Silvia. "I'm very good friends with the dean of Ashdean; I'm going to have a word with him when I next see him."

"We have a witness, a lorry driver, who saw Magdalena on Sunday, the fourteenth of October, the day she went missing, talking to a man by the side of the road," said Kate, ignoring her. "He says Magdalena was helping the old man change his car tire. This was close to the spot where her yellow scooter was recovered from the ditch."

"We asked the lorry driver to phone your help line and report this officially," said Tristan.

"Yes. And I think that this eyewitness evidence should at least warrant a search of some of the larger properties on the Shadow Sands estate and a search of the reservoir," said Kate. "And I will shout very loudly if this isn't done."

A look passed between Henry and Arron Ko.

"You have a colossal cheek, woman!" cried Silvia. "You don't get to dictate terms to the police."

"I was a police officer," said Kate. "And any body of water close to where a person has gone missing is always searched. And Kirstie Newett might be guilty of many things, but her description of the man who abducted her matches the description the lorry driver gave of the man who Magdalena stopped to help on the side of the road. I will also get Kirstie Newett to give an official statement, something you denied her before. So, I'll say again, the reservoir needs to be searched, as well as any empty or inhabited premises, of which we know there are several on the Shadow Sands estate."

Kate took a deep breath.

"You'll have your work cut out, Thomas," said Stephen. "He's your man. The lord of the manor, and the commercial premises are all in his name." There was a tinge of something in Stephen's voice—was it triumph or envy? Kate could certainly sense there was conflict between the brothers. Stephen went on, "Now, as much as I love standing around in the cold, talking bollocks, I have to get home to the kids. Jassy is expecting me."

"Will you do your job as a police officer and search the reservoir and surrounding premises?" said Kate to Henry, feeling like a madwoman but knowing in her gut that she had to keep pressing for this, however strange the forum.

"Yes, Henry, you should have the premises searched," said Arron, leaning on his stick. He looked exhausted. Silvia glanced back, and a look passed between her and Arron.

"The reservoir is complicated. It's a part-government-owned infrastructure project; there are different rules," said Thomas.

"Yes, we can't even landscape the visitors' center grounds on the side next to the power plant," said Dana, speaking for only the second time.

"Well. You can happily come back and nose around my shop," said Stephen, now annoyed and eager to leave. "I just own my shop, nothing else. I have nothing to do with the bloody estate and all this circus. Now, I really must go."

"Yes. This has gone on long enough," growled Dylan, who was still cradling the shotgun. "Henry, can you see that these two have a police escort off the premises?"

56

"Where is your car?" asked Henry as he marched them out into the car park.

"We came off the road, about a mile away, just before the reservoir," said Kate.

"So where do you want me to drop you?" he asked when they reached his police car.

"Back to my car. I can't leave it there. We'll need to call for assistance."

A moment later, the rest of the family emerged from the main entrance.

Silvia, Dylan, Dana, and Arron went to the Land Rover. Dana had to help Arron climb up into the back seat. Thomas and Stephen stopped to lock the door and then headed over to the other car. Silvia gave Kate and Tristan a nasty stare as they pulled past and onto the road.

———

Kate and Tristan rode in the car in silence with Henry, back to the point where their car had come off the road. When they pulled up at the shoulder, they got out, and Henry placed a call to the Automobile Association.

"I can wait with you," he said. "They're going to be here in twenty minutes."

"No, it's fine, thank you," said Kate. Henry went to go back to his car. "And you're going to search all the buildings on the estate?" she added.

"Yes," he said. He didn't look sure of himself. He got into his car and drove away.

Kate and Tristan stood in silence for a moment, watching as his headlights receded over the hill back toward Ashdean.

"I don't think anyone is going to search those buildings, are they, Tris?" said Kate. "Wherever Magdalena is, she's dead."

Tristan pulled the piece of paper from his pocket that he'd been working on while Kate was away with Jake at Great Barwell.

"I was going to show you this before, but we got distracted with the phone call with Dennis. It's the list of all the properties owned by the Baker family on the estate," he said.

Kate took the piece of paper and activated the flashlight on her phone. There was a list of addresses and buildings. Most of them were residential houses, like Ted Clough's. Something stood out on the list that made Kate stop in her tracks. She stared at the entry sixth down: FROME CRAWFORD OLD TELEPHONE EXCHANGE.

It was tucked in among several houses and a couple of farms owned by the estate. The building was registered as being owned by Stephen Baker.

Kate thought back to what Stephen Baker had just said to them. "*I just own my shop, nothing else. I have nothing to do with the bloody estate.*"

But when they had gone to the shop a few days ago, they were talking to Stephen, and his wife, Jassy, had been talking on the phone in the background . . . What was she saying? She was complaining to the post office about the boxes of stock that were delivered to the wrong place. She said, *"No, not the telephone exchange; it's Hubble on Frome Crawford high street."*

"Tris, have you got a signal on your phone?" she asked.

"I've got a couple of bars," he said, holding it up.

"Can you look up the old telephone exchange in Frome Crawford on Google Maps?" Tristan looked it up; it took a moment to load, but then it appeared on his phone. "Can you zoom in?" she added, wincing at the screen, which was dazzlingly bright in the darkness by the road.

"It's on an old industrial estate, outside the village," he said.

"Why would Stephen lie about it? When I was talking about searching buildings, he said he owned no other property, apart from the shop," said Kate. She looked at Tristan. His eyes widened.

"Jesus. It's Stephen Baker," he said. "And he's keeping Magdalena in that old telephone exchange."

Kate looked up and down the road, but there was no traffic coming in the distance.

"Damn this stupid car," she cried, kicking the back bumper. It lurched a little in the mud. "Can you call a taxi?"

"You know Ashdean. They won't come out this far anymore," said Tristan.

Kate was pacing up and down.

"We need to get there now, Tris!"

"What about Myra?"

"She doesn't drive. What about Sarah?"

Tristan pulled a face.

"Tristan. Please, I know you and Sarah have issues, but I need you to phone her now," said Kate.

57

Stephen Baker felt sick on the journey home with his brother, Thomas. The car was hot inside. Thomas always had to have the heating on full blast.

"Can I open a window? I'm burning up in here," said Stephen, wiping at the sweat on his brow. Using the main controls at the driver's side, Thomas opened the passenger window a centimeter. The wind whistled through the tiny crack, but Stephen couldn't feel it. He put a hand to his mouth, feeling his stomach lurch.

"Jesus. Open it properly!" he said, pressing the button. The window slid down, and cold, fresh air streamed into the car. He breathed it in, feeling relief.

Thomas pulled the collar of his shirt up around his neck, his long fingers fussing primly.

He's like an old woman, always worrying about drafts, thought Stephen.

"I think that's enough," said Thomas, pressing the button on his console. Stephen's window closed.

The fog had dispersed, and the road ahead was clear.

"Are you going to let the police search the estate buildings?" asked Stephen, glancing over at his brother's serious face.

"Yes," said Thomas, staring grimly at the road. "I've already had plenty of tenants on the phone, worried after Ted Clough's death."

The car hit a bump in the road, and Stephen felt the jolt in his stomach. He put his hand to his mouth and bit down on his index finger.

"Do the police have any idea who it could be?"

"No. We think it's probably one of the other tenants. We've got plenty of dodgy types," said Thomas. "That's the problem with tenancy agreements being passed down through families. And there's so many of those 'Cash for Gold' adverts on TV at the moment. Someone got wind of Ted's twenty grand's worth of gold coins and jumped at the chance to rob the old man."

"What about the reservoir? Do you think the police will take that woman seriously?" asked Stephen, trying to keep his voice even.

"I don't know. Why are you so concerned about it all of a sudden? You made it quite clear when you married Jassy that you don't want to have anything to do with the estate."

"Yes. You have a short memory. I was forced to choose between Jassy and my stake in the estate, remember?" said Stephen. He gave Thomas a hard stare. Thomas stared back.

"You made a choice," said Thomas. "Are you all right? You look a bit peaky."

"I'm fine," he said quickly, feeling his stomach turn over again. "If you're going to be worried about anyone, it's Arron. He looked bloody awful."

"The doctor's given him six months."

"Jesus. Stress, that's what made him ill. The stress of juggling a wife and a mistress. I'm sure he'd be fit as a fiddle if he'd had some balls years ago and left his wife for Aunt Silvia. She's always been his true love."

"I don't know about that. Everyone involved has always turned the other cheek. My concern is when he kicks the bucket, I need his one percent of the corporation to stay in the family," said Thomas.

To Stephen's relief, they had reached Frome Crawford high street.

"Well. Here we are," said Thomas as he pulled up outside the cookware shop. "Give my best to Jassy and the kids."

"Yeah. Thanks," said Stephen. He got out of the car and went to the front door. He spun out searching for his keys in his pocket and put them in the door as Thomas pulled away.

When Thomas was out of sight, he withdrew the key. His phone rang and he pulled it out of his pocket. It was Jassy.

"*Shit,*" he said under his breath. He ducked under the awning of the shop, out of sight from the window above, and answered the call.

"Hi, love," he said.

"Hey, are you home soon? I wanted to know if I should tuck in the kids or wait," said Jassy, at the other end of the phone.

"Sorry, love, this is going to go on a bit longer. I'll be another hour or more," he said.

"Okay . . ."

Stephen could hear the disappointment in her voice.

"Love you, see you in a bit," he said. He ended the call, switched off his phone. Peering out from under the awning, he walked around to the back of the building to the shop loading bay, where his car was parked. He unlocked it and ducked inside, taking off the hand brake. Pushing with his foot on the road, he rolled the car out of the loading bay and onto the road.

Stephen winced at the effort to push the car and felt a burning pain in his chest. When he got the car to the main road, he closed the door and started the engine. He pulled up his sweater and saw a faint line of blood spots on his T-shirt and lifted it gingerly. The stitches across his chest had burst.

"Shit!" he shouted, slamming his hand on the dashboard. He dabbed at it with some tissue and stuck it to where the blood was seeping out.

Stephen couldn't fathom how she had gained the upper hand on him. He didn't want to admit it, but it scared him. He'd always been able to keep the others under control, down in the dungeon. They had feared him. Now *he* felt fear, and she had his gun, and that was unforgivable. After he got himself stitched up at the hospital, he should have just shown Jassy the wounds and made something up, but he hadn't.

"Fuck!" he said, hitting the dashboard again. He thought back to when Kate Marshall had emerged from the lift with her pretty boy assistant. Were they onto him already?

They're all lying in wait for me, but they're not going to get me; I'll die before they get me! he thought. His eyes stung. Sweat was running down his face. He wiped it with his sleeve, put the car in gear, and drove away.

58

Sarah pulled up in a car ten minutes after Tristan called her.

"Are you all right?" she asked, winding down her window. She peered past Kate and Tristan, to Kate's car wedged against the tree.

"We're fine. Thank God for airbags," said Tristan. He hurried to the passenger door and got in.

"What are you going to do with the car?" asked Sarah.

"I called the AA," said Kate, getting in the back seat and fastening her seat belt. She saw that Sarah had wet hair and was wearing a dressing gown and bunny slippers.

"Tristan, are you sure you're not hurt?" asked Sarah, ignoring Kate.

"I'm fine," he said. "Why are you wearing your pajamas?"

"I was in the bath when you phoned."

Kate leaned forward between the seats.

"Sarah, we need you to take us to the old industrial estate next to Frome Crawford, right now," she said.

Sarah looked at Tristan.

"What do you mean? I thought I was giving you a lift home?"

"We believe Magdalena is being held captive there," said Tristan.

Sarah looked at them both.

"You can't be serious?" she said. "It's late!"

"Sarah, this is serious. This is lifesaving serious. We need to go now!" said Tristan.

"Now, Sarah!" said Kate. The penny seemed to drop, and Sarah nodded.

"Okay, but I'm not breaking the speed limit. This is Gary's car, and he's still got three years' payments left on the finance plan."

"Now!" shouted Kate. Her slowness was infuriating.

Sarah put the car in gear and made an agonizingly slow three-point turn, and then they pulled away back toward Ashdean.

———

Magdalena's hands were sore as she spooled out the length of plaited bedsheets in the corridor. Math wasn't her strong point, but she'd estimated that the distance between the floor and the hatch was two meters. She would need double that to get a good purchase from above to lift the porcelain toilet bowl off the floor and up into the open hatch. Her problem had been that the mattress was very small, just larger than a double bed. She'd started to tear strips out from the middle and ended up with strips of material that broke and were too thin. A couple of times she'd thought she heard the lift whir into life, and she'd stopped to listen, but her ears were playing tricks on her. Her whole body was jangling with exhaustion and adrenaline, and she was worried that her tank was now empty and shortly she would crash out with exhaustion.

The rope measured just over two meters. It wasn't much, but it would have to do. It was plaited tightly with six strips, and she'd tied four sections together. She always plaited her sister's hair when she was at home, and she tried not to think about this as she made her length of rope. The thought of not seeing her family again was too much.

Magdalena looped one end of the rope through one of the holes at the back of the toilet and knotted it tight. She then looped the other end over her shoulder. Checking she had the sharp pieces of porcelain in her pocket, she climbed onto the toilet bowl and hoisted herself up and into the hatch.

The small square platform looked up to the underside of the lift above and down to the bottom of the lift shaft, where the lift would come to a rest before the doors opened. She threw the other end of the rope over the edge, and she carefully lowered herself down into the lift shaft, so she was standing on the other side of the lift doors. Gripping the other end of the knotted sheets, she started to pull. She felt the rope take the weight, and then she leaned back, using her weight to hoist the toilet bowl up toward the hatch. The rope strained. She had expected it to be heavier to lift. She gave a big pull, and she leaned back with all her weight and lost balance as the toilet bowl came up through the hatch, over the lip of the platform. She had to duck out of the way as it crashed down in the lift shaft behind her.

"Shit," she said, looking at the three broken pieces of porcelain that lay among the metal braces at the bottom of the lift shaft.

———

When Stephen drove up to the building, it sat, bathed in shadows, at the end of a long, deserted street filled with old warehouses and some abandoned terraced houses. The lights from the town glowed over a hill, but the street was shrouded in darkness. He parked to the side of the building and got out of the car.

The blood spots on the front of his shirt were larger, and he cursed her.

Stephen went to the boot of the car and opened it. He took out a blanket and some reusable shopping bags so he could lift away a square of carpet. In the round well that usually contained the spare tire were his night vision goggles, a handgun, and a box of spare bullets.

He opened the gun's magazine to check that the bullets were loaded. He then spun it round and flicked it shut.

He let himself into the building at the side door, which was the original entrance, unlocking the padlock.

Inside was a large, cavernous space, which could comfortably fit six large cars. For a time, he had used it as storage for the cookware shop, but this had become too risky, especially when the kids were older and Jassy had started to take an interest in running the business. The surrounding warehouses were in use during the day, but even then, the traffic was transient. This place had been his playground for the past twenty years, on and off, apart from the few years when he had gone to live in America.

He hadn't indulged his pastime when he was in the States. He didn't have the confidence to abduct and kill on foreign soil, with the death penalty and the strict law enforcement. And when he came back with Jassy and they had children, part of him thought he might change, but the urges came back, and with them came the realization that he had a fiefdom. As a member of the Baker family, he had access to land and money, and protection. He carried on, because he could.

The building was empty inside. He kept it that way so that if anyone broke in, they wouldn't have any incentive to hang around. He also had the only two keys for the lift. One was in his pocket, and the other was buried in a drawer at home.

She has a gun. The words had repeated over and over in his head. He had to be ready to shoot the second he got down there and the doors opened.

He checked the gun again, put the key in the lock by the lift doors, and turned it to the left. The doors opened slowly. He removed the key, got in, and then put the key in the lock inside and turned it to the right. The doors closed, and the lift started to slowly descend.

He pulled on the night vision goggles and activated them. Then he got ready with his gun trained on the closed doors. Would she be lying in wait for him right outside the doors, or would she be hiding in one of the rooms?

The lift juddered and came to a stop with a nasty squeal. He stood for a moment; that hadn't happened before.

He hesitated, took a deep breath, and turned the key to open the doors.

———

Kate, Tristan, and Sarah pulled up outside the disused telephone exchange.

"I don't like the look of this," said Sarah, peering at the shadowy buildings.

"Stay in the car. Lock the doors. And call the police," said Kate. If she were on her own, Kate would have waited to get inside the building before calling the police, but the stakes were higher now that Sarah was involved.

"Can you pass me the wheel lock from the back, please, Kate?" asked Sarah politely.

Kate found it in the footwell. "You're not going to put that on the steering wheel, are you?"

"I'm not that stupid. If he comes out and tries anything, I'll use it to hit him on the head!" cried Sarah.

Kate nodded. It was a good idea. She wasn't sure how far Sarah would get if she had to run for it wearing her bunny slippers.

"Good. Use a wide grip, and swing at him with the lighter end," said Kate. "Do you have anything else we can use as a weapon?"

"There's a crowbar in the boot," said Sarah, holding the wheel lock in her thin, pale hands.

They left the car. Tristan found the crowbar in the boot, took it out, and slammed the boot closed. Sarah activated the central locking, and they could see her pick up her phone and call the police. Kate checked she had the canister of Mace positioned correctly in her hand. She looked at Tristan. He nodded and gave her a nervous smile.

"Okay. Let's do this," he said. They went to the door at the side of the building.

An open padlock hung in the hooks on the door. Kate pulled at the door, and it opened.

"Is this too easy?" asked Tristan, sounding afraid.

"Yes," said Kate, and they stepped into the darkness.

———

Magdalena started to shake almost uncontrollably when she heard the lift activate above her. She had been waiting for a long time, sitting on the small platform above the hatch with the gun cradled in her lap.

The lift was so loud in the shaft, and she watched as the huge box moved down toward her. She thought at the last minute that it was going to crush her, it came so close, but it moved past the tiny platform where she crouched, boxing her into the space and plunging her into darkness again.

She had debated leaving the pieces of the broken toilet bowl in the lift shaft, so that the lift couldn't properly descend, but that could have meant she'd be stuck for longer, blocked in by a broken lift. And if he couldn't get in, she couldn't get out. Magdalena didn't know how long she had been down there with no food, and she was concerned that she would soon starve if left any longer.

The toilet had broken into three pieces when it fell into the lift shaft, which had made it a little easier to lift them back up onto the platform.

The lift squealed as it crushed the smaller pieces of porcelain, and it came to a stop. She sat up on her haunches and held the gun out, aiming through the hatch. Her hands were still shaking from the physical exertion and lack of food. She thought for a moment that the doors wouldn't be able to open, and then they did.

She was poised with the gun when he stepped out of the lift. She saw the top of his head wearing the night vision goggles and the gun in his hand pointed in front of him. She aimed for the top of his head and pulled the trigger.

The sound of the gunfire was deafening. She didn't know if her hands were shaking or if it was the gun's kickback, but she missed, and the bullet hit the floor beside him. In the split second before she fired again, he looked up at her through the hatch. This was the first time she had seen him. In her mind he was an old man. He was younger, but she recognized his nose and the full lips and teeth from the man who had abducted her on the side of the road what seemed like a lifetime ago.

Something snapped inside Magdalena. The feelings of fear and hunger vanished, and she felt a huge wave of anger and hatred toward this man who had taken so much from her. With the last of her energy, she gave a warlike yell, and she launched herself through the hatch and jumped down onto him. Her foot caught on the edge of the hatch, pulling the lid closed with a slam. When they both hit the floor, the corridor was plunged into darkness. She wanted to kill him. She felt his body under hers, and she started to hit him with the gun and claw at his face. She could feel his hot breath and the way his muscles contracted as he yelled and threw her off him. She landed hard on the concrete floor, but she kept hold of the gun. There was a flash and two deafening bangs as they both fired.

———

Kate and Tristan looked around the empty space inside the telephone exchange. The room was bathed in shadows, and there was only one small window high up at the front of the building. They activated the flashlights on their phones. It smelled of mold and damp, but it was neatly swept. The concrete floor clean. They moved closer to the lift doors at the end. There was a muffled bang, and then another.

"What was that?" said Tristan.

"Gunshot," said Kate. "Shit. We're too late." She looked to see if there was a set of stairs, but there were just the lift doors. Kate hurried to them and pressed the button to call the lift, not thinking about who might have the gun. "You should stay here," she said as they heard the lift slowly crawl its way up.

"No way. I'm coming with you," said Tristan. The lift finally arrived and they got inside. It was dim, and there was a nasty smell, like rancid meat. There was a key in the left-hand side. Tristan turned it to the left and then the right. The doors closed, and the lift dropped with a rumbling lurch.

As they got closer, they heard a shrieking, screaming sound and another gunshot, which made the hairs stand up on the back of Kate's neck.

Tristan held up the crowbar, and Kate did the same with the Mace. When the doors opened, the flashlights on their phones lit up the corridor and two figures on the floor.

For a second, the two figures looked up at the bright light. It was Stephen Baker, with blood coming from his nose, and he was on top of a filthy, emaciated woman with long, dark, greasy hair. He had her pinned down, and he was strangling her.

"Magdalena?" said Kate. She didn't have time to process the fact that Magdalena was alive and she was down here with Stephen Baker.

A pair of night vision goggles lay beside Stephen's leg, and a few feet away from them was a handgun on the concrete floor.

The next part seemed to happen in slow motion. Kate ran for the gun, diving to the floor. Her hand closed over it, and Stephen's hands closed over hers. He yanked their hands up and under Kate's chin, hitting her hard in the jaw. She held on, but his powerful hands were prizing at her fingers.

Kate could smell his sweat, and he gripped her hand and started to bend her fingers back. Just as she lost grip of the gun, Stephen let go and went limp, crashing to the floor. Kate looked up and saw that Tristan had hit him over the head with the crowbar.

There was a moment of silence, and then came a scream from Magdalena. She picked up a second handgun, which was lying on the other side of the corridor, and she started to fire at Stephen's unconscious body on the floor. A bullet exploded into the wall with a spray of plaster, and then another hit him in the left shoulder. She staggered to her feet and limped toward Stephen, holding out the gun.

"Magdalena! Stop!" cried Kate. "We're here for you. You're safe. Please, stop!"

Magdalena screamed and moved closer to Stephen, placed the gun against the back of his head, and pulled the trigger. It clicked. The gun was empty.

"It's okay, you're safe," said Kate, managing to get the gun from her hands. She passed it to Tristan, along with the second gun. Kate didn't take her eyes off Stephen Baker, who was still lying facedown on the floor. Magdalena continued to scream hysterically. It was bloodcurdling and chilled Kate to her bones as she tried to control the situation.

"Empty the second gun, Tristan," said Kate. He fumbled with it, managed to get the chamber open, and tipped out the remaining bullets onto the floor.

Kate now had Magdalena in her arms, trying to calm her down.

"You're safe. We're here to take you home," Kate said.

"He took me! He kept me here," cried Magdalena. "He kept me here . . . in the dark and the cold." She started to talk rapidly in Italian.

Tristan knelt down next to Stephen. He was moaning, and blood was pouring from the wound in his shoulder.

"You need to put pressure on his shoulder. I don't want him bleeding out and dying on us," said Kate.

In the chaos, they hadn't heard the lift climb back up to the top floor. The doors opened.

Henry Ko emerged from the lift with Della Street, two other officers, and two paramedics. They stopped for a moment and stared at the three of them next to Stephen Baker.

"You finally got here," said Kate. "This is Magdalena Rossi. She was abducted and kept prisoner here by Stephen Baker," she said triumphantly. "Magdalena shot him in self-defense. He's bleeding badly."

Henry Ko was very pale. His mouth dropped open. The officers and paramedics with him hurried forward. One called for backup, Della went to help Magdalena, and the paramedics took over from Tristan and started to work on Stephen Baker's gunshot wound.

Kate stood up and approached Henry Ko.

"Now do you believe me?" she said.

EPILOGUE
TWO WEEKS LATER

It was a sunny morning at the beginning of November when Kate and Tristan arrived at the Exeter morgue. Kate parked the car and switched off the engine. She looked across at Tristan.

"Are you sure you want to do this?" she asked.

He hesitated and then nodded.

"I feel like I need to see them. I owe it to them . . . I haven't had any breakfast, just to be sure," he said. Kate could see his face was already pale. She nodded and took a deep breath.

They went to the main entrance, and they were buzzed in. Alan Hexham met them in the small reception area as they signed in.

"Morning," he said, his usually jovial face solemn. "You'll need to suit up, overalls and face masks, please."

When Kate and Tristan were ready, they came through to the morgue. A row of three bodies lay on the stainless steel postmortem tables. They appeared almost mummified. They had no hair, and in places the leathery, dark skin was missing. A nasty tang of decay and standing water permeated the room.

"These three poor souls, all female, were recovered in the reservoir from a depth of forty meters," said Alan. "They'd been weighted down and wrapped in material. The cold and lack of oxygen at that depth slowed decay, as did the sheets they were wrapped in . . ."

Kate stepped closer and looked at the first body. She felt sadness and revulsion that the reservoir had hidden these bodies for so long. She glanced at Tristan. He had his back pressed to the wall, and he looked pale.

"I don't know if you've heard the latest body count?" asked Alan.

"It was seven the last I heard," said Kate.

"Ah. The dive team have now recovered twelve bodies from the reservoir, and I know that another team are due to go down later today. I've already conducted nine postmortems. These three, all female, arrived late last night."

Kate knew from her time in the police that diving to a depth greater than twenty-five meters was complex. In some parts of the reservoir, the water reached a depth of forty or fifty meters. At these depths, police divers had to use special mixes of oxygen, and they were limited in the time they could spend underwater.

Alan went on, "From the six different types of DNA the police found in the basement of the telephone exchange in Frome Crawford, it's matched six of the bodies found so far, including Sally-Ann Cobbs and Ulrich Mazur."

Kate looked back at Tristan. His face was like chalk.

"What about the other six bodies?" he asked with a quavering voice.

"I spoke to Della," said Kate. "They also found residues of several types of bleach and caustic soda down there, which means Stephen Baker could have washed it down many times, destroying DNA . . . But they'll keep looking. And, of course, the police have now tested DNA found on Ted Clough's body. It matched Stephen Baker."

Stephen Baker had confessed an extraordinary story while in custody. He'd told the police he'd abducted and killed sixteen people, but, he said, that was when he'd stopped counting. He also admitted to killing Ted Clough. He'd said this to try and cut a deal with the police for a reduced sentence, but as Della had told Kate, if you admit to killing seventeen people, you aren't in much of a position to cut a deal.

"I think we've seen enough," said Kate, taking a last look at the bodies lying on the postmortem tables.

"Yes. How about a cup of tea?" asked Alan.

When they were settled in his office with steaming cups of sweet tea, they carried on the conversation.

"I can't understand why Stephen Baker felt so secure dumping these bodies in the reservoir," said Alan, sitting back in his chair. "Over the years, two of them floated—Fiona Harvey and Becky Chard—and their cause of death was covered up by Dylan Robertson."

Kate blew on her tea and sipped it.

"Stephen Baker told the police that Arron Ko and his aunt, Silvia Baker, have been romantically involved for many years," said Kate. "They would throw wild parties when Arron's wife was away on business. One night, when Stephen was very young, and after a long drinking session, Arron was driving Silvia home, when he knocked over and killed a young man. He was about to make superintendent, and if this ever came out, it would have ended his career. So Silvia asked Dylan to deal with the body. He weighted it down and dumped it in the reservoir. Stephen overheard Silvia and Arron talking about this late one night, when he was still a teenager . . . Years later, when Stephen started to develop his own obsession with abducting young women, he knew that as long as his aunt Silvia and Arron Ko were alive, no one would ever get permission to search the reservoir. They had given him the perfect place to dump the bodies."

"So they had no idea about Stephen and all those bodies in the water?" said Alan.

"Dylan was arrested two days ago, but the police are still trying to determine if he knew anything about Stephen dumping bodies. They didn't believe he did. He was only ever protecting himself, Silvia, and Arron when he'd prevented the reservoir being searched," said Kate.

"Henry Ko's been suspended, pending an inquiry," said Tristan, cradling his tea. A little color had come back into his face.

"He's saying he knew nothing of the watery graves in Shadow Sands. He's told them that his father had always insisted that the reservoir never be searched because of the cost involved to the company," said Kate.

"You think he's dumb enough to believe that?" asked Alan.

"It seems he was dumb enough to take his father's word for it," said Kate. "His father was the reason he kept getting promoted. Did Arron Ko pull the strings and ask for a different coroner to conduct Simon Kendal's postmortem?"

Alan sighed.

"Yes, it was him. I wasn't at liberty to tell you before, but in light of all this, yes . . . Do you think Stephen's wife suspected anything?" he asked.

"She's already filed for divorce and taken the three children back to America to be with her family," said Kate. "The police didn't stop her, so she's not a suspect."

"Why do you think Stephen did it—abduct them and keep his victims for so long before killing them?"

"I've spent so many years trying to understand what drives serial killers. It often comes down to a lack of empathy and the desire for power and control. From what Magdalena has told the police, Stephen derived great pleasure from keeping her in the dark and torturing her. If he survives prison, then I'm sure there will be psychologists lining up to study him."

"And as for Simon Kendal?" asked Alan.

"He was in the wrong place at the wrong time. Della told me they think Simon came across Stephen about to dump a body—they think it was a young woman called Jennie Newlove, who went missing in late July. Little was known about the circumstances of her disappearance, until now."

Alan nodded solemnly.

"Jennie Newlove was one of the bodies we identified during the postmortems," he said.

"They think that Simon got up in the night, went for a walk, disturbed Stephen dumping her body, and they got into a fight," said Kate.

"What about the tent peg?" asked Alan. "I flagged that he was stabbed by a tent peg when I looked at the case file."

"His friend Geraint was released from custody and cleared a few days ago," said Kate. "Geraint says that one of the tent pegs is missing from the tent that the police seized from his flat. The police think that Simon was carrying a tent peg for self-defense. The campsite was in the middle of nowhere, and the toilets are often used by drifters. Stephen could have stabbed Simon with the tent peg. Simon was then cornered, jumped into the water, and started to swim. Stephen pursued him in his boat, far up the reservoir. Simon lost a huge amount of blood and drowned, and then I found his body floating by the church tower."

———

Kate was glad the sun was out when she and Tristan left the morgue. The cold inside had seeped into her bones, and seeing those dead bodies had chilled her even more.

They stopped at her car for a moment, standing in the warmth.

"You okay?" she asked. Tristan was leaning back with his eyes closed, enjoying the sun on his face. He opened his eyes.

"Yes. I think so," he said.

"I got an invitation to Sarah and Gary's wedding," said Kate, changing the subject.

"She said she was going to invite you," he said.

"What changed her mind?"

"I think she secretly admires you, the fact you went for it to find Magdalena."

"*We* went for it," corrected Kate.

"And of course, Sarah can now tell the story, because she drove the getaway car," said Tristan with a knowing smile. "And in Sarah's version, just to warn you so you know, she drove us at high speed, and it's thanks to her that we got there in time and saved Magdalena's life. Oh, and she wasn't wearing her dressing gown and bunny slippers."

Kate laughed. "She's given me a plus-one on the invitation, and I was thinking of bringing Jake. He's going to be staying with me that weekend."

"That'll be cool. Is he okay after everything, meeting Peter?"

Kate shrugged.

"I don't know. He's asked to write to Peter, which I'm not thrilled about, but he seems under no illusions about who his father is," she said. "Time will tell . . . How about you and Sarah?"

"She's coming around to the fact that I like guys."

"And what about you? Are you okay with it?"

"I'm happy that I've been honest with myself. I'm a bit nervous about dating," he said with a smile.

"Oh my God, you are going to have no problem finding dates," laughed Kate.

They got into the car. Kate went to switch on the engine, then hesitated and turned to Tristan. She knew there was one more thing she had to tell him.

"Listen, I've been thinking a lot about the future, and I'm going to hand in my notice at the university," she said.

"Why?"

"My dream job was being a police officer. We know how that turned out, and since then, I've enjoyed lecturing, and it's been a good thing over the past eight years, but I want to be a private detective. Full time. Do it properly. I don't quite know *how* I'm going to do it yet . . . And don't worry, I'm going to stay for the rest of the academic year, and I know of several other lecturers who would take you on as their research assistant . . ."

Kate exhaled, relieved that she'd said it but concerned for Tristan.

"What if I came in with you and we went into business together? I know I would need to take some courses, and I might have to carry on part time at Ashdean for a bit until we get up and running."

"That's great to hear," she said. "But how would it work?"

"Let's go for coffee and make a plan," he said. "Mine's a caramel macchiato."

Kate nodded and smiled, and they drove off through the sunny streets in search of a coffee shop to plan their future as private detectives.

Author's Letter

Dear Readers,

Thank you to everyone who got in touch to say they enjoyed *Nine Elms*. Your lovely messages and feedback mean the world to me; they've kept me going and given me such a boost on the days when the writing process has been tough, and it's been great to hear your feedback about Kate, Tristan, and all the characters. In the first draft of *Shadow Sands*, Peter Conway was absent, but I received so many messages saying how much you loved to hate Peter, and so many people wanted to know what happened to him next, so I decided to include him in *Shadow Sands*, and I think the book is better for it. Thank you. Keep the messages coming; I love to hear from you all.

As always, thank you for choosing to read one of my books. If you enjoyed *Shadow Sands*, I would be very grateful if you could tell your friends and family. I've written this at the end of every book, but a word-of-mouth recommendation remains the most powerful way for new readers to discover one of my books. Your endorsement makes a huge difference! You could also write a product review. It needn't be long, just a few words, but this also helps new readers find one of my books for the first time.

As I've written previously, the UK seaside town of Ashdean, its university, and its inhabitants are fictitious, as is Thurlow Bay, where Kate Marshall lives on the cliff top. If you would like to look up the location on a UK map, I imagine Ashdean occupying a place on the south coast of England, next to a beautiful town called Budleigh Salterton.

I will also add that the Shadow Sands estate, reservoir, and power plant are also fictitious, as is Great Barwell Psychiatric Hospital, where we got to visit Peter Conway for the second time.

The other locations used in the book are real, but as with all fiction, I'll hope you forgive me for using a little dramatic license.

To find out more about me, or to send me a message, you can check out my website, www.robertbryndza.com.

Kate and Tristan will return shortly for another gripping murder investigation! Until then . . .

Robert Bryndza

Acknowledgments

Thank you to the brilliant team at Thomas and Mercer: Liz Pearsons, Charlotte Herscher, Laura Barrett, Sarah Shaw, Oisin O'Malley, Dennelle Catlett, Haley Miller Swan, and Kellie Osborne. Thank you, as ever, to Team Bryndza: Janko, Vierka, Riky, and Lola. I love you all so much and thank you for keeping me going with your love and support!

The biggest thank-you goes out to all the book bloggers and readers. When I started out, it was you who were there reading and championing my books. Word of mouth is the most powerful form of advertising, and I will never forget that my readers and the many wonderful book bloggers are the most important people. I hope you enjoyed reading *Shadow Sands*. There are lots more books to come, and I hope you stay with me for the ride!

About the Author

Photo © 2017 Petr Kozlik

Robert Bryndza is the author of the Amazon Charts bestseller *Nine Elms*, the first book in the Kate Marshall series, and the Detective Erika Foster series, which includes the #1 international bestseller *The Girl in the Ice*, *The Night Stalker*, *Dark Water*, *Last Breath*, *Cold Blood*, and *Deadly Secrets*. Robert's books have sold three million copies and have been translated into twenty-nine languages. In addition to writing crime fiction, Robert has published a bestselling series of romantic comedies. He is British and lives in Slovakia. For more information, visit www.robertbryndza.com.